Brenna
Lyons

Maher
Men

Night Warriors
Warriors, Book 5

Fireborn Publishing Copyright Statement

This book is written in US English.

PUBLISHER

Glossary of Warrior Terms:

Beast- Beasts are what humans erroneously refer to as vampires. The stories humans tell are obviously not correct, but you can't expect a human to get everything right.

Blutjagd- The "blood hunt." Warriors crave battle with the beasts, as the beasts crave blood. Warriors are tied to beasts in that they sense many of the beasts' special powers. A Warrior can feel the use of coercion, feeding, and other controls of humans. They also feel other Warriors engaged in *Blutjagd*, the death of beasts and Warriors in their range, and the presence of nearby beasts that are not fully ghosted. Rigorous battle training will quell the *Blutjagd* for short periods of time.

Elder- One of the original beasts, the Stone stealers who were damned for their crimes against the Stone and the Warriors. The elders are gifted with powers turned beasts are not, including the ability to reproduce with a *Blutjagdfrau*, the ability to turn other beasts, and the inability to be killed by anyone but a Warrior.

Endspiel- The point in printing when a Warrior must either seal printing or go insane. A Warrior who feels printing may not progress should break printing long before this point. Note that they are rarely smart enough to do so.

Fluch- The Warrior's curse, passed from father to son or daughter. The *fluch* may be removed from a daughter but never a son. If the *fluch* is not removed in the *Zeremonie der Freiheit* by the time the menses begin or the *Zeremonie des Schutzes* is performed before freeing, the daughter is cursed to become *Blutjagdfrau*, a female Warrior. Because elders target *Blutjagdfrau* as mates, Warrior fathers will go to any lengths to free a daughter not marked by the Stone.

Ghosting- A talent that both beasts and Cursed Warriors learn to harness. Ghosting can hide the physical form of Cursed Warriors or beasts and all they hold or carry from each other and humans. In a lesser strength, it can "blur" the image of the user so that humans do not note the passage in particular but still see a person there, which avoids accidental collisions. Even a ghosted beast cannot hide uses of power that a Warrior can track.

Krankheit- The "sealing sickness." In the final stage of the transformation between human and Cursed Warrior, at or about the sixteenth birthday in males and a year after the start of menses in females, the sickness strikes. The young Warrior will suffer nausea, vomiting, a high fever, disorientation, dizziness, and may become incoherent. It is usually the only time in a Warrior's life that he or she becomes ill, save morning sickness in a *Blutjagdfrau*.

Printing- Like imprinting, a Warrior becomes tied to his mate for life. He cannot choose another if she's lost, cannot be unfaithful while she lives, and cannot ever divorce or otherwise dissolve the union. A printed Warrior is the most stable of men, unless his mate or children are endangered or lost. Then, he will suffer the printing madness and may have to be killed by his house. Likewise, a Warrior who breaks printing, even early printing, will suffer for it. A Warrior who breaks printing too close to *Endspiel* will face the madness.

The Stone- At the beginning of the first Beast War, Ani—the premiere goddess of the Warrior world—placed a portion of Her essence in a stone. The Stone speaks to the Stone lord to advise and lead Her Warriors in their continuing battles. Sacred Weapons are bathed in the blue light of the Stone, which allows them to render beasts powerless and kill all beasts, including elders.

Veriel- The mad elder. The destroyer of lives. The mad deceiver, who led the traitors and freed the elders from the Stone. The most hated and hunted of all the beasts. Fixated on one woman, he would destroy the world to own her. Or... At least, that's what the stories say of him.

Warriors- Also called Cursed Warriors, Krieger der Nacht, Soldat der Nacht or Sons of the Stone. The Warriors were an ancient race of protectors who spawned the beasts and now are driven to hunt their former brothers to extinction.

Gods and Goddesses of the Warrior World/Stone Marks:

Ani- the goddess of birth/the mother goddess and leader of the Warrior gods, protector of women and children; mark of the mother of the great beast-killers

Baroo- god of thunder

Dobler- twin brother god, known as the peace-bringer

Fih- twin brother god of war

Geil- god of iron

Hir- god of the cool wood

Iol- god of immovable ice

Jee- god of justice

Kor- god of the bear

Len- god of the mountain

Mul- god of flowing water

Nul- god of stealth of the night

Ori- god of the sun

Pol- god of the horse

Reg- god of the intensity of the fire

Syth- god of precious stones; mark of the Stone lord

Tes- goddess of the stars, moon, and wishes fulfilled

Vin- god of the wind

Wul- god of the wolf

Zel- goddess of endings and death; mark of the Stone vessels

Section One:

Kord
and
Julia

Once Bitten

A Note About this Story:

In the original *Night Warriors* and again in *Hunter's Moon*, I hinted at what happened when Kord Maher took his mate. Kord demanded to be heard, of course, because there was a lot more to the story than the jokes other Warriors tell about the events.

In the end, I learned the Stone had very specific plans for the Maher family, plans that resulted in everything from making Lewis Maher a Stone lord to making Adam Maher the powerhouse Warrior he turned out to be...to creating Curt Maher, a Warrior equal to the task of taming Erin.

The Stone needed the right Warriors in the right places at the right times. That all started with one young Warrior daughter...and her brother's attempt to save her life.

Hope you enjoy!
Brenna Lyons

Prologue

August 20th, 1952

"What is it?" Maman's voice was a whispered plea.

Julia opened her eyes, stretching beneath the light spring quilt on her bed.

"You know what," her father commented. "Stay here. Paul and Jack will go with me."

That simply, Julia was wide awake. Jack was going somewhere with Father. They would take her along if she was fast enough. Father would take her with them. Father never denied her anything.

She slid from her bed and pulled her shoes on over her bare feet. She strode down the hall and out the back door, turning the knob with both of her tiny hands, then bolted across the lawn to the garage. She stumbled, her nightgown catching on her shoes; Julia lifted it and ran on. Father would demand she dress before they left, but if she took the time to dress first, they might be gone before she reached them.

Julia stopped in the doorway to the garage, looking around in confusion. Her father and brothers weren't there. She couldn't have missed them. All four cars were still inside.

She turned back to the house, confused. Where could they have gone this late at night?

"Juu—lia."

She turned to the sound of the whisper, her brow furrowing at a dark outline disappearing

13

into the tree line. Julia smiled. Jack was playing with her as he often did after her nap. Was it a game of tag, then?

She rushed into the trees, following the faint rustlings and movements from tree to tree until the tree house rose high above her. "Jack?" she called, looking up the slats nailed to the tree trunk.

There was no answer.

Julia looked around; Jack was nowhere to be seen. He couldn't ghost from her while she wore her amulet. She touched the disc to assure herself it was still there. No, he wasn't ghosting, so he had to be teasing her. She scowled. Father didn't allow the boys to tease her.

"Jack," she demanded. "Show yourself, or I'll tell Father." Julia planted her fists on her hips.

Still, her brother didn't show himself.

"Father will hear—" She stopped, taking a step back in surprise.

A man stepped from the trees, but it wasn't Jack. "There you are, Julia," he greeted her in a heavy accent she couldn't place. "I've been looking for you."

She shied from his offered hand.

The man chuckled. "Come now. Don't you recognize me?"

Julia shook her head shyly. This man looked like a Warrior, save his clothing, but it was no Warrior she knew. Who else would come here? Strangers didn't come to their estates.

As if he read her thoughts, the man knelt down a few feet from her. "You needn't be frightened. Could anyone harm you on *Landwirt* soil?"

She laughed at that, pressing her chubby fingers to her mouth. It was true. No one would dare harm her here—not while her father was Lord Farmer.

He smiled wider.

"Do you know Father?" she asked.

The man settled on the grass. "We have met each other many times." He leaned closer to her. "I would ask your help, Julia," he whispered in a conspiratorial tone.

"You need *my* help?" No one ever asked for Julia's help. When she offered, people patted her head and sent her to play. "What kind of help?"

"I have lost my amulet." His eyes were pained, much as Alan's had been when he'd broken Maman's favorite vase with his wooden practice blade.

Julia smiled. "I can get you one. Father has a whole drawer—"

"No!" He put up a calming hand as she startled. "Your Maman might see you. How would you explain your actions?"

She bit her lip, working at the problem and at a loss for an answer to it.

"I would be in even more trouble then," he confided.

"Then how can I help?" she asked in confusion.

"If you give me *your* amulet..."

Julia fingered the metal disc over her chest uncertainly. "Father says—"

"Never to take it off?"

She nodded.

"Your Maman has told me you've lost yours before."

Julia winced. She had lost it twice. Once, the chain broke while she was swimming. The other time, she lost it while she and Jack played in the woods.

"Did anything bad happen to you, Julia?"

"No," she admitted.

"Do you think anything bad *could* happen here?"

"No." That was said with more conviction. What could happen? Maman called this their sanctuary, and Jack said that meant it was their safe place.

"Was your father angry with you for losing your amulet?" He smiled a knowing smile at that.

Julia giggled. He knew Father well. Father was *never* angry with her.

"Will you help me, Julia?" His eyes were serious, hopeful.

She fingered the amulet. She'd never lied to Father. If she told him she lost the amulet—

"Julia," he whispered.

She looked at the doll in his hand with a gasp of surprise. "Babette."

"Yes. It is very like your Maman's Babette, but this one has dark curls like you do and not golden like your Maman's."

Julia nodded, touching the doll's beautiful pink dress.

"Trade with me," he offered. "I will give you this Babette for your amulet."

She nodded again, incapable of begging for the beautiful doll. It was even prettier than Maman's Babette. Julia had longed to play with Maman's doll for as long as she could remember. The man set the toy in her outstretched hands, and she hugged it to her chest.

"Julia," Maman called. "Julia, where are you?"

"Quickly, Julia," he urged her. "I must be well away before your Maman arrives."

She pulled off the amulet and handed it to him. It slipped through his fingers and fell to the grass. Julia laughed, looking to him, intent on commenting on his clumsiness.

She went still, caught in the red glow of his eyes. Fangs sprouted in his mouth, and claws took the place of the fingernails on his hands.

Julia turned and ran, dropping the doll at the base of the tree and scrambling up the slats toward the tree house. Strictly speaking, she wasn't allowed up there without Jack or Paul, but there were worse things in life than a broken arm.

"Julia," Maman called again, annoyance in her tone.

A hand fisted in the back of her nightgown and yanked Julia from her perch. She screamed as she fell, kicking as fingers bit into her upper arms.

"Julia!" Maman was closer now, her voice panicked.

Julia screamed again at a sharp pain in her shoulder. Her body went leaden and her mind disconnected from the world around her.

Memories danced in her mind: playing with Jack, riding on Father's shoulders, cuddling in Maman's arms when she was ill.

"No!" Maman screamed.

A shockwave coursed through her body, forcing her back. Maman fisted the front of Julia's nightgown and dragged her forward again. Julia whimpered as her shoulder exploded in pain. Then Maman's arms were around her, soothing her.

She forced her eyes open, trying to understand the warm liquid plastering her nightgown to her back and cooling in the night breeze. Julia shivered, the night suddenly colder than moments earlier.

Another shockwave forced her hard against Maman's chest. Julia closed her eyes again as her shoulder throbbed, even breathing painful of a sudden.

"Release her," the man's voice growled.

"Never. Leave us," Maman ordered. "My amulet will protect us both as long as it touches her. Leave us or face my husband."

The growling was louder, a fierce animal sound that made Julia shiver again.

"Hold to me, Julia," Maman whispered. "You must not let go. Never let go."

Julia fisted handfuls of Maman's blouse, her hands trembling wildly. Why was it so cold?

"I said release her!"

"Never let go," Maman repeated softly.

Then they were falling to the ground. Julia sobbed at a strange heavy thumping sound. It came again and again. She wrapped her legs around Maman's waist.

"Julia," the man whispered. "Come to me."

She shook her head, holding to Maman.

You must not let go. Never let go.

"Juuu-lia." His voice was calming, soothing. "Come to me, Julia."

"Never let—" she gasped, her mind muddled.

"Julia." His voice was sweet and pure.

She sighed, her muscles warm and relaxed. She was supposed to touch him, wasn't she? Julia relaxed one fist, trying desperately to focus on reaching out to him.

A roar split the night, making her head ache.

Never let go!

She fisted Maman's blouse, shaking her head. Julia gagged at a horrible smell, burying her face in Maman's chest.

"Julia," Jack choked. Was the smell too much for him, as well? His hands pulled at her.

"No!" she screamed, tightening her fists. "Maman said—"

"Julia, let go," he ordered.

Jack forced her hands open, dragging Julia from Maman's chest. She fought him, pleading for Maman to hold her. She grasped at Maman's skirt as her oldest brother pulled her away. He placed his body between them, and Julia beat at his chest.

His hand traced her neck. He cursed, dropping an amulet over her head. Then Julia was moving, wrapped in Jack's arms, sobbing into his chest and calling out for Maman.

"Jack!" Paul shouted. "Is she all right?"

19

"Call Damien. She needs a doctor." His voice dropped to a whisper. "I'll take her."

There was an uneasy moment of silence.

"Now, Paul," he thundered.

Julia grasped at his shirt, trying to ask what he meant. Who needed a doctor? Why? Was Maman hurt?

A scream of rage seemed to shake the stars. Julia met Jack's gaze, then everything went dark.

****

"A few more minutes," Jack promised, though he was certain Julia couldn't hear him. He touched her face, wincing at how cold her skin felt. He tucked his jacket around her, muttering a prayer that she would survive. If she didn't, their father was as good as lost, and Jack would be Lord.

I am too young to be Lord. I don't want it. Not now. Not this way. Certainly not because of the loss of his sister.

Damien met him at Julia's door. "Is it true?" he asked urgently.

Jack didn't answer immediately. He lifted his sister out of the car and headed for the cramped office in Damien's home with the doctor at his heels.

"Is it true?" he asked again.

"Is what true?" Jack snapped. "That my mother is dead and my father is in the throes of printing madness? That my sister is seriously injured? Yes to each of them, Damien."

The doctor nodded, motioning him to a high table. Damien pulled back the jacket, wincing at the little girl bathed in her own blood and that of her mother. Julia was pale, even her lips nearly colorless. Her breaths came in shallow gasps of air.

Damien cut her nightgown away from the wound, turning on Jack with a stricken look. "My God! What did this? I mean, how could—"

"The beast fed, and the wound tore away. We will not lose her, Damien."

He listened to her heart, grimacing. "Jack, I—"

"If we lose Julia, we lose my father," Jack growled. *I will not allow it.*

"I cannot treat this effectively. It's too late."

"It can't be."

"The hospital is too far."

"What can't you do here?"

"She's lost too much blood, Jack. This is a small clinic, and I'm not equipped to—"

Jack stripped off his shirt.

Damien shook his head in horror. "Warriors transfuse their own," he squeaked. "You're not—"

"Human," he finished acidly. "She is my sister. We will match well enough." Jack pulled a chair over and offered his arm.

The doctor hesitated. "What will this do to her?"

"I don't care, as long as it saves her life."

Damien stared at him, his mouth working as if he intended to argue. "Your blood—"

"I gave you an order, Damien." The doctor was bound to obey. Jack prayed he'd obey. Julia didn't have time for more arguments.

Damien nodded and set to work. He repaired the damage while the transfusion ran.

Jack stroked Julia's hair, murmuring his assurances that she would live to run and swim with him again. He caught Damien's hand, as the doctor reached for the needle in his arm. "Not until she's strong enough. My body will replace what I've lost. You know that."

Damien ran a shaking hand through his hair. "The damage is done," he agreed.

By the time the needles were removed, Jack shook in exhaustion. "Will she survive?" His words were slurred, and his vision jumped and blurred.

"Blood rejection happens quickly," he replied. "We'll know within the hour."

"Jee willing, there will be no reaction."

****

August 21st, 1952

Robert opened his eyes to the harsh morning light. He swallowed, wincing at the raw ache in his throat. How many hours had he howled over Merilee's grave? Probably until the sun was a gray line on the horizon.

He fisted a handful of the dirt in his trembling hand, then pressed his forehead to the freshly filled grave. Would that he had a lifetime to lie here and grieve, he would do so, but it was not to be. Robert and Merilee had six children, and he owed it to his wife to see them through this and everything else that came their way.

Robert pushed to his feet, stiff and aching. The walk to the house seemed to take ten times as long as it had the day before. Merilee no longer waited for him. What was there to rush for?

I failed her. I followed a false trail and left my family unprotected in the face of an enemy I grossly underestimated.

Paul looked up as he entered. He paled and dropped his gaze, then passed a glass of milk to Alan. He nodded Patrick toward his plate of eggs.

Robert touched Nikolaus's hair, biting back tears. "Eat up, boys," he offered in a hoarse voice. His own stomach twisted at the smell of food.

His gaze passed over then returned to the doll in the trash. Robert ambled over to it and picked it up, searching out his memories of the night before.

The doll had lay beneath the tree house in the clearing where he'd discovered Merilee's body. It wasn't a doll he'd seen before, certainly not one of the hundreds his daughter owned. Robert knew every one of those dolls by sight and name.

The truth stung him. "Damn that beast," he growled. "He used—"

Robert turned to the table abruptly, scanning his gaze over his assembled children, his heart pounding. "Julia? Paul, where are Jack and Julia?"

Paul placed his fork next to his untouched plate. "With Damien."

Robert dropped the doll, weaving on his feet as the china face shattered against the polished wood floor. "Oh... Oh, gods. I have to go, Paul."

"Yes. You do," his son informed him.

He hesitated long enough to kiss his younger sons goodbye, then sprinted for the garage.

Damien's home and office were almost twenty miles away. That gave Robert ample time to analyze what went wrong.

He'd told Julia she was safe. He'd never told her what there was to fear in the world. He'd led her to believe nothing could harm her. He'd hidden their mortal enemies from her.

Robert sobbed at the depth of his errors...and the cost of them. It had been too easy for the beast. The damned thing had simply walked up to a four-year-old child who trusted implicitly that she was safe.

How long had it taken him to coax her amulet away from her? What lies had he used to convince Julia to give away her protection?

I never even explained how the amulet protected her. To Julia, it was nothing more than a prized possession that meant I love her.

Robert hadn't questioned anything the previous night. He hadn't had a truly logical thought from the moment he saw Merilee's body until the moment he'd held that damned doll.

Now that he had a reason to search for answers, the answers seared him. The beast had used the doll. For whatever reason, Julia had taken off her amulet.

24

The beast fed. On Julia.

And killed Merilee with a tree branch, probably in an attempt to take Julia from her.

He pulled his car into the slot next to Jack's, trying to ignore the tang of human blood seeping from his son's vehicle. In a heartbeat, he was bolting through the door and into the treatment area. Robert went still at the sight of them.

Jack sat in a chair, bare-chested, his shirt crumpled at his feet, his head pillowed on his crossed arms next to Julia's hip. Sweat coated Julia's face, and a thick bandage enveloped her shoulder. A light blanket covered her to the chest, and she was very still.

Too still. Julia is never still, even in sleep.

Robert staggered to her, touching Julia's face with a dirt-caked hand. A fever raged in her. "Damien," he thundered.

Jack startled, training a weary gaze on his father. Robert's breath caught in his throat at how drawn his son was, shaking...pale. He glanced at Julia and then back to his son. Fevering or not, Julia looked better than her oldest brother did. "Jack?" *What have I missed? I know Jack wasn't injured. None of my sons were.*

His son averted his gaze, his jaw tightening.

"What have you done, Jack?"

Damien rushed in and laid a hand on Julia's throat. He shook his head, then shot Jack a look of pure misery. "I think your Jee might have failed you."

Robert grasped his son by the back of the neck, considering murder. "What did you do?" he demanded.

"She would have died in my arms," Jack pleaded. "I couldn't let that happen."

"What—"

"She needed blood. It couldn't wait. It was her only chance."

"Yours?" Robert asked, feeling faint.

"Yes. Mine. It was mine or death." His voice was sure in conviction.

Robert nodded, releasing Jack and turning back to his daughter with a clearer mind to the situation. "There is another possibility."

Damien looked up in surprise, a new bag of IV fluids in his hand. "Robert?"

"Check her wound."

"But only last night—"

"Check it," Robert repeated carefully.

Damien set the IV solution on the bedside table, eased Julia to her side, and started cutting and peeling away blood-stained bandages. He stared at her shoulder, barely breathing.

The urge to reach across the bed and shake him was strong. Robert tapped it down and forced a calm voice. "Damien?"

His emotions rioted. Robert wasn't sure if he should pray that she was simply ill in the aftermath of the attack or that Jack's blood had caused some of his healing to pass to her, no matter what it might mean in years to come.

"Well on its way to being healed." The doctor let loose a nervous laugh. "At this rate, there may not even be a scar. It's a miracle, Robert."

"*Krankheit,*" Jack grumbled. He winced, most likely in the realization of what he'd probably brought down on their heads.

Robert nodded his agreement. "I'll call Carrick. We have to know."

His son didn't meet his gaze. "And if I have somehow managed to curse her?"

"Then she will be *Blutjadgfrau*." Just the thought of it made Robert shiver in apprehension. "But she will be alive, Jack."

                    ****

A hand stroked at her hair. Julia groaned. Her entire body felt sore and feverish.

"Julia?" her father called. "Julia, please open your eyes."

She forced her eyelids up, trying to focus. Without success. Julia licked her dry lips.

"Julia?"

"Juice." Talking hurt, and she coughed in the effort to. "Please." *Maman says to always say please.*

A cup touched her lips. It held water, but even water tasted sweet and cold. It soothed her abused throat. Julia drank deeply, until her stomach complained. The cup retreated, and her father wiped her face with a cool cloth.

"Better?" he asked.

She nodded, and her stomach clenched. "Feel sick."

"I imagine you do."

"Maman," she requested. Maman always held her when Julia was hurt or wasn't feeling well. Julia couldn't remember ever feeling this bad before, and she wanted Maman.

Father didn't answer.

"Maman," she repeated.

"Do you remember why you're here, Julia?"

Her memories were muddled, fractured images that didn't make sense in conjunction with each other. "A man. A man who knew you. I ran from him to the tree house, but I fell...I think. I— It hurt."

"Do you remember anything about the man?" he asked gently.

"Dark... Like a Warrior. He was a stranger, but he knew me. He knew all of us."

Her father seemed to glow in anger, an aura that surrounded him. She'd heard Maman and her brothers talk about *Blutjagd* before, but Julia had never seen it. She hadn't known you *could* see it.

He glared at her, and his jaw tightened. Julia edged away from him on the bed. Father had never been angry with her before, but she suspected he was now.

Very angry.

He grasped her by the waist and lifted Julia from the bed, cradling her to his chest. She tensed for a moment, but Father didn't seem angry anymore. His chest shook in sobs, and his tears splashed on her cheek. For a long time, he didn't speak. Father rocked her, humming the lullaby Maman sang to her every night.

Julia sank to his chest, barely noting the words wrenched from his lips. He wove the tale of an old enemy who'd killed Maman and injured Julia. He pleaded with her not to risk herself again.

She had no idea how long Father kept talking. Sleep won out all too soon.

****

"Was that wise?" Jack asked solemnly.

"I will not allow Julia to feel responsible for her mother's death. It isn't true, you know. I never told her what dangers there were. She didn't know, and that is my fault. All of this is my doing."

Jack nodded. Even if it wasn't true, on some level, any Warrior father would believe himself guilty for allowing his wife and children to be harmed or killed. "What will you tell her?"

"What I already have." Robert sighed. "And we have to tell her what we are and what we fight. Julia can never remove her amulet now."

"Will you tell her why?"

Robert tensed, his *Blutjagd* burning fiercely again.

"You have to," Jack opined. "Julia has to know the risks she—"

"Perhaps someday," Robert conceded.

"Father—"

"Do you wish to terrify her?" he demanded. "The beast fed, Jack. It fed on *her*."

"I know."

"Can you tell a baby that she was fodder for a demon?"

His gut twisted at the thought of saying the words to Julia. "No." Jack chanced a searching look at his father. "Have you reached the Lord Armen?"

Robert nodded. "The Stone assures us that the changes are not what we feared. It isn't like a beast giving his blood. Julia may be stronger than the average woman, faster, more sensitive to the beasts. In fact, she may become a sensitive, for all we know. But she won't be cursed."

Jack sighed in relief.

"Your gamble paid off. I owe you your sister's life."

It was the highest honor a Warrior could pay another, owing someone the life of his precious daughter...or his mate. Jack just wished he felt worthy of it.

Chapter One

May 12th, 1967

Julia patted the amulet settled in the inside pocket of her suede jacket nervously. When her father learned she had ditched her brothers again to get laid, he'd have her shackled to Alan and Jack for the rest of her life.

She grimaced. *Until he manages to foist me off on James Armen, that is.*

Was it her fault that Julia didn't fit the mold of the perfect Warrior daughter? Her father was Robert Lord Landwirt, and Julia was the youngest child in a family of five brothers. That in itself wasn't unusual. The fact that Robert had a daughter at all was a blessing on him and their house.

It was a blessing for her father but a curse for Julia. Her brothers had been given a duty to protect her. In short, that meant any hopes of a normal life were smashed to bits. Dating was impossible. Losing her virginity meant running away from home, and the two other men she'd slept with in her short life were no better.

Julia smiled wryly and sipped her beer. She would get laid tonight. It was a moral imperative that she succeed before her brothers tracked her down. Father intended to marry her off to James Armen, to convince her that marrying the Warrior was the best option for her.

Her hope was that James would decide a mate who was as much trouble as Julia intended

31

to be wasn't worth the trouble. A Warrior as dull as James certainly wasn't worth Julia's time. Even if Robert somehow forced her to accept this marriage, Julia would make a statement to James tonight that he wasn't going to forget soon. The Warriors took their pleasure whenever they cared to. Julia would take back seat to a Warrior when the Christian hell froze over!

"Buy you a drink?" a male voice asked.

Julia glanced at the man beside her. He was a few inches taller than her five feet seven, blonde, slim, and clean-cut. In short, he was the antithesis of everything she liked. It was ironic that Julia loathed the Warrior attitude but lusted after their general look.

"Sorry," she commented. Let him think what he wanted. Julia wasn't in the mood to offer explanations to anyone. Realizing that she wanted to fuck a Warrior was disconcerting enough. Hell, it annoyed her.

An arm draped over her shoulder. "What about me, Honey?"

Julia stiffened, turning to face him. This one was more like it. He had dark brown hair and dark eyes, muscular arms and chest, and stood over six feet tall. Unfortunately, he was also a presumptuous jerk, which placed him in the bad attitude category.

"Take your hands off of me unless you are invited," she growled in warning, imitating Jack's detached battle face as perfectly as she could.

"Nice accent, Baby. You're not from around here."

Julia smiled sweetly. "No. I'm from somewhere where men know what happens if they touch me when I've asked them to leave me alone."

The man drew her closer to his chest. "What happens, Sweet Thing? You sic your brothers on me?"

She sipped her beer again and set it down on the bar. Her elbow crashed into his chest, knocking him several feet back. Julia stepped away from the bar and sent her fist into his jaw. The man hit the floor with a resounding thud that shook the wood beneath her feet.

"I don't need my brothers," she informed him coldly. Women weren't trained as Warriors, but Paul and Jack had decided she needed some form of training if she was going to keep sneaking off on them.

"Hey," another male voice protested.

Julia knocked him off of his feet with a solid kick to the solar plexus, then swung around to aim a punch at the third man in their group, closing on her with what she assumed he thought was stealth. She almost laughed at that, at the stealth humans thought they were capable of. They needed an education in Warrior stealth, in her not so humble opinion.

Another fist landed before hers, and Julia nearly fell on her face in surprise. It was fast— too fast—and her heart raced in denial. Strong hands steadied her, and a large body stepped between Julia and her attackers.

"Stay at my back," a deep voice whispered to her, the traditional Warrior order in battle.

33

Julia felt her lungs seize in dismay. She took a single step back, taking in the long, black leather jacket, dark jeans, and armored boots. *Not a Warrior,* she begged. Julia ran her fingertips along his waist, covering the hilt of his sacred weapon with a shaking hand.

He covered her hand, squeezing lightly in comfort—or in warning. "Now Chuck," he chided. "You know I can't allow you to attack a lady—especially from behind."

"You call that wildcat a lady?" he protested.

"She is a woman, a beautiful one at that. Wildcat or not, three men against her is deplorable."

Julia felt her cheeks heat. *Beautiful?* She shifted against his back. Whoever this Warrior was, she liked him. He was irreverent and kind...and had a sense of humor, nothing at all like James Armen.

"Get her out of here, Kord," a new voice spoke up. "You can trust him, miss. Kord will see you to where you need to go."

She nodded. "I know."

The Warrior backed to the door, his hand stroking her knuckles in a calming gesture. He didn't turn to her until they were on the street.

Julia feasted on his rather unconventional looks. His dark hair reached his collarbones and laid more like a mane than a proper cut. She gasped as she reached his eyes. He was a Maher. The deep blue eyes were unmistakable, and no house but Maher had them. Kord was of average height for a Warrior—six feet three or four—but leaner than most.

Her body tingled as he continued to stoke her knuckles. Wild ideas of enticing Kord to take release with her filtered through her mind. This might be her only chance for it. Any Warrior who knew who she was wouldn't dare touch her without her father's permission. Kord didn't know who she was, and so he could and probably *would* take her up on an offer of a night with her.

Kord's mouth curved up, and he arched an eyebrow at her.

Julia felt her cheeks heat. He was most likely waiting for her to tell him where to escort her. "Sorry," she stammered. "Thank you, Kord."

"Is your hand all right? That was quite some punch."

"Fine. My older brother believes in women being able to defend themselves." *After the way we lost our mother, that is to be expected.* Merilee hadn't known how to fight. Julia would never allow herself to be so compromised.

He raised her hand to his mouth and kissed the rising bruise that would most likely be gone by morning. "Where can I take you?"

Now or never. Julia stepped into the shelter of his body. "Know any close hotels or motels?" she purred.

****

Kord hardened as her body pressed to his. She smelled of sweet arousal and a musk-laden perfume. He sensed her, smiling at the fact that she was nowhere near high cycle.

35

"You don't owe me this," he whispered. Honor demanded that he make sure she knew that. "You were doing fine on your own."

"I know. I want you, Kord."

He nodded, relieved. He'd bagged his prey just before dawn, and there was no sign of beasts he might have to engage in the area. Taking release would be the perfect way to blow off excess tension before he returned to his own range.

But that left one more thing he had to know. "What's your name?"

"Julia." Her fingers trailed down his stomach to the belt at his waistline.

The burn of needing took up a fever pitch in his blood. Kord shivered in response. The need to take release had always been particularly strong in him, as it was in most Mahers, but the need to taste more of this fiery woman was near maddening.

Kord stroked at her hip. "You would willingly go to a motel with a man you just met, when you know he's armed?" He reminded her of the danger inherent in the situation, though Kord posed no danger to her. On some level, he worried about Julia. What she was doing wasn't smart.

Julia smiled widely. She guided his hand to the small of her back. Kord played his fingers over the hilt of a small knife.

"You want to go to a motel with a woman you just met, who is also armed?" she teased. Her voice held a lilting tone, something that smacked lightly of Old World, but it was muddled, as if she had traveled extensively during her formative years.

Kord slid his hand under her jacket, encircled the hilt, then pulled her closer to him with the grip. "Let's go. My car is this way."

She nodded slowly. "Please tell me you're not the once a night type."

"Never. If I was, I think you might be able to cure me."

Julia laughed. Kord escorted her to his Corvette and got her settled inside, the glow of sexual promise circulating through him.

He couldn't keep his eyes off of her for long. Julia was stunning. Her black curls were caught up in a ponytail behind her head. They shimmered in the light filtering through the car windows and from the dashboard. Julia wasn't rail thin; her curves were ample and inviting.

She turned her dark gaze on him, making his cock throb all the more. He snapped his gaze back to the road. It wasn't just that luscious body and eyes that cut through him that made Kord want her. There was something about a woman capable of taking out three large men that fired Kord's interest. Julia *would* have taken them all down. There was no doubt of that.

At the motel, Kord ushered Julia up the outside stairs and into his room. He was always welcome to use one of the Armen homes when he trailed a beast into their range, but Kord preferred a hotel or motel for the solitude. There were no lords to hassle him at a hotel, no pressure for him to conform to anyone else's expectations of him.

Kord rushed over to the bed and grabbed the jeans he'd worn to breakfast before he fell into bed that morning. He tossed them on top of his duffle, his cheeks heating at the sight of Julia hiding a smile behind her hand. No rules had definite down sides.

He cleared his throat. "Sorry about that. I wasn't expecting company."

She pulled off her jacket and tossed it on the same chair. "It's refreshing. My brother is so anal, it's disgusting. I prefer a little chaos, personally."

"Hmmm... One point against your brother. And he was doing so well," he mused.

Julia laughed outright and started peeling her shirt toward her shoulders.

Kord crossed the room to her and pulled her hands away from the fabric. "Let me."

She unbuttoned his shirt, while he stripped away clothing to uncover every inch of tanned skin he could. He stroked his hands over her body, clothed and unclothed.

Her bra and panties set nearly submarined any remaining self-control he possessed. Kord had expected something racy, but the red lace set, so insubstantial that they were see-through, all but brought Kord to his knees.

He stood, transfixed, as Julia slid his jacket and shirt off his shoulders and let them fall. She laid a kiss against his ribs, while nimble fingers went to work on his belt. Julia dropped it to the floor with his jacket, then went to work on his jeans.

Kisses rained down on his shoulders and chest, while she peeled his jeans away. Julia closed her hand around his cock, stroking him. She sucked in her breath. "Oh, yeah."

It came out a wisp of air against Kord's chest, and he swallowed a groan. He sought out her mouth urgently. Julia didn't disappoint him. She was the embodiment of the fire in his blood.

Too long. Kord had been without release, save self-release, for ten days—the entire time he'd been on trail. It was longer than his usual, but not long enough to make him this crazy, he was sure. It normally took between two and three weeks to make him this hungry for release. Of course, it took the normal Warrior well over a month.

"Do you want me to use a condom?" he offered. Kord hoped she would refuse it. Kord knew she was safe, but Julia probably didn't. If she asked, he'd do it to make her comfortable.

Julia shook her head. "Not unless you like them. It's not the right time for me to get pregnant," she dismissed his concerns.

Kord nipped at her chin, pulling at the upper edge of her panties, fighting back the fever—so like the tang of *Blugjagd* that drove the hunt and yet so different. In Kord, the urge to release was even more powerful than his need to hunt.

"Now," he growled. "I need you now."

"Yes." Julia grasped at the panties bunched in his hands and ripped the side seam. "Now."

He hissed out a breath as the material dropped away, ringing one thigh like a garter. She spread her legs in invitation. Kord lifted her up his body, smiling as Julia shivered and pressed her body to his. Her nipples were erect against the lace teasing his chest.

Kord lowered her around the head of his cock. "You've had sex before?" he inquired, belatedly remembering to ask.

Julia met his gaze. "What?" Her voice was thick in arousal.

"Are you a virgin?"

She shook her head. "No. I'm not."

"Good." Kord thrust into her, pushing down on her hips as he forced himself into her heat and tightness.

Julia wrapped her legs around his hips, and her fingers tightened on his arms. She cried out as he thrust again. "Yes, Kord. Oh, please."

He took her hard and fast, losing himself in the look of rapture on Julia's face. She climaxed. Kord uttered several curses as he followed her over. He hadn't climaxed so quickly since he'd been a first night.

Julia kissed his chest, nuzzling a male nipple. She bit lightly, and his cock jerked against her inner walls.

****

"What are you doing?" Kord asked in a voice comprised of one part arousal and two parts amusement, by her estimation.

Julia bit again, moaning as he hardened further, filling more of her, stretching her around his girth. "Testing your stamina," she teased.

He marched to the bed and settled Julia on the mattress. With her knees pushed wide, he seated himself even deeper inside her. "And the verdict is?"

She scraped her fingernails over his nipples, smiling as his cock pulsed inside her. Kord had incredibly sensitive nipples. He also had the most impressive cock she'd taken, though she admittedly lacked the experience Warriors had with sheer numbers of partners.

"I'll let you know after the fourth or fifth time," she informed him.

Kord went rigid, his eyes narrowing. "You're not a—" He shook his head. "No. You're not."

"Not a what?" she prodded him.

"Why didn't you question my weapon?"

Julia blushed. "I've... Well, I've met a few Warriors in my life, Kord."

He swore viciously and pushed away from her, leaving her on the mattress, empty and confused.

Kord started pacing the floor, his cock going soft. "Of course. I should have realized. You're a Warrior nymphette." He swore again.

"Excuse me?" Julia demanded. "I'm a what?" *What did you just call me?*

Kord shot her a look of mistrust. "Nymphette. They're also called Blade Chasers. I'm sure you've heard the term before."

Julia gaped at him, stunned that he was saying something so crass to her.

He kept going, now that he was on a roll. "So how many of us *have* you bedded? What is your personal record for number of times in a night?"

Kord stopped and waited for her to form an answer to his accusations.

"How dare— None. Well, you. That makes one Warrior and one time."

"What?" Kord asked, his brow furrowing and his fists unfurling.

"One, you stone-deaf creep." Julia pushed off the bed and started collecting her clothes. "I'd said I *met* Warriors, not that I'd fucked them." She pulled her shirt on over her head. "Honestly, I'd never been interested in it. They were always too strait-laced for my tastes. They were jerks. Should have known that you were all alike underneath."

"Now, just a damn—"

Julia pulled off her torn panties and aimed them at Kord's head. Kord ducked them and caught them in one hand.

She turned away, frustrated that even that went wrong. "Souvenir for you, *Warrior*. What's your record? How many women have you bedded? I'll put my money where my mouth is. You were my fourth. My first Warrior. And my last, I assure you." She stuffed one leg in her jeans.

Kord's hands wrapped around her waist, and he nestled his thigh to her buttocks. "I apologize."

"As well you should. Now take your hands off me," she warned.

He trailed his lips down the line of her throat, making her bite back a moan. And a protest.

"Don't leave, Julia." His fingers inched up her abdomen under her shirt, and he teased her nipples through her bra. "Let me prove that I'm different."

Julia took a calming breath. "No man is different."

"If that was true, Billy or Chuck would be here with you." He pinched one nipple lightly, then nipped at her neck. "You're excited."

Julia couldn't deny that. Her body was on fire for him. She shifted, moaning as his erection pressed to her lower back. Julia reached back and closed her hand in his hair. "Prove to me that you're different," she invited.

"What do all Warriors have in common?" he whispered. He took her earlobe between his teeth and nipped lightly.

She shivered and licked her lips. Thinking was abruptly difficult. "Giving orders."

"Okay then," Kord purred. "Command me."

Chapter Two

May 13th, 1967

Kord smiled at the sight of Julia sleeping next to him. He was tempted to wake her to make love to her again.

He furrowed his brow. When had he stopped thinking of it as taking release and started thinking of it as making love? Certainly not when he offered to be her love slave.

He shivered at the memories. What a splendid imagination Julia had!

No, it hadn't been that early. Kord had wanted her when he made the offer. Her candor and temper excited him. It still excited him, but he had considered it sex then.

Kord let Julia order him through three increasingly heated romps. Then, he took control.

That was when it was. Everything had changed in that moment.

There'd been no rush, no games. Kord had lay over her, his fingers threaded with Julia's, as he took her in slow, sensuous strokes. His kisses had been tender and his body completely relaxed into the loving.

An idea took shape, an idea that heated his arousal again. Julia knew what the Warriors were. She was obviously a saved, though—just as obviously—not a survivor of feeding. Julia bore no feeding marks and didn't wear an amulet.

44

Kord palmed a breast and stroked it, distracted by visions of something more with Julia. Would she agree to see him again? Would she agree to marry him, if Kord asked her to? If this *was* printing, of course.

He licked at the nipple straining into the air, as Julia's mouth curved in a smile.

Yes. Kord could easily picture this as printing. The idea of never wanting another woman came readily to mind. Most Warriors didn't print nearly this young—at least not since the first days of the war—but Kord's weakness, if he could be said to have a weakness, was his need to release. Release and printing were so intertwined that increased need for one could indicate increased need for the other.

Julia turned toward him and started stroking him. She purred in seeming contentment. "Warriors sleep during the day," she reminded him.

"With you naked in my bed? Never."

She squinted at the clock on the nightstand, then dropped her head back and groaned. "I have to go. My brother is going to kill me."

"Strike two against your brother." Kord nipped at her breast. "I need to ask you something."

Someone pounded at the door, and Julia stiffened. Kord laid his head on her breast with a grumbled curse. Five minutes! He'd only needed five minutes to make it clear to her that he wanted more. Whoever was at the door was a dead man.

The pounding started again. "Kord! Open the damn door. I need to talk to you."

"Coming," he shouted back. Kord grimaced. *Not anytime soon.* He laid a kiss on Julia's lips. "Be right back."

He dragged his jeans on and buttoned them over his insistent cock. Then he stomped to the door and yanked it open. "This better be good, James," he growled. Anything that took him away from the goddess in his bed had damned well better mean the extinction of the beasts, as a whole. Belatedly, Kord noted the strange Warrior at James's side and nodded to him stiffly.

"Can we come in?" James asked urgently.

Kord dropped his shoulder against the door frame as James started to move. "No."

The Warrior with him grimaced, most likely at the implications of his half-dressed, mussed, sex-scented state. "Sorry," he grumbled.

James rolled his eyes. "Don't be. If there wasn't one in bed with him, it would only be because she left already."

Kord scowled at him. "If you're quite through, would you mind getting to the damned point?" he groused. He prayed Julia wouldn't hold the crass comment against him.

James motioned to his tag-along. "Jack Farmer, this is Kord Maher. He's the best tracker the Warriors have to offer."

Jack nodded grimly. "Your grandfather has offered your services, while we're in Armen range."

Kord bit back a smile. He wouldn't have to return to Maher range today. He could see Julia again. "Who am I tracking?"

James sighed. "Lord Farmer, Jack, and Alan are all visiting Armen range—the manor house. Jack's sister snuck out sometime during the night and hasn't come back."

Kord winced. "Does she do this often?"

Jack shook his head. "Only three times in as many years. Well...four now."

He sighed. "Where would she go? Where has she gone in the past?"

"To pick up a man for the evening, but she normally has her fun and comes back while we're still searching for her. Our father doesn't make dating easy, as you can imagine. We've been searching pool halls, bowling alleys, bars—"

"Doesn't she realize how dangerous that is?"

Jack darkened a few notches. "Julia is almost as deadly as a Warrior is."

Kord's heart stuttered. His mind whirled, as bits of information fell into place.

Julia is highly trained. She carries a knife.

She has a muddled European accent.

She's slept with four men, counting me, and Jack's sister has disappeared to find a man to sleep with four times.

Oh, shit. No.

She doesn't wear an amulet.

No, I didn't see an amulet.

"Kord?" James asked. "Kord, you still with us here?"

"Stay here. I'll be right back." Kord made his way back into the room and ambled to the chair.

He picked up her jacket and started patting down the pockets. His *Blutjagd* stirred as he pulled the amulet from an inside pocket.

He glanced at Julia, unsurprised that she'd dressed while he'd been talking to James and Jack. She'd probably started dressing the minute he'd left the bed. Julia groaned when he threw the amulet onto the mattress next to her.

"Maybe I'll get lucky and he'll kill me," Kord mused. *When has fate ever been that kind to me?* He snatched up his boots, belt, t-shirt, and jacket, then stormed back to the door before Julia could form a response.

James looked up, backing off a step in shock. "Kord, you can dress before—"

Kord handed his belt off to James, then dragged his shirt over his shoulders. He pulled his jacket on. James tried to hand his weapons belt back, and Kord shook his head. "Give Jack your keys."

James hurried to do so, shooting Kord a look that said he thought he'd gone insane. "What is going on, Kord?"

"I place myself in your custody, James. Deliver me to Lord Farmer. Jack—" Kord swallowed a sour wave. "Get your sister out of my room before I forget the Rules of Sanction and throttle her."

Kord turned on his heel as both men paled. He headed down the stairs to his Vette as Jack launched through the door to the motel room. He'd pulled on his boots by the time James joined him. Kord handed over his keys to James, avoiding the other man's gaze.

James sighed. "She didn't tell you who she was. Did she?"

Kord glanced up at the room, just in time to see Jack slam the door shut. He led his sister toward the stairs, Jack red-faced in fury and Julia crying. Her brother's *Blutjagd* spiked, and Julia cringed. Jack reined it in.

He looked away, his heart aching. "No. She didn't tell me. I may be stupid, but I'm not that stupid, James."

"Good. Then Lord Farmer has to show leniency."

Kord snorted. "It would be kinder if he killed me. My grandfather is going to kill me, and he won't be as nice about it as Lord Farmer will."

James didn't reply to that.

Kord stared out the window. *It would be kinder if he killed me. In five more minutes, I would have proposed to her.* He swallowed a lump of pure pain.

****

Julia stared at her hands as Jack drove, trying to ignore his seething anger.

"Do you have any concept what you've done to him?" her brother demanded.

She sobbed.

"Do you?"

Julia nodded. She knew Warrior law well enough.

"Even if Father is lenient with him, his own house will not be. The Mahers aren't kind to their own. They are ruthless. You've *destroyed* him. He will never recover from this; he'll be a laughingstock forever, thanks to you. For what? So you could enjoy a piece of Warrior cock?"

"It wasn't—"

Jack glared at her. He had always been the one who understood her best, the one who bent the rules for her. Lying to him was impossible.

"In the beginning, it was," she admitted.

"In the beginning? Then what?"

"I don't know. Have I ever chosen to spend the night before?" She hadn't, and they both knew it. Her usual MO was a quick fuck and then hurry home before her father could get too angry about it.

Jack's hands tightened around the steering wheel. "You don't *know*? Saying it's different now than it was when you hooked up with him implies something changed. Are you falling for him?"

Julia squirmed uncomfortably. She'd felt something beyond her libido in that room. When Kord took her the last time, something in him melted her. Julia never dreamed the tireless lover with a taste for kink could be so gentle. There had been something unexpected in his eyes, and when he'd said he wanted to ask her something, she'd hoped—

Jack's eyes widened, and he shook his head in disbelief. He swore solidly for several minutes.

"Six languages," she noted miserably. "You usually restrain yourself to three. You even threw in curses in the language of the ancients. I must have really screwed up." It was an old joke between them. Warriors seemed incapable of

50

sticking to one language when they were on a roll.

"You have to tell him. Kord thinks this is all some sick game you're playing."

"It won't matter. He hates me. He hopes Father kills him."

"He *needs* to know. Kord is too proud to admit it, but you hurt him. Give him the courtesy of knowing you're hurting too."

She nodded, but she wasn't convinced that Jack was right this time. Julia had hurt him. She saw it in those beautiful blue eyes when he threw the amulet at her. Then, his expressive eyes had gone cold and hard. Nothing she said would touch him now.

****

Kord strode into the manor house with James at his heels. He nodded to Carrick Lord Armen stiffly.

Carrick smiled grimly. "Thank you for coming, Kord."

Kord's face flamed. "Don't thank me, Lord Armen. You may well banish me from your range in five minutes."

"Why would I—" He stopped on a gasp as the door opened again.

Kord stiffened, resisting the urge to look at Julia.

Jack stepped up next to Kord. "We need to talk," he whispered.

Kord shook his head. "There's nothing to talk about. I humbly submit to my judge."

Maher Men

Brenna Lyons

"You did nothing wrong," Jack pleaded with him. "It was Julia's fault."

"Listen to him, Kord," James urged him. "There's no reason for you to take the punishment for this."

Kord raised his chin. "That is not your decision to make. Or mine, for that matter. Lord Farmer is my judge. It's a matter of honor that I face him and submit to it. You know that."

Carrick's eyes narrowed. He looked from Kord to Julia and back. "Inside," he growled.

****

It didn't take long for the Armens to call in their men and her family.

Not long enough. When Jack and James hadn't managed to talk Kord down, she'd tried appealing to Lord Armen.

His answer had been short and sweet. "I'm not Kord's judge in this matter."

While it was a good sign that Lord Armen wouldn't be adding charges on, it was unlikely that he was going to intercede.

The moment her father and Alan entered the room, Julia ran for them. Robert enveloped her in a hug.

"This is my fault," she blurted out before he could ask if she was well.

Her father settled her on her feet. "What?"

"I didn't tell Kord who I was. My amulet was in my pocket. Blame me. Not him."

52

His eyes narrowed, and *Blutjagd* simmered in his skin. Julia took a step backward. Had she pushed him past his limits?

"Alan, take Julia to her room."

Her brother's arms closed around her.

Julia fought him. "Wait! I have to give testimony."

"To. Her. Room!"

"As you wish," Alan vowed. He hauled Julia to his shoulder and started walking.

She beat at his shoulder, trying all the while to talk sense to him. *Who am I kidding? Alan has always been too strait-laced for anyone's good.*

He lowered Julia to her feet at her assigned room, then opened the door for her.

There was time for one more plea. "This is wrong, Alan. You know it's wrong."

"He's lord. Not you. Not me. You know that."

Julia bit back a sob and stepped inside. No matter what happened next, she was sure there was no way for her to undo what she'd done. She also knew she'd never see Kord Maher again. Her father would see to that.

"One more thing," Alan offered.

She looked up at him, hopeful that Alan would show his human side for once.

"Take a shower. You won't get a kind glance from Father until you don't stink of your night with Kord."

The door closed between them.

Julia pulled at her blouse, indecisive. On one hand, the outfit was a reminder of a wonderful evening. On the other, it was a reminder of the worst morning of her life. Not to mention, it reeked of Kord, and that was likely to drive her crazy, given the time to.

She stripped off her jacket and clothes and tossed them down the chute to the furnace. Then she reached in and turned on the shower.

****

Kord didn't watch Alan drag Julia away. He couldn't bear to.

She tried to argue his innocence—to the limits of his hearing and beyond, he was sure. It warmed Kord's heart that she would do it. Maybe she felt something for him after all.

A glace in Lord Farmer's direction made it clear he was unmoved by the display. Kord turned his attention to Carrick instead. He couldn't read the old man, but it was better than the cold hate directed at him by Robert.

His judge's *Blutjagd* drew closer. "Where did you meet my daughter, Maher?"

"I interfered in a bar fight she was involved in." Would that help or hurt his cause?

He turned around Kord's body, coming face-to-face with him. "About?"

"She turned down a man who didn't appreciate being turned down. He and his friends decided to take offense."

"Did you act as judge, in my place?"

"I didn't know she was protected. Her amulet was—"

"In her pocket," he growled.

He nodded. Julia had already admitted that. *No help, by the looks of it.*

"What then?"

"She made an offer I had no reason to refuse."

"And you took her to...? Gods help you if you say you fucked my daughter in a car."

Kord shook his head. "I have a motel room. We went there." Not that he'd never fucked a woman in a car, but Kord had known Julia was higher-classed than that right away. *Besides, she asked for a room somewhere. I wouldn't have refused her.*

Robert's sour scowl said he didn't consider it good enough. "How many times?"

Kord's throat closed up, and he cleared it before answering. "Five," he reported.

The first two punches came in quick succession, both to his left cheek. The next three were to his midsection.

I'm probably lucky he didn't take a groin shot as well. Kord stood there, doubled over, gasping for breath.

He did the mental math. Five sexual encounters and five blows. Did Robert intend to let Kord pursue printing with Julia?

Do I want to pursue it? He certainly was a lot more open to the idea now than he'd been on the drive to Armen manor.

Before Kord could work his way to an answer to the question, Robert started issuing orders.

"You touch my daughter again— You come within a hundred yards of Julia, and I will gut you and deliver your balls to your lord."

Kord nodded. "I understand." He straightened tenderly, swallowing a groan.

"Be out of the city within an hour and a half," Carrick added. "Don't return until Julia Farmer is gone."

"Agreed." At least he wouldn't have to answer to Jason for being banned from Armen range entirely.

James handed his weapons belt back, and Kord took his leave with a dip of his head. It took all his fortitude not to glance at the top of the stairs on his way out.

****

Kord unlocked his motel room and pushed through the door into it, looking around in misery. He still had an hour of the time Lord Armen had given him to clear out.

Not that I need that much time. He could have all his gear collected and be on the road in ten minutes.

At the same time, what was the hurry? It wouldn't be a welcome homecoming. Not even his successful track would be acknowledged. By the time Kord arrived, Lord Armen and Lord Farmer would have spun their side of the story to Lord Maher, and his grandfather and father would take it out of his hide within minutes of him walking through the door.

He didn't want to waste time. Kord's resistance to the idea had nothing to do with honor or the concept that the sooner he took his beating, the sooner he would heal from it. Simply put, he wanted to get away from Julia Farmer as soon as possible. The further from her he was, the better for his sanity...and hopefully, the sooner he could try to forget the woman ever existed.

Kord ambled around the room, grabbing his clothing and gear. With each item he shoved into his duffle bag, he endeavored to bury the reason he was packing up a little deeper.

Until he came to the ripped panties on the floor. Kord stared at them, reliving the moment when Julia tore them off. His cock stirred, and he was abruptly aware of Julia's scent permeating the room. *More than just her scent. Her arousal. Her climax. Our mixed scent from sex.*

Fuck this. If her brother had seen the torn panties, I wouldn't have even made it to my true judge. Kord snatched them up and stomped to the closest waste basket, determined to throw them away.

He hesitated with his hand over the waste basket, his muscles refusing his rightful order to open. Kord pleaded with the gods to give him the strength to do this. He couldn't have something of hers as evidence of the truth he wanted to deny. He had feelings for Julia, and focusing on her scent and memories of her might well send him to a mad cabin. If that happened, he would definitely never hear the end of it.

Kord tried to toss it away again, but he couldn't do it. Muttering curses the whole way, he returned to the duffle bag, stuffed the panties inside, and finished packing. With one last look around to assure himself he hadn't forgotten anything, Kord closed the room behind him and headed for his Vette.

He glanced at his watch. *Twenty minutes. I can be halfway out of the state by the time my hour is up.*

He sighed. Kord would like to claim it was in relief, but he knew he'd be lying to do so.

****

It didn't surprise Kord to see his oldest brother waiting for him when he parked his car at the side of the manor house. Falken stood at the top of the stairs, glaring down at Kord, his arms crossed over his broad chest.

Kord ignored Falken's unspoken warning and hefted his duffle out of the back seat. He climbed the stairs to the side entrance, feeling weary in a way that had nothing to do with lack of sleep or a long track.

"What the hell did you think you were doing?" his brother growled at him.

"Did Jason and Calvin both die while I was gone?" he replied acidly.

Falken's forehead crinkled in confusion. "What?"

"Well, if they haven't, you aren't my true judge. Not only do I *not* have to answer you, I really shouldn't, and you should know better than to ask."

Falken shoved against Kord's shoulder. Kord didn't take the bait. He scowled at Falken, rounded him, then kept walking.

Kord had only made it three steps inside the foyer door, when both his father and grandfather appeared on the library side of the room. Berne came through the kitchen doorway, and Falken came in behind Kord.

He sighed and shook his head. "I don't suppose you'd let me get a shower before we do this?" he asked.

Jason shook his head. "I don't see why I would. You're just going to have to shower again later."

Kord abandoned his duffel on the floor, then unclasped his weapons belt and dropped it on top of the pile. He waited for some indication of what would come next.

Calvin strode to him and laid a two-fingered slap against the overlapping bruises on his cheekbone. "Robert took his pound of flesh, I see."

He nodded.

"You never thought to *ask* who you were sleeping with?"

As if you've never picked up an anonymous woman in a bar room. "It's more accurate to say I didn't think to ask if a woman *not* wearing an amulet was a visiting Warrior daughter I didn't even know was in town."

"Well, now you know, don't you?"

In other words, the fact that she hid her amulet from me doesn't mean a thing to them. "Yes. I do."

Jason snorted at that. "You'll know better once we're done with you."

Kord forced his hands not to fist. "You're the judge."

"And I won't be nearly as kind as Robert Lord Farmer was."

I knew that. "I am at your whim."

His grandfather walked toward Kord, every muscle strung tight. "You have blackened the name of Maher. Before I'm done, you'll learn never to do that again."

Kord opened his mouth to offer another platitude from Warrior law. It never emerged. Jason's punch knocked him off his feet, and he slid a full body-length across the marble floor. He pushed himself up, wiping blood off his mouth and jaw. Kord turned back to Jason, waiting for the next blow.

Maybe I'll get lucky, and he'll *kill me.* Kord knew better. There were too few Warriors in Maher range to kill him over something that wasn't a capital offense. He would live, and he would regret living.

Chapter Three

May 20th, 1967

Julia gasped at the feeling of fingers skating between her thighs. Long hair teased at her throat, and two fingers thrust home. She moved, bringing her neck in close contact with soft lips.

She didn't question who was in bed with her. "Kord." He'd come back to Armen range for her.

"Be quiet, Julia," he breathed. "You don't want anyone to hear us."

She didn't. Gods forbid her father overhear them having sex in the Armen manor. *Or anywhere else, for that matter.* Kord would lose his head, for certain.

He thrust his fingers in and out, massaging her toward release. She swallowed moans of delight she dared not vent.

"Let me know when you want more." His voice was pure seduction.

Julia nodded.

"Yes?" he teased.

"More, Kord. Please." It came out a series of fractured gasps.

His hand retreated, and he shifted. His cock slid home.

Julia teetered on the edges of a potent climax, her breathing going ragged.

And snapped awake, tangled in the sheets. Her body protested the whispers of climax she wouldn't be able to claim. She knew that from the last two nights. She dreamed of Kord and woke up wanting him, over and over.

The door flew open and someone stepped inside the room. "Are you all right, Julia?"

"Go away, Jack." What part of her not wanting to talk to any of the men in her family didn't they understand?

He didn't comply. Her brother closed the door and came to the side of the bed. Julia didn't doubt that he could smell her arousal, but hopefully he wouldn't comment on it.

"Taking release to memories of Kord?" He seemed amused by that.

I wish. That would at least be enjoyable.

She wanted to claim outrage that he would say such a thing, but it wouldn't be believable. *When has Jack ever walked on eggshells around me? Wait!* "Why do you think this has anything to do with Kord?"

He smiled. "I heard you say his name from the hallway. Guess you didn't know you have a tendency to talk in your sleep."

She didn't lie to say she was stroking off...or offer the truth, either. It was none of Jack's business.

"Or maybe it was a sex dream. Printing Warriors sometimes have sex dreams where they can't climax." He sniffed loudly, no doubt noting that she hadn't. "Hmm... This could be serious. Maybe I should inform Father—"

"Don't you dare!" Julia reasoned that her father couldn't do any worse to Kord. The damage had been done and judgment rendered.

"My sex life is none of Father's business. Or yours, for that matter."

"If Father knew—"

"What? He would offer me to Kord, like some consolation prize on a television game show? It won't matter, Jack. Even if I wanted that, Kord has washed his hands of me." *Warriors are notoriously proud. He won't relent now that he's made a decision.*

"I think you're wrong about that, and I think you're lying about not wanting Kord."

Her oldest brother knew her too well. Lies stuck in her throat. "Go away, Jack. Get out of my rooms."

He sighed. "Don't do something stupid, Julia. Just...don't." He left her room and shut her in again. As she expected, he didn't move away.

They have a guard on me at all times. It was unacceptable. The whole situation was intolerable.

Now Jack thinks I'm printing? *Is that even possible?* Her state of unease said it was.

Realization came in a flash. Kord had refused her. She just had to break printing to escape this madness. If she couldn't have Kord—and that was a given—breaking printing was the only choice she had left.

I can't go to a mad cabin. That would snap her father. He would probably get himself killed trying to make Kord pay for a situation that had never been his fault.

Not to mention, her father would try to interfere in the process, and Julia was sure she wouldn't deal well with that.

He has no right to order me around this way. There were limits to what a Warrior could order a freed daughter of the house to do. But as long as she stayed with the Warriors, her father would force the laws to his whims. *Or Jack will...or whatever Warrior husband I end up with.*

Run.

The thought was seductive, simple... *Perfect.*

Just run. Break printing and then forge a life for yourself, outside the Warrior world.

Julia got out of bed. She didn't need to be quiet for this part. She had to make Jack think she was having problems sleeping.

That isn't a lie. He knows that as well as I do.

She pulled out two sets of clothes: one set to wear and the other to carry in her purse. Julia double-checked everything while she packed the clothes into the purse; if she couldn't come back, she couldn't risk leaving something important behind.

That accomplished, she took everything to the bathroom. With the shower blasting, she dressed quietly, hung her amulet on one of the towel hooks, then left by way of the bathroom window.

She wished she could actually ghost, as the Warriors ghosted. Ghosting was just a matter of wanting to be unseen, she'd heard. Julia wasn't going to have a problem with that part. She wanted to be unseen more than she wanted anything else right now. *Well, almost anything.* Kord was the only thing she wanted more, but Kord had been warned away on threat of death.

On the ground, Julia took off at a run. She was known for long showers. It would take forty minutes or so for Jack to realize she'd been in there too long and investigate the reason. By the time the search started in earnest, she'd be on a bus or train.

America was a big place to lose herself in, and she was carrying twice the Warriors' usual 'pocket money' of five hundred dollars. That would be enough to accomplish her task.

****

May 21st, 1967

Kord entered Jason's office. He'd been ordered to report to his house lord, and he dutifully reported. Still, he wondered what snide comments about his recent dishonor he would have to endure this time.

The beatings he'd taken, back-to-back, from his grandfather and father, followed by trial with both of his brothers, had been more than enough to remind for Kord to be sure who he was sleeping with for years...or maybe life. It was also intended to remind him not to dishonor the Maher name again.

But it wasn't enough for Jason and Calvin. The bliss of forgetfulness was not to be his anytime soon, and every reminder of Julia was like another blow to his still-healing ribs.

"You asked for me, my lord?" he asked brightly.

Robert Lord Farmer and Jack turned their heads to track his entrance, and Kord went still, his heart hammering, his mocking smile fading away.

"I haven't gone near her," Kord blurted out. "I haven't contacted her, in any way." He bit back a grimace at how guilty that protest made him sound. And though he hadn't contacted Julia, he wanted to, with every breath he took most days.

"Too bad," Jack breathed.

Kord ground his teeth at that. "While I hate the thought of denying you my head, Jack—"

"Stand down," Jason roared.

Kord raised his hands in surrender. He tried to make sense of Jack's look of shock. Had he really thought Kord wouldn't respond to that threat?

"We don't want your head," Robert stated. "We want your help. You're a tracker, Kord. Without a question, you're the best tracker in North America...possibly in the world."

Kord waved him off. "No. If she's taken off again, she's *your* problem."

Jack darkened, *Blutjagd* burning in his skin. His shoulders and arms tensed beneath his shirts.

Kord glared at him. Jack knew better than anyone why he couldn't do this. Julia had played him. She'd nearly gotten Kord killed with her games.

Jason motioned for Kord's attention. "I've offered Maher's help."

"Then you go. Or my father. Or Berne or Falken. You're all trackers. I was ordered to stay away. I agreed to it, and I intend to live to that vow."

66

"I rescind that judgment," Robert inserted.

A surge of hope built in Kord. What was he offering? He shook that thought away. It didn't matter what the Lord Farmer was offering. Kord didn't want any part of Julia.

Liar. I want a whole lot of that woman.

But I don't want any part of her games.

"I made my vow. I stand by it," he decided. His life was complicated enough without a woman like Julia in it.

"Damn you," Jack exploded. "She's protected. You have a duty to—"

"She's Farmer protected," Kord countered. "I have to save your sister from a beast if she's in my proximity. I don't have to save her from her latest lay of the—"

Jack came to his feet, glaring at him, bloodlust in his eyes. "She surrendered her amulet. Julia left it behind in her rooms at Armen manor last night. She's never done that before."

Kord took a moment to center himself. Why did it bother him that she'd given up her protection? It was a good way for him to refuse to help. "Her stupidity is not my concern." It came out without the heat he'd intended.

Julia is unprotected out there.

It's her own fault. She chose to leave the amulet behind.

"She's been fed from," Robert stated in obvious misery.

Kord's stomach lurched at that. "What? When?"

"When she was four years old."

Jack's eyes filled with pain. His shoulders slumped, and his *Blutjagd* faded.

Kord faltered. Had her brother failed Julia somehow?

Another thought occurred to him. "She doesn't have a mark. She can't have been—"

"She was. Julia was hospitalized for three days after the attack."

Maybe it didn't leave a mark because she was so young? Kord pushed that thought away. He didn't need to know why she didn't carry a mark. He needed to understand Julia.

He caught Jack's gaze and held it. "Why?" he asked.

"Why what?" Robert jumped in.

"Why would she risk it again?"

Jack winced.

Kord let his *Blutjagd* loose. "Why? You tell me, Jack, and you tell me the truth. Now."

Her brother sighed. "Julia had no memory of the feeding. She was young, traumatized. She nearly died of blood loss, and then she was sick in the aftermath. High fever. She lost her mother. She was... My mother was holding Julia when the beast killed her with a null weapon. I wanted to—" Jack looked at his father, darkening.

Kord swallowed a scream of rage. He turned on Robert Lord Farmer, well aware that he was risking his life to confront him. "You never *told* her?" he thundered. "You left her unprepared for the fact that they can track her?"

Robert nodded. "I'd always intended to tell her, but it never seemed to be the right time."

Jason cursed fluently. "That was damned shoddy handling, Farmer."

Kord turned out of the office without a word. He wanted to tear Robert apart with his bare hands. Leaving the room was a smart move, one that might save both their lives.

"Where are you going?" Jack called out.

"To find your sister." *I only hope I find her before a beast does.*

****

Julia shifted the shopping bag on her hip, glancing up at the setting sun. She had intended to be back at the hotel room before sunset, but she'd missed her mark.

Her fear made no sense to her. Without her amulet, she was at no more risk than any other human woman.

Less, considering the dagger Julia carried and her limited training. Jack had Carrick Armen bathe the dagger in the Stone's glow before he gave it to her for her sixteenth birthday. It was as deadly as any sacred weapon was.

Still, she found her free hand fluttering to her bare throat and her gaze flicking to the colored clouds on the horizon. Julia's breathing was strangled, a nameless panic building in her chest. She quickened her step, all but bolting for her hotel room.

As if that will protect me from a beast.

It didn't matter. She had to reach the room. She was more certain of that now than ever.

The impact came abruptly. One moment, Julia was rocketing around a corner, her hand clenched on the bag of food. The next, she was falling, the food scattering, rolling and clattering against the pavement.

Hands closed around her upper arms and wrenched her to her feet before she could crash to the ground. Julia struck out blindly, the pains shooting up her arm from the effort increasing her panic.

That should have driven someone away.

"Settle now." His voice was soothing, calming.

Julia's muscles went warm and lax, as if she hadn't slept in days. Her breathing and heart rate slowed.

He eased her backward, his blue eyes bright in something she suspected was amusement. "That's right."

The brick wall pressed to her back. Julia sagged against it, dimly noting her mounting arousal. The deep recesses of her mind argued that she wanted Kord. A warm wave of sensation washed over her mind, and Julia moaned, trying to grasp at the thoughts slipping through her mental fingers.

His lips closed on hers, claiming her mouth in a heated kiss. He cupped her breast, testing the already-hardened nipples. Visions of him taking her—here and now, thrusting into Julia against the wall—danced in her mind.

"Now," he agreed. His pulled at her jeans, impatient, baring her stomach to the chill evening air.

Julia bit lightly at her lower lip as his hand snaked inside her clothes, his hot fingertips circling her clit, his pace matching her pounding pulse.

She would have screamed when his fingers parted her slit, were it not for the odd tightness in her chest. Only a strangled sob escaped her. It felt wonderful, better than Julia ever dreamed foreplay could feel.

"You're mine, Julia. You know that. Don't you?"

She nodded. She did know it. No one had ever mastered her this way. Another face floated at the edges of a hazy memory, then was swept away.

"Mine," he repeated. That stated, he stripped her jeans partway down her thighs.

Julia touched his chest, marveling that he was nude and ready. Her body pulsed against his fingertips at that.

His cock slid between her thighs as his fingers retreated, taunting her with the promise of a fierce joining. "First, you will scream for me." His voice rumbled out, darkly seductive.

She nodded, gasping as he closed his hands around her hips and positioned her for the first thrust.

His cock pressed to her body, and his mouth teased at the side of her throat. "Then, I will feed. At the height of your pleasure."

Feed? Images of him spreading her legs and sucking at her slit, his tongue delving inside her—

He stiffened.

71

Julia's mind cleared abruptly. The smell assaulted her, the rotting stench that clung to her brothers after a successful hunt. "Beast," she choked.

Her position became clear to her, half undressed and his cock spreading her nether lips. Julia shoved at him with a cry of dismay.

The beast was tossed aside, not by her push, but rather by whatever Warrior had just killed it. She met her savior's gaze, fully expecting to see her father or Jack. Even Alan would be a pleasant relief.

Julia sobbed at the sight of Kord. She pulled at her jeans, finding them shredded from the waistband to the top of the thigh. She tried to turn away from him, her hands shaking. She couldn't face him. Not after that beast touched her.

I let *it touch me.*

Kord wrapped an arm around her. He threaded an amulet over her shoulders with the opposite hand. Julia shook her head, trying to extricate herself from his arms. She held the tattered remains of her jeans together with one hand.

Kord wrapped his leather jacket around her and pulled her to his body by the grip. He hefted her over his shoulder without a word, and she felt him slip the hotel room key out of her back pocket. The warm wash of ghosting enveloped her, crackling under the strain of his *Blutjagd.*

He didn't say a word until the door closed behind them. Kord placed Julia on her feet. He cupped her chin and forced her face up, so he could look her in the eye. She couldn't hold his gaze for more than a moment, and a sob escaped her lips.

Why Kord? Julia would rather have had Jack see her being screwed by a beast than Kord. On closer consideration, she was glad her father hadn't, but Kord was even worse than her father.

He eased his jacket off her shoulders. "Take off your clothes," Kord ordered, his voice low and his expression strained.

Julia tried to flee his grasp, abruptly fearful, though she couldn't state why she would be.

"Julia! You have beast blood on you. Do it in the bathroom before you bathe, if you need to, but get those clothes off so I can get rid of them."

She nodded, backing away slowly. He sighed, releasing his grip on her arms as she calmed herself. Julia retreated to the bathroom and closed the door behind her. She removed her clothing with wildly-trembling hands, then pushed them out the door. From the sounds of it, she guessed Kord was depositing them in a trash bag.

"Bathe, Julia." His voice seemed oddly tense. "I'll be here."

She swallowed another sob. Better that Jack would have seen what happened than Kord.

****

Kord cycled his fist opened and closed, reining in the urge to punch something. *Hard.* Every time he closed his eyes, visions of Julia in the beast's arms seared him.

He ran a shaking hand through his hair and glanced around at the Spartan hotel room. Kord would have to check in soon, and he was no more sure what he was going to tell them about how he tracked her than he'd been when he'd started driving.

She'd done everything right, as far as thwarting a tracker like himself. Julia had obviously squirreled away cash. She'd used public transportation instead of renting a car. She hadn't touched her bank accounts. He'd had nothing to track, as he usually would.

I had her *to track.* But what difference that made, he wasn't sure.

I have to check in. The Hunters would have felt the kill in their range. When all of their own checked in, they would know he'd entered their range.

I don't remember *entering their range.* Something had led him on, something nameless. He'd almost swear a voice had been whispering directions to him, but that made no sense. The Stone didn't speak to Warriors, save the Stone lord. Kord wasn't one. He didn't even have the mark of Syth. All the same, if pressed, Kord would have to admit the only reason he'd found Julia was the intervention of the Stone.

Julia's sobs intensified, then quieted.

She's trying to stifle them. She doesn't want me to hear her cry.

Kord checked his watch. Julia had been in the bathroom for more than half an hour, and she'd refilled the tub twice already.

"Julia—" He snapped his mouth shut, mindful of what he'd nearly asked. *Who am I kidding? She's further from okay than any saved I've ever met.* And he'd met more than his share.

She mumbled something, an answer he didn't consciously note.

Kord went to the door. "Julia? Do you need my help?" *Gods, what will I do if she says 'yes' to that?*

Help her, of course. It was a duty. He would have to follow through.

"Please just go away," she choked out. A muffled curse followed.

He hesitated, torn between his duty to his grandfather and her father and the soul-crushing need to comfort her, no matter what it cost him. Cursing himself as a dead fool, Kord opened the bathroom door and stepped into the room with her, his gaze averted.

Julia gasped, and he flicked his attention to her face. Kord lingered, battling back black rage at the sight of her red-streaked cheeks, swollen eyes, and scrubbed skin. She shook her head, breaking the moment.

Kord walked to the tub, then knelt at her side. He grimaced at the sight of fresh tears rolling down her abused cheeks. "What is it?" he whispered. *What can I do?*

She stared at the washcloth in her hands, her lower lip trembling. "I still feel it." Her voice was a broken whisper. "I still feel the beast's hands on me, touching me. I—I can't—" Her breathing came in ragged ins and outs of her chest.

75

"Shhh." Kord laid a kiss on her forehead, then another over her eyes.

He pulled gently at the cloth clenched in her hands, massaging her knuckles to ease it away from her. Kord wet it in the hot water and started bathing skin she'd rubbed an angry red. He caressed her, as gentle as the beast had been brutal.

Julia opened her eyes, her brow furrowing. "What are you doing?" There was no protest in it. Her voice sounded of a mixture of confusion and exhaustion.

"Washing away the beast's touch," he promised. "Close your eyes." If she kept up the silent pleading with him, he would push for something she wasn't ready for.

Julia closed her eyes; she dropped her head back as he stroked the cloth down her throat. Mentally, he replayed the moment when the beast tasted her, his arms tightening down in frustration.

No. Wash it away. The beast can't touch her again. Never again.

Kord washed her shoulders and arms, paying special attention to her hands. *Forget that they were covered in beast blood*, he pleaded with her silently.

He lingered over the amulet he'd given her, repeating his duty over and over again before he caressed his cloth-covered hand around one full breast and started washing it. Julia's nipples tightened, and her eyes flew open. He went still, waiting for her protest that he'd gone too far. Far from delivering it, she arched into his hand with a groan.

Kord bit back one of his own as his cock lengthened. The press of his jeans against it was sweet torture.

He talked himself down. If he took her, it meant his life. Whether Lord Farmer took it or Lord Maher did was immaterial. One way or the other, Kord would die if he bedded her again.

If I don't take release... If he gave Julia pleasure without sating himself, the punishment would be nothing more than a beating. The beating from Jason might well come close to killing him, but one look at Julia convinced Kord it would be worth it.

He met her gaze, stroking the sensitive tips of her nipples until they came to hard points for him. Julia nodded, encouraging him.

Kord ran his hands down her ribs, then lowered his mouth to her breast. Julia cried out softly, tangling her fingers in his hair the way Kord loved. He played at her body: suckling and licking, nibbling and stroking. Kord urged her thighs apart, bathing the soft flesh between, seeking out the rising heat tipping up to him in anticipation.

Julia's hands tightened in his hair as the soft cloth brushed over her clit. She whispered his name, a clear request for him to continue.

He tossed the cloth away, then eased two fingers into her. Her body clenched at him, inviting him in. Kord released her breast with a groan and sought out her mouth for a kiss.

Just my fingers. No matter how powerful the indications that she wants my cock, I can't give her that.

Julia met him feverishly, her hand dragging up at his black t-shirt as if to pull him into the tub over her.

Maybe into her body.

He left the kiss. "We can't," he reminded her.

She nodded, her face a study in shared torture. Julia didn't beg him to take her, though she surely wanted it. Kord thanked several of the ancient gods for that small favor. The fact that he would willingly forfeit his life if she asked for him again taunted him.

His mind screamed at him to make this memorable, to do something he hadn't done the last time he'd had her. If this was going to be the last time Kord touched her, neither of them would ever forget it.

Julia tightened her grip on his shirt as Kord lifted her out of the tub, cradled in his arms. He ignored the water pouring off her body and down his jeans, striding to the bed of a purpose.

She didn't question his intent when he lowered her to the edge of the mattress, though her gaze strayed to the bulge in his jeans. Kord shivered at the stark hunger in her dark eyes. He knew she wanted to ask him to have sex with her, but she didn't dare to.

Ask. I won't deny you. I can't.

She didn't. He pushed her knees apart, then sank to his knees between them. Julia pushed herself up on her elbows, holding his gaze as she draped her knees over his shoulders.

Unable to hold back, Kord leaned forward and tasted her, his tongue gliding over her, then swirling inside her the sweet depths behind her slit. Julia moved restlessly, twisting and tilting her body around his questing mouth. She tightened her thighs around his face, then edged them apart to give him greater access. Julia grasped at the back of his hair, her breathing going choppy, her breasts shaking with each ragged breath.

Kord felt her climax coming mere moments before she pushed up on her hands, screaming wildly for him. Her taste made his head spin. Kord pressed his cheek to her inner thigh, swallowing the urge to seal his fate by bedding her properly.

Julia groaned his name, her body open to him in offer of more.

He eased away from her, employing the last of his self-control and self-preservation to accomplish it. He lifted her further onto the bed and wrapped the blanket around her. If he didn't do that, common sense might desert him and leave him to die.

That accomplished, Kord turned and picked up the phone from the night stand.

"What are you doing?" Her voice was weighed down in sleep.

"Checking in. Your father—"

Her eyes opened and went wide. She shook her head in seeming terror. "No. You cannot tell my father what happened with the beast. You can't."

"Julia—" *What am I going to say? She's panicked, and I won't survive trying to calm her a second time.*

Tears filled her eyes and spilled over. "No. Please. Just...not that."

"I have a duty." Kord had to file his report. Her father had to know what his shoddy handling had caused. On one level, he had to because he would have to see to Julia's trauma, but Kord took fierce satisfaction in the fact that the Lord Farmer would suffer for his poor choices, just as Kord suffered every time he thought of Julia in the hands of the beast.

Julia shook her head.

Kord dropped the phone back onto the cradle. "You want me to lie to him?" he demanded.

She didn't answer, but she deliberated so potently, he could read her wish to ask that of him on her face.

"I can't lie to them," he asserted. *How dare you suggest that!*

Julia turned from him on the bed, silent sobs shaking her form.

Kord snatched the phone up, his fingers hovering over the dial. His heart ached at her continued games. He should call Maher manor and report to her father immediately.

No. Don't do that.

Kord shook the voice away. It was crazy. It was enough to make him think he was losing his marbles.

Julia is enough to make any man go insane.

Still, he hesitated to dial his home number. Kord sighed. *Fine.* He dialed the Hunter manor instead. The phone rang twice, and the click of the line opening followed.

"Hunter," a young man stated.

Too old to be Stephen. The voice isn't deep enough to be Colin. "Corwyn?" Kord guessed.

"Ah. Kord. We were wondering if the kill was yours."

"It was. There was no time for me to notify you first."

"No problem. Maher let all the North American ranges know you were on the track. Do you have her? Is she unharmed?"

He hesitated, looking at Julia out of the corner of his eyes. He didn't have to tell Hunter anything. "Yes. Tell the Lord Farmer we're on our way."

"Tonight?" Corwyn asked, seemingly confused by that pronouncement.

"The sooner, the better." *Then I can wash my hands of her.* "I'm rested. Tell him... Tell him his daughter will be in his custody as soon as I can get her there." It would take most of the night, but it would save Kord's head to get her out of his hands before he either throttled her or fucked her.

"Done."

"Thanks, Corwyn." Kord set the receiver back in the cradle. He hesitated a moment, then scrubbed his hands over his face.

His heart pounded in outright fear, and he avoided looking at Julia again. How far would he go to protect her? He was already trying to find a way to avoid it.

I have to get out of this before I do something terminally stupid.

"Get dressed, Julia. It's time to go back."

Her expression said she might argue with him.

Or run again. Kord offered her a hand up. "Don't run. Please don't ever take your amulet off again."

She opened her mouth to respond, and he cut her off.

"They can track you, Julia."

"I wasn't fed on," she replied hotly.

"Yes. You were."

She shook her head in denial.

"When you were a toddler, you were. Do you remember when you were sick after your mother died?"

Her face lost much of its remaining color, and she stared at his outstretched hand.

"They never told you. It was wrong of them to hide it from you, I know. You were fed on, and the beasts can track you."

Julia swallowed hard. "How— How did *you* track me?"

"I don't know," he admitted. "I just did."

She nodded. "You should change your clothes too. You're soaked."

Except his clothes were in the car, and Kord didn't intend to leave her alone long enough to get them. "They will dry on the drive home. It's just water."

"In other words, you don't trust me." Oh, she was perceptive.

He didn't trust her. He couldn't. His life depended on remembering that Julia liked games. Kord didn't answer the accusation. Instead, he curled his hand in offer.

Julia pushed the blanket away, rose without his help, and marched across the room to her duffle bag. Kord focused on her delectable ass, then turned his back.

I have to get her back to her father as soon as possible. He took one last peek back at her. *Even then, I may need a mad cabin.*

****

May 22nd, 1967

Julia walked into the Maher training house at Kord's side, forcing herself not to wince at the glares and raised eyebrows of the Warriors in attendance. *My family, his family, and— Oh, joy! The Lord Armen is visiting too.*

Kord was all business. It was hard to reconcile the hard Warrior with the tender man he'd been the night before.

Don't stare. Julia snapped her gaze aside...just in time to catch Jack's look of exasperation.

Her father came down the stairs at a run. He caught her at the base of them in a breath-stealing hug.

"It's...okay, Father," she gasped out. "Let go."

"Are you injured? Injured at all?"

"Can't breathe," she quipped.

His grip loosened, and she dropped to the flats of her feet with a sigh.

"A couple of bruises. Nothing more." *Until Kord tells you the rest. Who knows what will happen after that?*

Her father fired up at her attempt at an assurance, and Kord followed in his wake.

Before either of them could speak, she did. "Which is *your* fault." She'd wanted to say that since Kord told her how she'd been lied to. It was a relief to vent it.

Both of them gaped at her, and her father let his hands drop away from her in seeming shock. He found his voice first. "What?"

"How dare you not tell me I'd been fed on! I have a bull's-eye on my back, and you never told me." She pushed him.

Not that her father moved a millimeter from it. He made an expansive motion with his hands. "You're my daughter. Of course you're a target."

"A target they *shouldn't* have been able to track. You lied to me."

"I didn't," he protested.

"A lie of omission, but a lie all the same."

"Actually, you did lie to her," Jack informed him, his voice cool. "I called you on it then, and you said you would tell Julia later. Always later...every time I asked."

Her father went pale. He moved his mouth as if to speak, and nothing came out.

"You didn't explain the danger she was in when she was young, because you didn't want to scare her. You didn't tell her what the amulet did for her. As a result, she was tricked and fed on.

You didn't tell her she was fed on, and she left the amulet behind. It was a stacked wager, and the odds were in the beasts' favor, which she didn't know, because you lied. As wrong as Julia is to take off her amulet, your lies force her to make rebellious choices she's ill-informed about, which puts her in greater danger. You. Are. Endangering. Her."

Her father's stricken expression was nearly enough to make Julia want to comfort him. *Almost. Not quite.*

Carrick Lord Armen stepped forward, his expression grim. "I can have the Council of Lords convene within the day."

Her father didn't argue it.

"Is that really necessary?" Julia asked, aghast that it had come to this. She'd thought she could raise the subject with him, give him a verbal thrashing, and it would be done with. He could be stripped of his title for this if they convened a Council of Lords.

"It's been necessary since you were four," Jack opined.

"I agree," Kord jumped in.

"While I agree as well, it's not your place, Kord," Jason Lord Maher snapped at him.

Kord opened his mouth—most likely to retort, and Julia overpowered him. "Since Kord had to save me, I'd say he has every right to his opinion about the situation."

She looked around at the males, noting that Alan had joined them at some point during the argument. "For that matter, I want to know who decided not to tell me I'm a sensitive."

Julia had replayed her reactions before the beast attack, again and again. The only reason for her to run in panic the way she had was that she knew a beast was stalking her. She just hadn't known what the sensation meant consciously.

The Warriors went deathly quiet. None of them moved a muscle.

At last, her father stammered out an answer. "We didn't know. I swear it."

Julia crossed her arms over her chest. With all the lies so far, she wasn't sure she should trust her father again. Something told her he was lying to her, so she challenged him to tell her whatever he was holding back.

"They didn't," Carrick confirmed.

"The Stone told you that?" she asked.

"The Stone didn't have to. Your father called me after you were fed on, seeking answers from the Stone. She wasn't overly forthcoming with answers, but she did supply the one Robert was most interested in."

The Stone wouldn't answer? That's always a bad sign. She started to question him.

Jason beat her to it. "And what answer was that?"

Carrick didn't hesitate to offer it. "If Julia would be *Blutjagdfrau.* She isn't, of course."

Julia's patience snapped. "I'm not an ignorant child. Being fed on doesn't make a woman a *Blutjagdfrau.*"

Carrick focused on her. "You are correct, but it wasn't the feeding that your father was afraid of. A simple feeding? He would have assumed you wouldn't be overly-affected."

Her father and both brothers found blank spots on the wall to fixate on.

Her head whirled in what she would like to believe was lack of sleep. Julia's mouth went dry. "What *did* concern him enough to call and ask you that question?" Surely, the beast hadn't tried to feed her on his blood. That would do something much worse than make her a *Blutjagdfrau.*

Jack cleared his throat, but he didn't look at her. "You were bleeding out on Damien's examination table. The only chance I had to save your life was a transfusion. My own blood." He smiled weakly. "I can't regret that choice, Julia. You're alive."

His smile dimmed into a wry shadow. "But my blood did something else to you, and the Stone wouldn't tell us what it did. I had hoped your ability to sense *Blutjagd,* your faster healing, your sexual nature, and your minor successes with light ghosting were the extent of it, but they're not. Not if you're sensing beasts."

Julia grasped at the balustrade, abruptly dizzy. If that wasn't all— *What would have happened if the beast finished? Was the beast who attacked her an elder?* There'd been no indication of that. Surely, Kord would be treated like a hero if he'd killed an elder. *But what if it* had *been an elder and he'd finished? Am I changed enough to carry for them?*

Her father reached for her, and Julia batted his hands away with a grumbled curse. It didn't satisfy her sense of outrage, and she punched him across the cheek. He fell back in seeming shock.

"Don't you dare touch me," she warned him. *Is my temper another side effect of Jack's blood? Is it my version of* Blutjagd? Julia didn't want to know. *Yes, I do want to know. I need to know.*

The tension in the air was too much for her, and Julia made her way up the stairs, her knees shaking.

"Do you want my help?" Kord offered with an air of formality.

Julia looked back at him, her heart aching. She did want Kord's company, almost more than she could bear. *It's just another trick of the blood, my sexual nature.* "Thank you, but...no. I need time. Space." *I need to know what I am.*

Kord tipped his head and retreated.

An insistent voice in her head urged Julia to follow him. She ignored it and walked away.

****

May 23rd, 1967

Kord stood at one side of the room with his father, brothers, and Alan Farmer. Across from them, Julia had been afforded a comfortable chair. Between them, Robert maybe-soon-not-to-be Lord Farmer stood with Jack. At the head of the room, the six remaining lords stood as judges.

They'd been questioning Jack and Robert for the last half hour, and every exchange sounded more damning to Kord. There was little question that Robert wouldn't be lord, given much more testimony. The only real uncertainty was what else the lords would do to him.

"Why didn't you bring this to the Council earlier, Jack?" Gunther Lord Crossbearer challenged.

Jack stiffened a notch. "I knew my father planned to marry Julia to a Warrior if he could. I *thought* he would be honest with Julia and her intended mate, when that happened. Given his reaction when Kord told Julia she'd been fed on, I knew he'd hoped to avoid her finding out, even then. The only reason he told Kord at all was that he was refusing to track her; my father had no choice but to tell him."

"But your sister disappeared four times prior to this time," Carrick pointed out. "For her safety, shouldn't you have sought judgment earlier?"

"This is the first time Julia left her amulet behind. Wherever she disappeared to before, she was still protected by the amulet."

Julia shifted in her chair, and her face went crimson. Kord felt his lips twitch in a scowl. Despite Jack's tactful handling, most—if not all the men in the room knew the reason Julia had disappeared the earlier times.

Finding a man to fuck.

And I'm jealous, damn it! Kord cursed himself as a fool for it. It made no sense for him to be jealous. Julia wasn't his; she would never be his.

"I see."

Kord snapped his gaze away from Julia and focused on Carrick. The old man was staring at Kord, his eyes narrowed.

Carrick moved his attention to Julia with exaggerated care. As Stone lord, he'd taken it upon himself to lead the questioning. "And you, young lady."

Julia cringed, then straightened to meet whatever comment or question he was about to make.

"Why did you run *this* time? Were you seeking yet another cock?"

Kord stamped down his *Blutjagd*. This was unseemly. They knew she wasn't.

What am I thinking? I don't know what she was doing any more than the lords do.

Carrick smiled.

He's taunting me. Because I was the last man she was with, he's taunting me with her drive to find another.

I don't know what she wants any more than Carrick does. Unless the Stone is telling him. Some days, Kord envied Carrick Lord Armen that certainty.

Not always. The Stone likes Her games. He shifted his gaze away. That brought him to Julia again.

She had gone pale, and her hands were gripped tight on the arms of the chair. "What? No! How dare you insinuate that!"

"Then why don't you tell us what you *were* doing?"

"I don't know. I just ran."

Oddly enough, Kord believed her.

"How did you expect to survive without accessing your accounts?" Carrick pressed her.

Julia rubbed at her temple, a tremor working through her hand. "I didn't think that far in advance. Get a job, I guess. I'm educated. I could do that."

"You just ran. No forethought at all."

She nodded.

"Why? I don't understand you."

Neither did Kord, but browbeating Julia over it seemed beyond the pale to him. *It's not my place to say that.*

Julia slid a glance at Kord, then focused on Carrick again. Nearly in unison, all seven of the lords and Jack turned their heads his direction. A peek out of the corner of his eyes revealed that his brothers and Alan had followed suit. There was no animosity in their expressions, but Kord knew they were balancing the fact that she'd run *away* from his position against that glance his direction.

Please, Tes, don't let them think I traumatized her somehow during that first night together.

She snapped. "I ran to get away from overbearing, opinionated males who let me have no say over my own life. You all act like you own me, and I'm sick of being property."

Carrick's expression went pained, though Kord wasn't sure why it would. "I see," he repeated.

Kord was really starting to hate that refrain.

After a moment of silence, Jason stepped into the void. "What did you feel your father was denying you? Or the rest of us were?"

Kord shifted forward a few inches, anxious to know the answer to that. Had *he* made her feel denied? Or was it her father? *Why did she run away from my direction? Was it chosen by chance? The first bus or train she could find? Or was it personal?*

Does it matter? He'd like to claim that it didn't, but it did.

Julia hesitated, and the air went heavy in anticipation. She glanced around the room, pausing momentarily on Jack...then again, in Kord's general direction. It seemed she was staring at the wall above the Warrior's heads.

At last, she met Jason's gaze. "A lot of things I couldn't name until I learned the truth about myself. I don't think I'm built to be a meek Warrior daughter who follows commands from the men."

Kord's heart melted at the truth of it. Julia had a Warrior's drives but a protected's rules. She likely felt shackled by them, smothered.

"Certainly not after your brother gave you his blood," Carrick agreed.

"Not before," Robert corrected. "Julia has always been headstrong. She's always been more of a handful than the boys were. All the more so after the transfusion."

Carrick cocked his head slightly, focusing far away.

He's asking the Stone if it's true. It wasn't unexpected. If Robert felt his son might also be punished, he might be lying to try and save Jack. Since he was already accused of lying, he was just adding a few more blows onto the list.

92

Maybe not. He'd be lying to the Council of Lords, now.

"Yes, I see that," Carrick breathed. He glared at Robert. "Still, you risked your daughter."

Robert tipped his head in acknowledgment. "I was blind, I know. It was cowardly and beneath me to do it. A father should never be unaware of the needs and protection of his children."

"Or a lord of his protected. You know you cannot be lord of your house after this." Carrick stated it as if it were a foregone conclusion.

The nods of the other lords announced they weren't going to argue it.

Robert ground his teeth, then sighed. At last, he drew his sacred weapon, turned the hilt to Jack, and went to one knee before his oldest son.

Jack took the weapon. He didn't waste time. "I am Landwirt now."

His father bowed his head deeply. "I stand, a Warrior of Landwirt. My blade is yours, my duty at your whim. You are my Lord Farmer."

Alan came forward and repeated the ceremony. Jack unsheathed his former weapon and put the lord's weapon in its place. He didn't hand the other weapon to Robert, a sign that he realized the lords hadn't announced they were done with his father yet.

Robert stood and faced his judges again. Jack moved to join them, taking his place as part of the Council.

Carrick nodded grimly. "It occurs to me that, in our rush to call in the Council of Lords, Kord never gave us a full account of his track. I think we should know, in order to properly punish Robert for his trespasses against his daughter."

Out of the corner of his eyes, Kord saw Julia go an unhealthy shade of gray. She trembled wildly, but she didn't try to catch his eye or to beg off.

Does she fear what will happen to her father, if I give my report? Or what will happen to her?

It doesn't matter. It is my duty to report it.

"Kord?" Jason prompted him. The edge in his voice warned Kord that he wasn't happy at instructing him to answer a query posed by the Council of Lords.

He cleared his throat. "I tracked Julia to Hunter range."

"How?" Carrick interrupted him.

"I don't know...precisely. It seems sacrilegious to suggest the Stone had a hand in—"

"Oh, She did. I simply wanted to see if you knew it and if you would admit it. Why do you think the Stone led *you*, when She wouldn't assist any other Warrior, including her family or me?"

"That, I don't know." Would Carrick think he was lying? If he did, what would the punishment be for it? *Probably severe.*

Carrick waved him on.

"The Stone got me close, but the coercion drew me the rest of the way."

"What was the coercion?" Jason asked.

Kord shook his head, though he knew very well what the beast's true aim had been. "I would assume keeping Julia docile. By the time I got there, she wasn't fighting the beast anymore, and her weapon was sheathed." He hadn't lied to them. What he'd said was true. *Just...incomplete.*

It's a lie of omission.

Carrick interrupted his inner argument. "What was going on when you got there?"

"The beast was going for her throat. I ended him as quickly as I could. I didn't even challenge him or ask for a name."

Another half-truth. If Kord kept this up, he was going to lose his head.

It's my duty to report. Honor demands I do so completely and truthfully. I told her I wouldn't lie for her. Why am I doing this?

Two answers popped into his head, neither comforting.

The first was that he'd expected to give this report to four Warriors. Tops. Those numbered her father, her two brothers, and Jason. He knew it didn't matter if it was one Warrior asking or a dozen. His duty was the same.

It matters to Julia.

Which brought him to the second answer. Despite the lies and deceptions, despite her asking him to forego his duty, Kord *cared* what Julia thought and felt.

"Kord!"

He winced at the sound of Jason's warning. "Sorry. Replaying the mental movie," he lied.

"I asked," Robert Farmer growled, "if the beast laid hands on my daughter."

"He ripped her clothes. Between the damage to them and the beast blood, I had to burn them, but I gave her my jacket until she was safely in her hotel room." *And burned the jacket as well, but that's not important.*

Robert's *Blutjagd* spiked at that, and Kord braced himself for the explosion.

Jack's gaze narrowed. "What aren't you telling us? What did the beast do to my sister?"

Kord grumbled a curse. "He didn't have time to do anything. I ended his foul existence. I'm sure he *intended* to do more. He ripped her clothes. That *says* he intended more, but he didn't get it."

Julia's eyes went wide and wild. Kord forced his gaze from her to her brother.

Carrick raised a hand for silence, and Jack closed his mouth with a snap. The other lords fell silent as well.

The Lord Armen stared Kord down, his gaze piercing. "Is there something else you should tell this Council, Kord?"

Damn it. Why couldn't the old man leave it alone? He'd asked the one question designed to test Kord and to damn him, if he lied in response to it.

"Well?" Carrick challenged.

Kord glanced at Julia, conflicted. On one hand, he had a duty to protect her. That duty wouldn't normally extend to lying and hiding things for her, of course. That directly conflicted with his other duties.

He focused on the lords, the truth choking him. Jack opened his mouth, and Kord started speaking.

"I want the right to pursue printing with Julia." It was true, and yet Kord had no idea why

96

he'd blurted it out that way. *Maybe so Jason and Calvin won't pummel me too badly before I head to a mad cabin?*

The room went deathly still. There was no answer or question, no burn of *Blutjagd*... It seemed the assemblage was holding a collective breath.

Jack recovered first. "Did you bed my sister again?"

"I don't believe you would be my true judge." It wasn't smart to antagonize him, but Kord couldn't seem to help himself.

Robert pounced on his response before Kord could continue on to denying it. "I want the truth," he demanded.

Carrick interrupted before Kord could seal his fate with a flippant response. "Speaks the Warrior who still hasn't faced up to his own dishonor for lying."

Robert glared at him.

Jack snorted. "Since you handled Kord's punishment so badly last time, perhaps you should leave it to me this time."

His father gaped at Jack. "Badly? I took a single blow for each offense, as you well know."

"And ordered Kord away from Julia. You recognized how important it is for Julia to be under the personal protection of a Warrior mate, but you ordered the only Warrior she'd shown an interest in away from her."

"He didn't ask," Robert protested.

"You didn't give Kord a chance to. You didn't even ask him what hopes he harbored, if any. You heard what happened, ignored Julia's pleas and deceptions, and punished Kord out of frustration and without thinking first."

Kord marveled at Jack's defense of him.

As if Jack saw the thought forming, he motioned to Kord. "You're not free of me yet," he warned. "If you had grown a pair of balls that morning and said something, I would have attempted to talk my father down for you. But you were too busy licking your wounds over the fact that my sister put you in the situation you were in to admit you felt anything for her."

Kord nodded grimly.

"Why didn't you tell me?" Calvin demanded.

"Not your place, Calvin," Jason countered.

"It damned well is. Kord is *my* son, not yours."

Jason glared at him, then waived Calvin on.

"Why didn't you tell me?" Kord's father repeated.

"You weren't in a listening mood," Kord offered simply. "If the fact that there was no way I could have known who Julia was didn't make a difference, what difference would printing make?"

"You should have just broken printing," Berne offered acidly.

"Don't you think I tried?" Kord shot back.

"Shut up, Berne," Calvin snapped. He shot a warning look at Falken for good measure. Then he locked gazes with Kord. "It would have mattered," he reasoned.

"Now you tell me," he grumbled.

"I would have taken your place tracking her if I *knew* why you were refusing to go. I wouldn't have done that to you."

"The Stone wouldn't have led you to Julia," Carrick interrupted them. "I imagine She would have pestered Kord into going after Julia anyway. Used his printing against him, possibly."

"I still want to know what happened *after* Kord saved my daughter," Robert spoke up, seemingly reminding everyone that the question was still on the table and unanswered.

Kord sighed. "I. Didn't. Bed. Her." *Not that I didn't want to.* He motioned Robert to silence. "I admit comforting her went further than it should have, but I took no satisfaction from her." If Robert decided to take another blow for it, Kord had earned it.

Jack looked toward Julia, and Kord followed his line of sight. The color had returned to her face in a rush.

Her brother grumbled something unintelligible. "Considering you're printing, and *we* sent you after her, I think we should forgive that blow."

Robert's expression said he wasn't ready to agree with that.

"At least Kord told the truth," Gunther intoned.

"I've got the blow coming to me," Kord admitted.

Without missing a beat, Robert marched across the room and punched Kord in the face. His eyes watered, and pain exploded in his head. Kord took a series of calming breaths, and his vision cleared slowly. Robert offered a tense nod and returned to the middle of the room.

"Is that a 'yes' to pursuing printing?" Kord pressed him. He wasn't going to let the chance to ask pass him by a second time.

"Yes, damn you. If Julia is willing to allow it, of course."

All eyes turned to Julia. She gaped at them, and Kord's heart sank. She was going to refuse him.

Hello, mad cabin.

At last, she nodded shakily. "Yes. I...I'm willing to try that."

Kord smiled.

****

Julia didn't know what to make of it. If Kord was just saying he was printing to avoid telling them what the beast was really doing when Kord killed it, what was the smile for?

Encouragement? Thanks for going along with his plan?

What if he's really printing?

That was just too much to ask for. More likely, this was just a way to get both their necks off the chopping block.

Lord Armen broke the silence. "Well, Robert. What are we going to do with you?"

Her heart stuttered at the many possibilities. She hadn't considered the cost when she made a public show of calling her father out for lying. "Is this really necessary?" she asked again. "I know the truth now, and he's been stripped of his place as lord for it." For the rest of his life, he would have to take orders from his sons...grandsons, if Robert lived that long.

"His lack of honor has harmed more than you," Jack responded crisply. "It has caused every Warrior in Landwirt stress. It caused Armen *and* Maher to expend resources when you disappeared. Not to mention, it's a gross breach of trust with you and with the other houses. He brought a *marked* protected in, without warning the other houses he was doing it."

"Precisely," Lord Armen agreed.

"I'm the one who ran." Something told Julia they would ignore that.

Jack rolled his eyes. "Tell the truth, Julia."

"I am telling the truth."

"When you ran... Whenever you ran, you needed to. You were driven to."

Her face heated. "I guess so." Even when she'd escaped from James Armen to go to the bar, she'd been driven by anger so fierce, she couldn't stand it.

"That's the truth. Had you understood your drives earlier, had they been given the respect they deserved by our father, running wouldn't have been necessary."

"It *is* necessary that your father pay for the full extent of his crimes," Lord Armen agreed.

Lord Smith motioned for attention. "I suggest a blow from each of the lords for each of his offenses."

Her father winced, but he didn't protest it.

One by one, the other lords agreed with the idea.

Jack turned toward the Mahers. "Kord, will you take Julia out? She doesn't need to see this."

"Why not Alan?" Robert argued.

"Because I additionally impose a blow from each Warrior of Landwirt for each adult year that Warrior has had to live to your decision not to tell Julia the truth. Alan and I will give our blows now. The others will give theirs when you return home."

"Kord is also owed a blow for me misjudging him."

"Now you think about that?" Jack pointed out. "Not before you laid yet another blow I suggested you skip?"

"Waived," Kord offered.

"I don't accept that," Robert argued. "Maybe Calvin—"

Jack snapped. "You gave Kord permission to pursue printing with Julia. Stop torturing the man, and let him get to it."

Robert grumbled something that sounded vaguely affirmative.

"Kord?" Jack jerked his head in Julia's direction.

"With pleasure." In the blink of an eye, Kord was at her side, offering his hand.

Julia took it, her heart tripping in excitement at his proximity. She rose to her feet and accompanied him out of the room.

In the foyer, Kord smiled down at her. "A walk or your room?"

The idea of the two of them in a bedroom was appealing. *Too appealing. I don't even know if he was telling the truth or lying about printing yet.* "A walk, I guess."

His smile didn't dim in the least. "As my lady wishes."

The door was halfway closed behind them when a shout of pain rattled her nerves. Kord hurried her along.

They were in the woods before he spoke again. "He'll be okay, you know. It's just a beating. It won't kill him."

"I know. It will just make him *wish* he was dead. I've heard that about it, anyway."

"Yes. It does." His voice was subdued.

Julia didn't doubt that he was remembering the beating he took when he returned home from Armen range. "Did it hurt that much?"

Kord didn't offer an answer.

"I am so sorry, Kord. I tried to stop it."

His hand closed around hers in a little squeeze. "I know. Thank you for that. It meant...means a lot to me that you tried."

"I shouldn't have asked you to lie for me." The beating for that was sure to be worse. Based on the punishment they'd imposed on her father, it would probably be more than Kord could bear.

Kord stopped cold, stiffening. "I didn't skip the details for you because you begged me to."

"I don't... If not that... Why would you risk it?"

He brushed a hand along her cheek and shifted closer to her. His lips closed on hers. Julia gasped in surprise, then met him avidly.

The passion between them scorched at her nerves. In a moment of clarity, she knew why she'd left her amulet and run away. If she couldn't have Kord, she didn't want anyone.

He guided her to the side, then slightly uphill. The light got brighter, and the wind kicked up. Julia guessed they'd left the trees behind.

She eased out of the kiss and looked around at their surroundings. The lake was breathtaking. Julia didn't have to ask how far it was to the nearest neighbors. When Warriors owned land like this, they owned it all.

"How about a dip in the lake?" he offered.

"What if someone else comes up here? Looking for us or something?"

"They'll be busy for quite a while."

Beating my father to a pulp.

"If one of them *does* follow us, I'm sending him back with scars." He trailed his lips along the line of her jaw. "But if it makes you feel better, I'm wearing boxers today. Underwear aren't *much* different than swimsuits."

Julia nodded her agreement.

Kord didn't waste any time. In a few heartbeats, he had his armored boots unbuckled and off. His jeans and socks followed. He looked up at Julia from his crouch and raised an eyebrow.

It took her a moment to decipher that. "Oh. Yes." She kicked her shoes away and went to work on her jeans.

By the time she straightened, Kord was stripped to dark blue knit boxers that matched his eyes and a black t-shirt. He reached out and started working the buttons on her blouse open.

Julia licked her lips, and Kord's erect length pulsed against his boxers. Her blouse disappeared in a rush. Kord captured her mouth again, then guided her backward into the cold waters of the lake.

She placed her hand on his chest, giggling into his mouth at the cloth beneath her fingertips.

He broke from the kiss, his brow furrowed. "Something amusing?"

Julia pulled at the t-shirt and let it rebound against his chest. "You forgot something."

His pained expression raised a lump in her throat. She grasped the lower edge of the shirt and lifted it. Kord wrapped a hand around her wrist, bringing her to a halt. He shook his head. Julia grasped the shirt in her other hand and dragged it as far up his chest as she could.

The skin beneath was a patchwork of purple, green, and yellow. Here and there, she could spot signs that ribs had been broken but were well toward healed.

"It was just a beating," he assured her.

"But you said—"

"I shouldn't have. It will be gone in a week or less. I promise."

But I did this to him. Right now, my father is facing the same. Because of me. Tears welled in her eyes.

"Julia? Would you rather wait until I'm healed? I can wait."

What next? On the off chance he was printing—*really* printing, if she didn't feel the same, breaking printing would make his broken ribs feel like Disneyland. *If we continue. If I don't end it right here and now.*

If he's not printing, he lied to the Council of Lords. The beating he'll take for that will be the stuff of legends.

Either way, I risk hurting him worse than I already have.

"Julia?"

She released his shirt and waded toward the shore, heartbroken at the choice she was making.

Kord followed her; his hands closed on her shoulders. "Julia? What is it?"

"We shouldn't do this."

"What? Why? We have your father's permission to."

"I'm bad luck for any Warrior saddled with me."

He circled her body, performing a visual assessment of her expression. "What are you talking about?"

"I've already gotten two Warriors beaten half to death, and—"

"One. Your father made his own bed, and now he has to lay in it. And a beating won't kill me. I've taken all manner of beatings in my adult life."

"But this one was *my* fault," she pointed out.

"And you apologized for it. I accepted that apology."

She shook her head. "I'm bad luck for you."

"Shouldn't I be the judge of that?" His frustration bled through.

"I...I don't know."

Kord backed off a step, looking pained again.

I keep hurting him. I can't seem not *to hurt him.* Julia left the water, then collected up her clothes. She took one last look at Kord.

He knelt in the water, his head bowed.

I just keep hurting him. No matter what I do, I hurt him.

She ran for the trees. Halfway back, Julia took the time to pull her clothes on. Then she sprinted for the training house.

The sight of her brothers carrying her father through the foyer stopped her short. He was unconscious, bloodied...broken. His nose lay at an odd angle to his face, mashed and skewed. His breath came in fits and gasps.

And he's dishonored. Permanently. For the rest of his life, he will never be trusted.

I keep hurting everyone around me.

"Julia?" Jack questioned her.

She met his gaze. He'd handed their father off to one of Kord's older brothers, and he was edging toward her, his hands up in a calming gesture.

She ran for the stairs, and vaulted up them two or three at a time. Once she was in her assigned bedroom, she slammed the door behind her. The sounds of pursuit were impossible to miss; Julia locked the door, just in time for the rattling of the doorknob.

"Julia?"

"Go away, Jack."

"Julia, you weren't supposed to see that."

Her stomach lurched, and she swallowed it down. "I know."

There was a moment of silence. "Let me in, Julia."

She was tempted to. The urge to run or strike out or scream was stronger. "I want to go home, Jack."

"We can't. Not until Father recovers. A week. More likely two."

Julia laid her head against the door. *Two weeks.*

The knob rattled again. "Julia?"

"Two weeks," she conceded. She could avoid Kord for two weeks. She'd nearly done that at home, when her father or brothers pissed her off.

"What happened with Kord?"

"Two weeks," she repeated.

Jack hesitated a moment, then walked away.

Chapter Four

June 2nd, 1967

With his nerves hyper-sensitized by printing, the change in air flow indicating someone in the doorway was no more subtle than the acrid burn and squeal of brakes. The scent was male, which meant it was no one Kord wanted to talk to. That a given, he didn't invite the other Warrior in.

Just when he hoped the interloper would wander away, he entered the room uninvited instead. The door swung shut, closing them in together.

Kord shot a warning look...at Jack. Of the people in the world he wanted to see least, anyone from Farmer range topped the list.

Not anyone, he conceded. *Julia is welcome. Any time.*

Jack hooked his thumbs in his weapons belt and leaned a shoulder against the door frame. He tipped his head in greeting.

"What do you want, Jack?"

"I thought you said you want to pursue printing with Julia," he noted evenly. It was a false veneer, Kord was sure.

"Pursue what? Your sister won't see me, won't talk to me. She hides in her room all the time. What do you suggest? I'm sure you would *love* it if I broke into her room to force her to talk to me."

"I would, actually."

Kord stiffened, glaring at him, challenging Jack to take him on, if that was his intent.

Jack sighed. "I don't want your head, Kord."

"What do you want?"

"For the two of you to stop playing games and get down to what you both clearly want, so I can stop pretending my father can't travel and get back to running my range."

"Not my choice. I have an open-door policy. Your sister has no intention of walking through it." The truth hurt. *It hurts less than going to that mad cabin is going to.*

"Why?"

Kord ground his teeth in frustration. "Why don't you tell me? I thought it was the bruises, but she knows they've healed now. That means she either never wanted to pursue printing with me or she's changed her mind about it since your father's judgment."

"Nothing has changed. Nothing that matters, anyway."

Kord swallowed down a scream of rage and forced his voice to even. "So she never wanted to print with me." It wasn't a surprise, so why did it hurt so much?

"I didn't say that."

Kord stared at him, fishing for words in the murky depths of his mind. "What the hell *are* you saying?"

"Do you know *why* we were in Armen range?"

"To meet James Armen." Everyone knew that. It wasn't a secret.

"Actually, the Stone just told Carrick that Julia would meet her mate in Armen range.

Based on the ages of unmated men in Armen, my father *assumed* James Armen was that mate. No one counted on you being in Armen range while we were there."

A flicker of hope lit in Kord's chest. "The Stone said it?" If that was true, there was chance for them. *More than a chance.*

"Yes, She did. The Stone isn't known for letting people deny Her wishes."

Kord smiled. He wanted to laugh, to crow in triumph, but something told him claiming Julia wouldn't be that easy.

"By the way, I don't think your bruises are what sent Julia running for cover. She's seen bruises, broken bones, stitches..."

His smile faded. "You weren't there, Jack." She'd taken one look at the bruises and refused him outright.

"I think it goes deeper than that. I think whatever you refused to say when you redirected the conversation to your printing during my father's judgment is the key."

Kord didn't claim not to know what Jack was talking about. That would be an outright lie. He'd avoided that so far.

"I get it, Kord. She's your mate. Whatever you don't want to say—and I hope to the gods it's not the worst-case scenario—you're not saying it to protect my sister."

He nodded stiffly.

Jack waited for more.

"It's not the worst-case scenario. Just so you know. To put your mind at ease."

"Thank you."

"For giving you enough evidence to take my head?" Strangely, Kord didn't fear that, though he suspected Jack had no intention of doing it.

"No. But now I do have enough information to talk to my little sister." He disappeared before Kord could question that.

****

Julia cringed at the sound of the knock.

She'd shouted Alan out of her room less than an hour earlier, which meant he was still off somewhere, licking his wounds.

She'd made it clear she had no interest in speaking to her father yet, which meant it wasn't him coming to make peace or to find out why she was upset with Alan.

Kord seemed determined to prove he wasn't pursuing an unwilling woman.

Lord Maher and Lord Armen were off somewhere together, and none of the other Mahers seemed to have an interest in interacting with her.

That left one possible candidate. "I'm not in the mood, Jack."

"Are you decent?" he responded.

Based on how I've destroyed Kord's life, definitely not. She doubted that was what her brother meant. "Excuse me?" she challenged.

"If you're not, cover up, because I'm coming in there."

Julia dropped the book she'd been pretending to read and raced for the door. If she locked it before Jack got it open, he would be

112

stuck outside. Surely, he wouldn't risk offending the Lord Maher by breaking down a door in his house for less than an emergency.

The door opened before she got to it, and Julia stalked away, cursing. The door closed again, most likely with her brother on the wrong side of it.

"Happy now?" she asked brightly.

"No, and neither are you."

She turned to face him. "You could send me home with Alan. I promise not to run from him." Julia stopped short of suggesting Jack take her home and leave Alan to escort their father. At least Alan would likely keep his opinions to himself during the trip.

"Tucking tail and running. I never thought I'd live to see the day when you did that."

"You said it. I'm not happy here."

"Well, that is your own fault, and you can end it anytime you choose to."

Julia didn't deny it. *The cost is too high.* She sank to the bed, exhausted by this never-ending circular argument.

"What isn't Kord telling me?"

She shrugged.

"He already told me it's not the worst possible scenario, so you might as well tell me."

It was hard to breathe. If Jack knew Kord was derelict in his duty to report fully to the lords, she'd already failed.

"Julia, tell me, damn it."

"Don't take it out on Kord. I shouldn't have asked him to. It's my fault. All of this is my fault."

"You're saying he bedded you again? If that's all, I'll take a couple of blows for it and for him lying about it, but—"

"He didn't lie! He told me he wouldn't lie for me, even when I asked him to." She waved Jack off before he could protest. "I shouldn't have asked. I know it."

"So, Kord hasn't lied at all?"

Julia shook her head. The more she ran the scene at the lake through her mind, the more convinced she was that he hadn't lied about printing.

"Then what are you afraid of?"

She didn't answer him. Julia couldn't find the words to do it.

"I am Landwirt now...lord of the range. If it comes to light later—whatever *it* is—I'll already know. No one else will be able to stand as Kord's judge, and I give you my word to be even-handed with him."

Julia bit her lower lip, considering what he'd said. "Promise me."

"Do I really have to? My word isn't good enough without it?"

She glared at him.

Jack motioned for peace. "Fine. I think we can dispense with a blood oath, since my blood already runs in your veins, but... You have my solemn vow, as Lord Landwirt, that you and Kord are both safe from me. Acceptable?"

"Acceptable." Spitting out the rest was more difficult.

"Well?" he prompted her.

"Going for my throat wasn't the only thing the beast was doing." She peeked up at him, wincing as her brother's eyes went wide, and his face darkened.

"He said—"

"It didn't have time to...you know. Two more seconds and the beast would have, but it...didn't."

Jack scrubbed a hand across the back of his neck, shifting from foot to foot as he would before a fight. "He didn't want to say that in front of everyone, because of you."

"I guess so."

He nodded, then sank to the mattress next to her. "That's it?"

"Yes."

"Okay. I know. You have no reason to refuse Kord now."

He wasn't that stupid, was he?

"What is your reason now?" Clearly, his patience was running thin.

"Maybe that he's decided I'm more trouble than I'm worth," she offered miserably. "And he's right. I'm bad luck for any Warrior stuck with me. You know that well enough."

"I don't think so."

Julia shrugged. It was practically her brother's duty to make her feel better, if he could. It was ingrained in them. While she'd like to believe Kord still wanted her, chances were Jack was wrong.

He sighed. "For argument's sake, say I'm wrong."

She groaned.

"I'm not, but assume I am."

Julia hit him. "I'm more than willing and able to assume you're wrong, jerk."

He chuckled. "*If* I'm wrong, and Kord doesn't want you as his mate, there's still *something* that man wants from you."

Her cheeks heated as his meaning slammed home.

"I know you, Julia. You can't convince me you don't want another piece of that man."

"Admittedly, but how do I even start that conversation?" Jack was a guy. He might have an idea about that.

He stood and straightened his weapons belt. "Go to his room and see where it goes."

"Seriously? Just walk into his room with the intention of having sex with the man?"

Jack laughed. "He is male. Besides, Kord told me something very interesting."

"Which is?" And did she want to know?

Of course, I do.

"He has an open-door policy where you are concerned."

Her heart lightened. She sobered at the truth that she'd kept him waiting for a week and a half. "And he said this when, precisely?" If the information was more than a few days old, it was worthless.

Jack glanced at his watch. Just when she was sure he was going to claim he had a meeting or something, in an effort to deflect her question, he answered. "Twenty-two minutes ago." He smiled. "Kord hasn't changed his mind, Julia."

He let himself out of the room, leaving her reeling at the possibilities.

****

Julia watched Kord as he stopped cold in the doorway from the bathroom, his gaze ranging up and down her body. His eyes widened, and his cock rose behind his jeans. His weapons belt hit the floor with a dull thud.

She stood, sauntering to him, well aware of the show she was putting on for him. His button down shirt extended nearly to her knees, but she had buttoned it strategically, so it hid only the thick patch of curls at the apex of her thighs. Wide vees of flesh showed above and below the two buttons she'd fastened.

Kord's body was taut in anticipation. His gaze locked with hers, and her heart skipped in excitement. She went still, watching his reactions.

Jack was right. Kord is more than willing to sleep with me.

Of course. He's a Warrior. He's a sexual animal at his most potent.

Isn't that what I am, thanks to Jack?

He wrapped his hands around her hips and pulled Julia the remaining half-body length to his chest. Julia gasped against his lips, as they closed over hers. Kord ripped the few fastened buttons away.

She reached for his jeans, spurring him on. Kord was going to take her hard and fast.

117

Where? On the carpet? Against the wall? She didn't care as long as he didn't stop.

Kord dragged his t-shirt off, then pushed the button-down shirt off her shoulders. He guided her to the bed and lifted her onto it. Julia leaned back on her elbows, watching the play of muscles as he slid the jeans off over his bare feet, creating every bit the show for her she'd created for him.

He crawled up between her thighs, his fingers sliding deep inside her in mute promise of what they both wanted. Julia groaned as his body covered hers, his fingers moving in and out in long, slow strokes.

His lips teased at hers. "I'm going to make love to you," he whispered. "You want that. Don't you, Julia?"

She nodded.

"How much do you want it?"

Julia found it hard to put that into words. How many nights had she woken up, at the edges of climax, thinking of joining him? *Every night since the first night with him.*

"Julia?" he prompted.

She tangled her fingers in his shaggy hair. "Anything," she offered. "I will give you anything for one more night with you."

"Be my mate." His voice was little more than a whisper.

"What?" She couldn't have heard him right.

"Be my mate. Say you will. I don't care if you mean it," he moaned. "Just let me pretend you do."

"Do you mean it?" Could Jack have been right about Kord?

He pulled back and met her gaze, misery etched on his face. "I do. If you refuse me—"

Julia covered his lips with one shaking hand. "I won't refuse you. I'll be your mate, and I'm not just saying it. You have my vow that I want to."

His chest spasmed, as if he'd swallowed a sob. Kord kissed her fingers, then moved his face to uncover his mouth. "For all times?" he managed.

She nodded solemnly. "I'll be your mate. I'll bear your sons."

Kord's hand retreated, and his cock slid home. Julia gasped in surprise, as he pinned her hands to the mattress and took her in slow, deep thrusts, much as he had in his motel room, when he took control of their sex after agreeing to be her sex slave. His mouth teased at hers, left to explore her jawline, ear, or the column of her neck, and returned to taste her kiss again.

She moaned at that, closing her eyes and sinking into the sensation of Kord claiming her. "When will I be fertile?" she breathed. If she was on her usual schedule, it couldn't be long.

His teeth closed around her earlobe, and he sucked it in gently. He released it and nestled his lips to her ear. "Soon." His cock jerked inside her at that.

"How soon?"

"You'll be approaching cusp in a few days." Kord slowed, muttering a curse. He seemed to savor every inch of his cock brushing back and forth across the walls of her sheath.

Julia nipped at his throat. "Good."

His eyes opened wide. "Good?"

"I forbid you to go on trail for the next two weeks," she informed him.

Kord thrust deep inside her, crying out harshly as he climaxed. An expression of stunned fascination settled on his face.

Julia nodded, smiling at his reaction to the invitation. She rolled her hips back and forth, watching his eyes dilate in renewed lust. Oh, yes. Kord would be insatiable now.

He started to move again, that same maddening thrusting from before she made her offer. Julia's breathing went ragged. Kord's mouth closed over hers, thorough, savoring. The combination was too much, and she rocketed over into her own release. Kord groaned again as she pulled her head back and cried out, her fingers tightening on his.

"The way I wanted," he managed.

"Wanted?" Her voice was weak and her mind muddled. Julia licked her lips.

"To seal. To—" His eyes closed. "To ask you."

Her heart skipped a beat or two. "When did you—?" Julia choked on the words. She couldn't finish the question.

Kord's midnight blue eyes opened. "The first morning," he admitted.

Her heart ached at that. "I am so sorry, Kord."

"Don't be," he dismissed her.

"I didn't know how to tell you how I felt," she admitted.

"I'm glad to hear that."

"But—"

"You're mine, Julia. Say you're mine."

She nodded. "I'm yours. Always."

"That's all that matters," he assured her. In the next heartbeat, he was climaxing again.

****

June 5th, 1976

Kord stroked into Julia, smiling at her gasp. She knelt in front of him, his chest to her back. He stroked his hands up and down her body, cupping her breasts, playing at her clit, while they ground against each other.

She tangled her fingers in his hair, pulling lightly, urging him on. Kord took the hint, thrusting deeper.

Julia had become much more vocal since her family left for home, and their sex had done nothing but become more energetic and frequent. Of course, her approach to high cycle had a lot to do with that.

A heavy-handed knock at the door put Kord off his rhythm for a moment. He resumed with a groan.

The doorknob rattled. "Damn it, Kord. Jason wants to see you."

"Go away, Berne," Julia ordered.

Kord chuckled, then brushed his lips along her shoulder. "That's Falken."

"What's the difference?" she breathed.

Kord had thought the same thing many times. As far as he could tell, his two older brothers were cut from the same cloth. It was hardly necessary to differentiate them from each other.

Julia raised her voice. "Go away, Falken."

Something in her tone went straight to Kord's libido. Someday, Julia was going to be a great Lady Maher, if his brothers died before Kord did.

Julia shouted in pleasure at Kord's increased intensity.

Falken stalked away, hitting something made of wood as he went.

Kord ignored him. The only thing that mattered to him was Julia and the potential child they would have together.

It took only minutes for them to reach their fourth shared climax of the day. In the aftermath, they curled together on the bed, sweat-soaked and gasping for breath.

Julia laughed, long and hard. Kord couldn't help himself; he joined in.

At last, her laughter tapered off. She sighed. "You do need to go see Jason. Lords don't wait forever, and they don't like waiting at all."

"I know. I know." He scrubbed a hand over his face, then rolled to his feet. "I'll take care of this, and we can share a shower when I come back."

Julia mirrored his movements. "Add lunch to that. I'm starving."

Kord stopped with his jeans in his hands. He shot a smile at her.

****

122

It took a moment for his look to make sense to her. "Quit. I'm not craving or enjoying increased appetite." *Yet*. Warriors didn't usually take long to produce a child. "I've just built up an appetite since breakfast."

His smile widened, and Kord went back to dressing. He didn't do much of that. His jeans and the black button-down shirt were the extent of it. Kord didn't even button the shirt; he left it open down his chest, and he didn't brush his hair.

Julia took a moment to appreciate the view.

"Ready to go?" he asked.

She motioned up and down his body, momentarily at a loss for words. "Like that?" she managed.

He was barefoot, sex-mussed, sweaty, and half-dressed. It wasn't the way a Warrior reported to his lord.

"As I recall, I promised you two weeks."

"So you did."

"Then we are on vacation, and I intend to enjoy it."

She nodded. Together, they made their way out into the corridor and then down the stairs.

Falken stood outside Jason's office, his arms crossed over his chest, puffed up a like a cat in fighting posture. "Jason is waiting," he reminded them.

Kord's smile dimmed a bit. "Just let me get Julia settled in with—"

His oldest brother made for their position, malice in his expression. His *Blutjagd* singed at Julia's skin.

"When the lord calls for you, you go, Kord. Just because you want to get your dick wet again with—"

Kord's right cross took Falken down with a rumble of floor tiles. His *Blutjagd* didn't even flicker. "Go in the dining room, Julia." It was a command, if she'd ever heard one.

I've been expected to follow countless commands in my life. She might argue with them, if she understood what was going on between the brothers. Instead, she stood there and gaped as Falken levered himself off the floor.

"Apologize," Kord ordered him.

Falken's glare was enough to send Julia scrambling for the dining room doorway. Once she was there, she turned back to them. Something told her not to give the two Warriors her back.

The older Warrior spit blood into the palm of his hand, and what she suspected was a molar came with it. Julia wondered if Warriors could regrow teeth, and she suspected the next few weeks would tell the tale.

Falken motioned to Kord, slurring thanks to his swollen jaw. "You want *me* to apologize, when you knocked my tooth out? What the fuck—"

Kord punched him again.

Lewis and Jason were in the foyer and between the brothers before Falken could get up again.

"What is going on here?" Jason demanded.

Falken came to his feet and lunged for Kord. Kord pulled his fist back to punch his brother

124

again. Lewis tackled Falken to the ground, and Jason pushed Kord back.

"Stand down," the lord ordered.

Both brothers nodded, and Kord relaxed his arms, shaking them out as if at the end of a training bout.

Calvin looked toward Julia. "Are you injured?"

She shook her head, still a little unbalanced. "No. Kord told me to run."

He nodded and turned back to Falken. "You better have a damned good reason for this."

"Me? Kord has been beating the shit out of me and telling me to apologize for it."

Kord pushed against Jason's hold, clearly trying to get at his brother again. "I'm not telling you to apologize for me hitting you, you asshole."

"Stand down," Jason commanded again.

Kord complied, but his expression said he was going to take Falken apart at his earliest opportunity.

"Now explain why you're beating the hell out of Falken."

He glared at his older brother. "Julia is my *mate*."

"I know that," Falken protested.

"Then why would you think it was appropriate to say I just want to wet my dick in her like she's a blade chaser? I won't stand for that level of disrespect, and you better damned well know it, because next time I'm going to do a lot worse than knock out a tooth and leave some bruises. Next time, I'm leaving scars."

Julia gasped and pressed a hand to her mouth, shocked. She hadn't considered what Kord would make of that comment. She'd ignored it as just another Warrior barb. She'd heard thousands of them, tossed between her brothers.

All four of the Warriors looked her direction. To his credit, Falken went ashen, a sure sign that he realized he was in the wrong here.

She forced her hand down, then nodded to let them know she was okay. If they thought she wasn't, Falken might not make it out of the foyer in one piece.

Kord wasn't done with Falken yet. "For your information, my *mate* is high cycle. If our attempts to conceive a new Maher Warrior don't meet with your approval— I believe 'fuck you' just might be an appropriate response to it."

Calvin and Jason turned toward Falken, shooting him twin looks of disbelief.

"I didn't know!"

Calvin cleared his throat.

Falken ground his teeth, then executed a formal and antiquated bow to her. "My apologies, Julia. I had no right to say something so crass and unfeeling. It's been a long time since we've had a woman around the house, but my mother did teach me better manners than what I displayed today. I will promise to be more mindful of my manners, if you promise to have one of the other Warriors beat sense into me when I am out of line."

Julia laughed. Maher Men had a wit about them that was very charming. "I think I can take you," she countered.

Kord tensed.

"But I will make that promise," she conceded. No Warrior wanted to think of his mate fighting her own battles. Their instincts ran too high for that.

Falken nodded. "And I apologize to you, Kord. Producing young Warriors is your first duty."

"Correct," Jason intoned. "I estimate that Kord handled your punishment well enough already. But since producing young Warriors *is* his highest duty, you and Berne will take on trails whenever Julia is high cycle." He nodded to Kord. "Keep us apprised."

"I will."

Chapter Five

December 19th, 1967

Kord paced back and forth, the phone pressed to his ear. Every ring ramped up his heart rate. By the time James answered with a grumbled 'Armen manor', Kord was at the edges of self-control.

"I need Carrick."

"He's in the middle of something right now. I can have him return—"

"Interrupt him."

James hesitated. "Is it that important?"

"Let's put it this way. I can be there, demanding answers in person, in less than six hours."

"Understood. Hold on. I'll get him."

Kord bit back a half dozen ill-advised responses. James wasn't stonewalling him; there was no reason to antagonize him.

Besides, this isn't his fault. Only the Stone had the power to affect his life this way.

Carrick pulled the phone up with the clatter of Bakelite. "I know why you're calling."

"Do you?" Kord challenged. *There's a reason I'm calling him. He's the Stone lord. Carrick might know before I ask.*

"Jack called me last month."

He clamped his hand around the receiver. "And you told him what, precisely?"

"To be patient, which is less than I'm going to tell you."

128

Kord didn't smile at the idea of Jack stewing. "What are you going to tell *me*?"

"The Stone says the time isn't right yet."

"Not right for what? This is a baby we're talking about."

"I know what we're talking about, but I don't know what the Stone is."

"So my child or children are part of one of the Stone's puzzles?" That didn't bode well. It rarely went well for those involved in the puzzle.

"Sounds like it to me, and I don't like it any more than you do."

"When *will* we have children? Can I promise Julia that we will someday?"

"You can make that promise. The Stone tells me you will have a child when the time is right."

"But? Something tells me there's more to the puzzle than that."

"All of Maher's Warriors will descend from you, Kord. Falken and Berne will never find mates. They will never produce children."

Bile rose in his throat.

"Anything else?" Carrick asked cordially.

"No. I think that's it. Thank you, Carrick." Though the news wasn't good, he'd interrupted whatever the lord had been doing. He should be gracious for the expenditure of time.

"Take care, Kord."

"Yes. I will." He fumbled the receiver onto the cradle, his fingers numb.

Take care? That was the understatement of the millennia. If all the Mahers from here out would be his descendants, not dying before he sired them was essential.

A hand closed on his shoulder, and Kord snapped a look at his father.

Calvin went pale. "She can't have children," he guessed.

"We can, when the Stone decides the time is right."

A series of foul curses erupted from Calvin's mouth.

"It gets worse."

"Can it?"

"Apparently, Julia and I are going to produce the *only* heirs to Maher."

His father winced.

"Yeah," Kord murmured. "I know."

****

May 20th, 1970

Kord sighed at the shifting of the mattress. Julia yawned and made her way to the bathroom. The sounds of her using the toilet and sink filtered back to him, the soothing sounds of his mate in his life.

"Oh..."

The wrenching tones of Julia vomiting snapped Kord awake. His next clear memory was bolting across the room and dropping to his knees at her side.

Julia spit, groaned, then heaved again.

Kord's head spun, and he tried to figure out what to do for her. No one in the house had been sick since his *Krankheit*, and there was nothing to be done about that but let it run its course.

For all that Julia had a Warrior's blood running through her veins, she wasn't one. *If she's sick, she needs a doctor. David will know what to do for her.*

What if— He hesitated, his hand inches from her back. It had been more than a year since he'd stopped checking Julia's cycle every month. The waiting had been intolerable for them both, and they'd decided it would be less nerve wracking if they just let the baby come when the Stone decided the time was right.

Please, let it be that. The alternative was that his mate was sick, and Kord had no experience in dealing with a sick human mate.

He stroked her back, seeking out her cycle. The stillness was unsettling. Energizing. *Perfect.* He smiled.

Julia flushed the toilet, then laid her head on the toilet seat and groaned. "I don't know what's wrong with me. I can't even remember the last time I was sick."

That was probably true. Julia had faster-than-human healing, though not as fast as a Warrior's healing. She probably hadn't been sick since after the beast attack when she was a toddler.

"It will be fine. Trust me." Now that he knew what was making her ill, it was easier to think. *Easier to breathe.*

Kord grabbed a washcloth off the shelves and wet it at the sink. He bathed her face, refreshed the cloth, then carried her back to bed and tucked her in. He laid a kiss on her forehead, offering what little comfort he could.

"Be right back."

Julia nodded, then took the washcloth from his hand and settled it over her eyes.

He pulled on a pair of jeans and made his way down the hall. At Falken's door, he knocked and called out his brother's name. Berne was out on trail, but he'd heard Falken come in late at night.

His brother grumbled something Kord didn't catch.

"It's important, Falken."

He stomped across the room and pulled the door open. "This better be important. I've only been down for three hours."

"Sorry to disturb you, but Julia is sick."

Falken reached out and grabbed a t-shirt. "I'll get David."

"That can wait until later. I need a tray of—"

"You woke me up to cook for your mate? Are you serious?"

"She's throwing up. I don't want to leave her that long."

"If she's throwing up, she needs David, not a hot breakfast."

"I don't *want* a hot breakfast for her." What little Kord knew about pregnancy said that was a very bad idea, considering her state.

Falken braced one arm on the doorframe, his brow furrowed. "Kord, you're not making any sense. I know your mate is sick, so let me get David for her."

Julia started moving again.

Probably back to the bathroom to empty whatever is left in her stomach. "Look, I don't

132

have time to explain this properly. I need crackers or bread sticks, milk, fresh fruit, maybe plain croissants and cheese cubes. If we don't have it, buy it."

His brother's look of irritation melted into shock.

He gets it now. He's putting it together.

Sounds of Julia heaving reached them, and Falken winced.

Kord shifted from foot to foot, torn. He needed to see to her needs, but he also needed to make sure Falken understood him.

His brother stood, transfixed.

"Come on, Falken," he pleaded.

"I've got it. Get moving."

"Thanks." He turned back toward their rooms.

"By the way, good job, little brother."

Kord couldn't help it. He smiled widely at the idea of his son in Julia's womb. He offered Falken a quick nod, then rushed back to Julia's side.

He took the washcloth from her hand and refreshed it again. Kord bathed the back of her neck and shoulders.

"When is this going to stop?" she complained.

Kord sighed, wishing he could give her better news. *That would be dishonorable. This is something I can't control, much as I would like to.* "I understand the usual duration is two to three months."

Julia seemed to hold her breath. She turned to look at him, and Kord cleaned her ashen face. She didn't question him.

He smiled. "I guess the time is finally right."

She wrapped herself around him, trembling. Just when Kord was about to ask if she was all right, Julia laughed.

Sounds of someone approaching warned they wouldn't be alone for long. Kord reached out and swung the bathroom door shut. The last thing he wanted was Falken seeing his mate naked.

His brother knocked on the bedroom door.

"Leave it by the bed, Falken," he shouted.

Sounds of compliance filtered back, and he approached the bathroom door.

"Saltines and milk are by the bed," Jason reported. "We'll bring the rest when Falken gets back from the store. Calvin is on his way to pick up David. He should be here within the hour."

Kord's 'thank you' choked off when Julia turned around and brought up more into the toilet.

Where is it all coming from? She hadn't eaten in ten hours, and he could swear she'd already thrown up more than she ate.

Jason didn't inquire about her condition. "You are relieved of all other duties, Kord. Take care of her." He was in motion before Kord could respond.

Julia heaved again, and Kord placed a hand on her shoulder, aching for what she was forced to endure.

This is harder than fighting beasts. In this situation, there's no enemy to beat down. There

134

was only his mate in misery and whatever pitiful comfort Kord could offer her.

Chapter Six

February 15th, 1971

"Oh damn!" Julia's exclamation was followed by a full-throated scream.

Kord rubbed her back, whispering his assurances that it was almost over.

"No screaming, Julia," Celeste counseled in her deeply-accented English. "Push. Now."

Julia grunted and folded further around the mound of her womb. Kord helped support her trembling legs.

"End of contraction," Celeste announced. "Your son will be born very soon."

"Or our daughter," Kord purred.

"It will be a boy," Julia countered miserably.

He didn't argue with her about it. Since it had taken them three years to have a child, chances were the Stone would demand a son of them. *Not to mention, this child is huge.*

"Is Julia all right?" her father called out from behind the curtain.

Before Kord could order him out, Julia was barking a warning of her own. "Leave. Go far enough that hearing me won't make you want to come in, or I'll have Calvin remove you bodily. And *then* I'll take Kord's sacred weapon to you personally, removing your need to visit bars."

"Going." His footsteps retreated.

Kord bit back a laugh at her chosen threat.

"It's not too late for me to make you pay for this, too," she grumbled.

"Not saying a word," Kord promised.

Julia started huffing out breaths, adding curses to the mix as she leaned into the next contraction. When it eased, she leaned against Kord for support.

"How are you?" he asked. "Honestly?"

"Glad we didn't do this earlier," she quipped. Her humor let him know her condition wasn't as dire as he'd feared.

"I am sure it was not for lack of effort," Celeste offered brightly. As Farmer range's doula, Celeste was well aware of Warrior drives.

Not to mention she knows precisely why she was requested to see to Julia's pregnancy and delivery. While every Warrior family had lean times and flush, Crossbearer and Maher were both facing extinction. Kord was the youngest son of an only child, Berne was dead, and Falken hadn't found a mate, as prophesized by the Stone. It had taken Kord and Julia an inordinately long time to produce a child, as Warriors went. If Julia didn't provide an heir to Maher, their family might well disappear completely.

Would the Stone actually allow that to happen? He hoped not, but neither his family nor hers were taking any chances.

Jack Lord Farmer had sent Alan, Robert, and Celeste to safeguard Julia. Even now, Kord was certain Jack was sitting by the phone, waiting for an update on his sister and nephew.

Maher was even more protective of her. Every Maher Warrior had staked out territory close to home for the last month of Julia's pregnancy, and all of them were on the grounds now, in case any beasts were stupid enough to try and end Maher, here and now.

Then, in a stubborn show, their son had done what few Warrior babies did; he'd decided to come more than two weeks after his due date. The result was a lot of pacing, snarling, and more than one smacked face, when someone annoyed Julia to her breaking point.

Julia's stiffening body and shout of pain reinforced that the baby wasn't procrastinating anymore. Ever since labor started, he'd made it clear he was in a hurry to end his confinement.

Celeste started to speak, and Julia shot her a death glare. To her credit, the doula knew when to shut up.

The contractions sped, one starting nearly as soon as another ended. Julia's sounds fell off slightly, no doubt as she had more trouble catching her breath and the labor pushed her toward exhaustion.

Celeste worked between her legs, and Kord winced at the sight of her rocking the baby's shoulders in an attempt to help him deliver.

"One more, Julia," she instructed.

Julia's whine of pain ended abruptly, as their baby slipped into Celeste's hands. She panted, laying against Kord's chest, her eyes closed as if she might drop off to sleep at any moment.

Deciding which one of them to look at was an impossible task. In the end, Kord laid kisses on Julia's temple, whispering everything he could tell about their son at a distance to her.

Celeste gasped, her eyes going wide.

Kord tensed. "What is it? Is something wrong?" Was this the Stone's puzzle?

"He has a mark. I think I've heard—"

"Show me. Now," Kord ordered.

Celeste came to his side and placed their son in his arms, wrapped in a baby quilt that had serviced generations of Mahers. Julia opened her eyes and stared at the mark on their son's chest. Kord chuckled, relieved.

"No problem?" Celeste asked nervously, tucking a blanket around Julia's legs.

"We should invite our fathers in," Julia opined.

"Would you, Celeste?" Kord asked.

She nodded and disappeared behind the curtain. Grumbled complaints from the hallway said the other Warriors weren't happy at being excluded.

Too bad. This is our time and our choice.

Their son wriggled in Kord's arms, kicking the bottom of the wrap open to nestle his little feet to Kord's chest. He stuffed a chubby fist in his mouth and turned his head toward Kord, most likely looking for a full tit to sample. Kord laughed at that. Minutes old and already hungry. That was a definite mark of a Warrior baby.

"What should we name him?" Kord asked. He'd told Julia she could name their baby anything she wanted, and it was time to choose a name.

"Lewis. Lewis Lee Maher."

He pressed another kiss to her temple. "Perfect. Just like our son."

The door opened, and both of their fathers rushed through it and around the curtain to them.

"How are you?" Robert demanded.

"How's the baby?" Calvin's voice overlapped with his.

"Thankful for my advanced healing," Julia joked. "And starving."

Kord's cock tightened at the reminder. Julia would be healed from this and ready to exercise her drives in no time. In the meantime, every Warrior at the manor would be mindful of providing anything she asked for. Once their fathers spread the news that she was hungry, someone would be bringing her a tray of food.

"And Lewis is just fine," Kord inserted. "In fact, we not only have a future Lord Maher, we have a young Stone lord."

Calvin chuckled, then roared in laughter.

"Something is funny about that?" Kord challenged him.

"Not at all. If the Stone tortured us all with three years of trying before you had a son *and* marked him as a Stone lord... Maher isn't going to be allowed to die anytime soon."

Lewis yanked the fist out of his mouth and howled, most likely demanding his first meal.

Julia smiled at him. "I hear my cue. If you would give us a moment?"

The two older Warriors hurried to comply.

Kord handed Lewis off to her, missing his son in his arms already. It didn't take her long to get him settled on the breast.

"Afterward, I have to give him his amulet and blessing," Kord reminded her. Sunset was in less than two hours, and his instincts demanded Kord protect his son as soon as possible.

Julia nodded but was strangely silent.

He took notice of that. "What's wrong?"

"Do you think the Stone will let us have another child?"

Kord swallowed down assurances that She would. This had the distinct feel of one of the Stone's games. "I don't know," he admitted.

She snuggled into his chest and laid a kiss against it. "Then I guess we'll just have to keep trying."

Section Two:

Adam
and
Jo

The Black Knight

The Knight of Swords

Dedicated to...

My Aries husband, who is my Warrior in many ways.

About the card...

Tarot Card: *Knight of Swords*

Anyone who's met Adam of Maher in *Will of the Stone* and *Opposites Attract* will understand why he is the perfect choice for this card. Adam is blunt to the point of being tactless and unthinking. He doesn't spare the feelings of others and seemingly doesn't consider them very often. He's authoritative, overbearing, expects instant compliance to his orders, doesn't deal well with mutinous or disrespectful behavior, and commands attention in everything from his attitude to his sheer size. He is a man who battles verbally and physically with dexterity, but due to his other attributes, he puts his foot in his mouth more often than he is comfortable with. His prowess in battle contributes to his cocky demeanor and makes him less able to see when he's pushed too far with others around him, making it more difficult for him to interact naturally and form relationships.

On the surface, Jo seems like his perfect female counterpart, fire and fire. She's intelligent, pulls no punches, says things that hurt, and seems intent not to form relationships with the Warriors around her, but Jo isn't quite what she seems. Though...she is Adam's perfect match in many ways.

Chapter Seven

October 2nd, 2024

"I still don't think this is necessary," she stated flatly, in a voice that sounded like she was a woman who was accustomed to her orders being followed.

"It is," Kord assured her, firmly but kindly.

"I *have* an amulet." Her tone drifted over the line into sarcasm, and Adam winced, waiting for Kord to bring the hammer down.

What came down was more of a pillow than a hammer. "Which is of no use against a null weapon. They know who you are now, and this new plan of theirs to kill off the doctors..."

Ah, a doctor. That's why Kord is cutting her slack. But this was a lot more slack than Adam had ever seen him cut someone.

"But moving me two states? Really, Lord Maher!"

Adam scowled. There was nothing worse than a protected who wasn't capable of simply following orders. and *Kord expects me to babysit her for the next three weeks?* He'd thought he'd paid his dues and paid them well. *What did I do to end up back on scut duty?* He bit back a sigh. Maybe Kord just wanted the best he had to keep Miss Smart-Mouth alive that long.

"It's all arranged," Kord replied simply. "I'll oversee moving your belongings. The position in Mississippi is ideal. It's more money and a smaller community than Oklahoma City was.

The house is superior, and you have three weeks of leisure—my treat."

Her voice rose in near-warning. "Treat? With all due respect—"

Adam had heard enough. He pushed the door open and ducked inside. "With all due respect," he interrupted her in a gruff voice, "your protection must come first. Kord is being more than kind." *Much more kind than I'll be if you take this attitude with me.*

The woman turned to him. Her eyes settled momentarily at his chest level, where she would expect to meet any other Warrior's eyes, then she tipped her head back, following the line of his breastbone up to his face. He waited for shock to register in her expression. It typically took a few seconds for his sheer size to hit them full force.

This one rolled her bright blue eyes, scrunching her sun-pinked nose. "I take it this is your bulldog," she noted acidly.

"This is my grandson—"

"Adam," she inserted before Kord could, turning away and fluffing the short, blonde hair around her face. "Yes. I figured that out."

"You've met?" Kord asked.

Thankfully, no.

The woman snickered. "I've heard of him."

Adam stiffened at the implied insult. "Then you've heard I do my job well and expect a protected to obey my orders without argument."

She laughed outright. "Well, I've heard the second half, anyway."

"Meaning what, precisely? If you'd rather have another—"

"Adam," Kord warned.

"Right," he replied, fighting the tension in his jaw. "I assume you're ready to leave?" All he'd been told was that it was an emergency move he'd be overseeing, but Kord usually arranged even emergency moves to be handled smoothly.

She pointed over her shoulder. "My bag is right there."

"Good. I have my orders already, so I'll see you at the car, Miss..." *And the more time she takes getting there, the more time I'll have to calm down before she does.*

"Jo," she offered. "Joanne Wright of the Boston Wrights."

"Of course. How stupid of me." He turned and hoisted her bag, marching down the stairs.

Wonderful! He was stuck with the proverbial bitch from Boston for almost a month. *What did I do to deserve this one?*

****

Jo hesitated in the entryway, slipping her Gucci 2526 tiger eye sunglasses onto her face and taking a deep breath. She strode out into the New Mexico sunlight. The glasses were useful for more than protecting her eyes from the harsh rays; they masked her slow inventory of Adam Maher quite effectively.

The man was eye candy if she'd ever seen it, and with the company Jo had kept for the last three years, she'd seen more than her share, several of them up close and personally. She felt a sweat break out completely unconnected to the mounting heat of the day.

Adam leaned against a black MDX: Wave Killer sunglasses reflecting her image, six feet seven or eight of mouth-watering muscle, sporting one of those spiky top haircuts with some length to the back and a package between his legs big enough to keep almost any woman entertained.

She sighed and moved on. Too bad this candy was so sour. By all accounts, Adam Maher was nothing but trouble for any woman who had to depend on him...and most men.

He opened the door for her without a word.

Jo settled on the seat, grasping the seatbelt. She met Adam's eyes through both sets of sunglasses, wondering at his continued presence. "Thank you," she offered curtly, hinting that he should get moving.

"Oh, good. You know how to say it."

Before she could reply, he'd shut the door and started around the vehicle. Jo secured her seatbelt, determined to ignore him. Adam seemed inclined to do the same. The first twenty or thirty miles passed in silence.

"So, you're a little young to be a doctor," he noted.

"I'm a nurse practitioner, but considering Warrior healing, it doesn't make much of a difference."

"Of course. Why did you leave Cross range?"

She shrugged. Her real reason for leaving was none of his business. "Explaining Warriors to debutantes isn't all that easy, Mr. Maher."

"Adam will be fine." He didn't acknowledge the snub.

Jo considered her options for ending the conversation. All things considered, the less she talked to him, the better. "Adam?" she half-laughed. "Are you sure you don't want me to call you Conan?"

His hands tightened on the wheel, and he shot her a look that fluctuated between fury and disbelief. "Adam will be fine, darlin'."

Jo shivered, then scowled at his familiarity. Still, he was angry, which meant he'd likely keep his distance, and that was just what she wanted.

****

"So, who told you about Conan?" Adam's voice was truly conversational for the first time in their short acquaintance.

Jeez! Doesn't he know when to shut up? After eight hours in the car, the last thing Jo wanted was another reminder of who Lord Maher had saddled her with.

"Seriously, who told you about that name?" he persisted.

Well, Adam certainly wasn't easy to turn aside, not that she'd expected him to be. Jo turned the page in her book, steeling her expression. "I thought that was common knowledge," she stated calmly. It wasn't, but she wasn't about to let Adam off the hook that easily. He'd hurt too many people she cared about for that.

"Let me guess. You came from Cross range. Erin avoids doctors like the plague, and the Lords and Lady of Cross and König wouldn't pass those tired old tales on. That leaves Hunter."

She didn't answer him, feigning interest in the book.

"Ah. I see. It *was* Hunter." He didn't seem upset, which surprised her. What had happened to his anger? She'd been counting on it.

"I've met a lot of Warriors, Mr. Maher. They come from all over to see the Königs. They all have stories to tell, you know. and I've heard more than my share."

"I wouldn't have thought the society princess would spend a lot of time slumming with the help."

That's better. There's the annoyance, but admitting I've spent a lot of time with Warriors was a mistake. "I enjoy studying the dynamics of Warrior psychology," she offered without looking up. *How long have I been staring at this page? Maybe I should turn it.*

"Do you?" There was something of a taunt in that.

"I find your complete inability to ground yourselves fascinating. You are always at one extreme or another, always dependant on interaction with another to control you. Whether you find that centering in battle training, battle, or a woman, it cannot come completely from within."

He settled on the sofa next to her. "That's a very interesting observation. What does Daddy think of his darlin's research project?" Surprisingly, he stopped short of asking how in depth she took the study.

"Nothing." She pushed to her feet and headed for the larger bedroom.

"Trouble in Beantown," he mused, sounding entirely too smug. "That's why you left Cross."

"Not at all," she replied, covering her aching heart with an air of cold indifference. "But don't take my word for it. If a beast ever kills you, you can ask him yourself."

She glanced back at him from the bedroom doorway, noting his pallor in satisfaction. She closed herself into the room, heading to the bathroom to splash cold water on her face. Remembering her father always left a bad taste in her mouth and an empty ache in the pit of her stomach.

Chapter Eight

October 3rd, 2024

"I guess I owe you an apology," Adam offered, forcing out the foreign words. He only hoped this one would be better received than the last he'd attempted.

Jo looked up from her sandwich, searching his face as she swallowed. She shrugged, looking at her plate and picking a corn chip from the untouched pile. "You can't help it," she dismissed him.

He froze, his coffee cup halfway to his mouth. "Excuse me?"

"A very intelligent woman once told me that males were genetically predisposed to being thoughtless assholes. Oh, and arrogant. She definitely said arrogant. I have to admit that I've found her observations to be very astute."

He set the coffee down a little more forcefully than he'd intended to, sloshing it over the rim. "Really?" he asked, clamping down on the last of his calm. Did she set out to irritate him? It certainly seemed like it to him.

"Yes. From that frame of reference, you can't help sticking your foot in your mouth at every turn. I've come to expect it."

Adam rubbed at the tension in his temple. "Who do I have to thank for introducing you to this nugget of wisdom?" he managed with just a touch of sarcasm.

She smiled sweetly. "Erin König-Crossbearer."

He forced his annoyance back, abruptly suspicious that Jo's information had come from what he'd previously considered the least likely source. Usually Erin avoided doctors, but maybe that didn't extend to female doctors or to nurse practitioners. If her information came from Erin, there was no telling what bullshit Jo believed him guilty of.

"And who, pray tell, was Erin referring to when she imparted this advice to you?"

Jo chuckled, swallowing a mouthful of her fruit juice without spraying by the grace of whatever god she worshiped. "As I recall, she didn't mention names. Then again, Erin would have a hard time choosing. Every Warrior in existence seems to—"

"I must have missed the section in the Rules of Sanction that states Warriors are required to accept abuse from protecteds."

"Really? I must have missed the section that stated I have to like putting up with the Warrior's crap."

"You think I've been giving you shit so far?" Boy, was she in for a major surprise if she answered in the affirmative. If there was one thing he was sure of, it was that she had no clue how dangerous antagonizing a Warrior was.

She shrugged and sipped her juice again.

"You ain't seen the half of it, darlin'."

Jo rolled her eyes much as she had in Kord's office, going back to her sandwich, though with the same little shiver she couldn't quite suppress every time he slipped into a thicker-than-normal accent.

Adam found himself analyzing her fighting style much as he would any other beast. He winced at the comparison, then continued.

He replayed their discussions thus far. Was he imagining that she seemed to get more abrasive every time he tried to extend the hand of friendship? Jo wouldn't be the first woman who'd kept up a smart-ass attitude to hide that she was interested in him. *Maybe I need to pay less attention to what she says and more attention to when and why she says it.*

Chapter Nine

October 6th, 2024

Jo stiffened as Adam sat down beside her, looking up at him out of the corner of her eye. "Yes?" she asked coolly, trying to ignore the skip of her heart at his proximity.

"I thought we should go over the plan for when we reach Ripley."

"I know how to check into a new job, Mr. Maher, and Kord briefed me on the new house, complete with blueprints," she finished wryly.

He propped an elbow on the back of the couch, half turning toward her. "Why don't you ever call me Adam?"

"Is there a reason I should?"

"I asked you to," he pointed out to her.

"This isn't something I have to obey you about. My safety hardly depends on using familiar address with you."

She attempted to focus on her reading, but Adam's hovering made that a physical impossibility. Jo cursed it silently. They'd been cooped up together for four days, and she still found herself rereading every word she attempted several times before it stuck. The man was infuriating, but he was undeniably hot enough to drive a woman to distraction. She'd known that before she left Crossbearer range. Not that Erin had used that term for him, but her description of Adam, when he wasn't acting like a complete jerk, sounded hot to Jo just the same.

I knew coming here was a bad idea. I should have gone to Armen.

Oh, so Todd Armen could finally convince me?

Decidedly a bad idea! Hunter range...

No, there was more than one Warrior in Hunter that she'd like to get to know better. How many times had she argued this with herself before she decided that it had to be Maher range, where she didn't know any Warriors? Too many.

She bit back a sigh. Maher range was perfect. All she had to do was keep the Warriors at arm's length.

As if taking up the challenge, Adam shifted closer to her.

Jo edged away, trying to make it look innocent, maybe like he was blocking her light with his strong, hard, luscious—

Stop it! Hot or not, a Warrior seeking release is not what I want. I want—

She'd always wanted the depth of printing. Sure, sex with a Warrior was addictive, but Jo had already made that mistake. Enticing as it was, it wasn't enough.

Oh, and the light is over your other shoulder. Jo rubbed her forehead to hide a grimace at that thought. The last thing she wanted was to be transparent and give Adam any indication that she could be convinced.

"We're stuck out here together," he ventured. "There is very little in the way of amusement, and—"

"Get this straight, Warrior." She adopted the snap of Erin's voice when she was "officially ticked off." "I am not here for your *amusement*. I am only here because keeping this damned amulet depends on me obeying orders given for my safety, no matter how stupid I think they are." She pushed to her feet. What was the point of sitting here, when she couldn't concentrate? "And I'm starting to wonder if that's worth it." This man could drive her to drink, and Warriors in general seemed to be her personal weakness.

His look of male interest faded into concern, and his biceps bunched slightly. "You don't mean that."

"Why not?" she challenged him. "I haven't been fed on."

"They know who you are now! The hive mind has you on file. If one beast sees you, it's over. Without your amulet—"

"Give it a rest. Without the amulet, they'll know I'm not a protected professional in your service anymore. They'll know I'm not a threat to them anymore."

Adam moved so quickly, he had her by the arms before she noted movement. She shivered at the touch of such a powerful Warrior. She'd met many. She'd seen them train, and few were as fast as Adam was. To date, only the Königs matched him. Jo forced herself to follow what he was saying.

"No, Jo. They'll know *I'm* no threat to them. They'll take you down for the thrill of the hunt and the knowledge that they'll be hurting every Warrior who—"

"Hurting you?" she thundered, trying to pull out of his grip. "Why would it hurt you? I'm nothing but a duty to you. You don't know me or care about me. Or is failure that painful to you?"

He dragged her to his chest, his eyes narrowed like the predator they emulated, seemingly fighting back a murderous rage. "I will admit that you don't make it easy to like you, but if you think all you are is a duty to me, you have no understanding of the Warriors, at all. Yes, losing you will hurt. It will hurt me. It will hurt any Warrior who's ever met you, anyone who has ever protected you."

Jo stammered out the beginnings of a protest, all too aware of the press of his body to hers, but Adam kept talking.

"Not having your amulet is the worst thing I can imagine for you. Without it, you have no chance in the face of a beast. He'll kill you without question and without remorse. He will kill you without warning, and there won't be anyone protecting you."

She forced her breathing to even then answered him in a low, calm voice. "According to Kord, the amulet is useless. If a beast sees me, even if I'm still wearing it, I'm as good as dead. So, tell me why I should keep it."

His hands gentled, and he drew her the rest of the way to his chest, enveloping her in his arms. "I won't allow it," he breathed. "That is the difference. As long as you have the amulet, you have me."

Jo closed her eyes, relaxing against him, the feeling of being cherished warming her beyond the shared heat of his body. She winced at that. What was she thinking? This wasn't a profession of love! She was a protected professional. The Warriors wouldn't want to let her choose to leave them. They'd want to make Jo feel safe and important. It wasn't personal.

She bit her lip. But would they lie to get it? Their moral code would preclude using trickery to get something advantageous, but she couldn't be certain that all of them would live to that code.

"You should let me go," she suggested. She enjoyed being in his arms too much, maybe enough to make her ignore her discomfort with the life she'd lived with the Warriors thus far.

"Don't make this decision without thinking it through. Don't make it without talking to me. Promise me, please."

"Let me go, Adam." She wasn't making any promises, especially not to a Warrior with a sexual interest in her.

He backed away, the beginnings of a smile curving his lips. "As you wish, Jo."

She fluffed her hair, looking away. "What's so damned funny?" she asked.

"Nothing. It was just nice to hear you say my name."

"Don't get used to it."

Chapter Ten

October 13th, 2024

Adam hesitated then nearly growled in frustration. Second-guessing himself was becoming a habit where Jo was concerned. The woman was driving him crazy. He couldn't figure out if she was interested or not. Every time he thought he had her pegged, she did something that seemed to blow his assumptions out of the water. Dear gods, but he had to know for certain, and if the only way to do that was to push some buttons, he was going to do it and see which lights turned on.

He knocked on her bedroom door and waited for her to acknowledge his presence.

Jo opened the door, glaring at him. "Yes?" she asked in the superior Boston-bitch tone.

"Just checking," he informed her.

"Checking? Checking what?"

He smiled, ranging his eyes down her body, much as she had when he'd been inspecting his weapons at the table. "Just making sure you haven't decided to take off."

Jo darkened, and she opened her mouth and closed it twice before she forced herself to speak. "You know I hate you, don't you?"

Adam smiled at that. Her voice was breathless, and her eyes were locked on his bare chest. Her hand moved as if to touch him then fisted and returned to her side.

"Yeah, I know how much you hate me," he assured her.

"Good. Then you will remove yourself to your room and not bother me again tonight."

"You forgot one step, darlin'." He deepened his drawl, anticipating the demure Eastern shiver it would set off.

Jo didn't disappoint him. "What did I forget, Mr. Maher?"

"A good night kiss."

Her eyes widened. Jo placed a hand on his chest as if to push him away. "You think I'm going to—"

"Yes, I do, and I think you want to."

She didn't deny it.

Adam leaned toward her, giving Jo every opportunity to push him away. Her arm folded with his forward motion until it was snug to her ribs. Her eyes closed, and she tipped her head back to meet his lips fully.

The kiss was slow and solemn, a deep discovery in more ways than one. He'd known Jo would be different from the first time he touched her, and she was. No woman had ever kissed him like she did.

Jo threw herself into the moment, seemingly oblivious as Adam traced his fingertips up her side. He stroked the rigid tip of one nipple, and she sighed into his mouth. He broke off the kiss, giving her the opening she needed to make a coherent decision.

For a moment, she didn't move. Jo stood with her hand pressed to his chest and her eyes closed, enjoying his still-stroking fingers. "So good," she whispered.

Adam smiled. Oh, yes. Jo wanted him, and she was willing. Maybe she'd even decide he wasn't such a horrible person once he rocked her world a few times and she let him get more than five words out without taking his head off.

"Warriors are so good," she groaned.

He pushed away from her, running his hand through his spiked hair with a muttered curse. Why did the gods have to curse him this way?

"What is it?" Jo asked, confusion darkening her eyes to a stormy sea blue.

"You're a blade chaser?" he asked.

Her cheeks turned crimson, and her eyes were piercingly clear again. "I think it would be more accurate to say that every Warrior I meet is a skirt chaser," she countered hotly.

"Well, you hardly seem adverse to the idea." And that thought ate at him for some reason he couldn't begin to fathom. What did it matter if she was a blade chaser? He'd had a few. It was a fact that he hadn't enjoyed them nearly as much as some Warriors did, but he'd tried it. The fact that they existed had never bothered him before, and he'd found them useful for a quick fuck on more than one occasion. So, why now? Why did it bother him that Jo was a blade chaser?

Jo growled at him, fisting her hands as if she meant to belt him across the mouth. "Typical! You Warriors can be rutting pigs, but let a woman enjoy the ride, and she's the one in the wrong."

"Well, I wouldn't worry if I were you," he shot back.

"And why is that?"

"Because, I'm not like every other Warrior you've met. I—"

"Who said I slept with them all? I never said—"

"I am not a rutting pig, and I have no intention of becoming just another Warrior one night stand to you."

"I hate you," she repeated, slipping back into the bedroom and slamming the door between them.

"Good," he shouted through it. Adam ambled back to the couch, his jaw clenched tight. It was good that she hated him. He didn't need another empty fuck in his life. The fact that he didn't want her to be another one intruded on his fury, and he shoved it away. He wasn't going there, either. *Not with a blade chaser.*

But... His mind kicked in again, something he found difficult when he touched Jo. Just having her in his arms made his thinking mind take a quick holiday. He nearly groaned at that. What was it about her that made him lose IQ points?

Never mind that. You wanted to push buttons and you did. It's time to analyze what you learned from it.

She claimed that Warriors were unthinking assholes, completely incapable of living moderately. While he'd disagree about the first half, there was no denying that the second half was largely correct.

Back to the subject... What else did she say?

Jo believed all Warriors were skirt chasers. His gut rolled at that. If she believed all Warriors were skirt chasers, it was unlikely that she was a blade chaser. Blade chasers enjoyed the game; they played on the urges that drove the Warriors to get their kicks. If there was one thing he could bank on, it was that Jo didn't get off on Warriors bedding women indiscriminately.

It was much more likely that she'd thought a Warrior was serious when all the creep wanted was release. Adam fisted his hand at the thought of it, the drive to slit a throat strong in his mind.

Relief that her actions didn't support the image of Jo as a blade chaser slammed into him, forcing him to re-examine the reason why that belief burned as deeply as it did. He didn't want her to be seeking simple release, and he was what Calvin called "stupid for a woman". The more time he spent with Jo, the more certain he was about both of those facts.

He groaned, praying that he wasn't printing. While Kord would be more understanding about it than Calvin would have been, it wasn't a good thing to be distracted when he might have to protect her from beasts. He did have a duty to perform, and he wasn't certain how well he could perform it if he was thinking with the wrong head.

Adam turned toward her door, considering their situation. If Jo wasn't looking for release and neither was he, there was a chance for them yet.

Chapter Eleven

October 15th, 2024

Jo peeked up at Adam again. He sat on the grass, meticulously cleaning and sharpening a full arsenal of weapons in the dark, consecrated metal of a sacred weapon. She looked away, feigning interest in her book, visions of Adam wielding the broadsword dancing in her mind. It wasn't an image she needed to have; she needed to snap out of it. That was easier said than done.

He stood, swiping a cloth down the weapon's length and dropping the soiled material at his feet. Adam dwarfed even the huge sword. He hefted it in his right hand, the muscles in his arm and back tightening as he executed a practice swing.

Her gaze ranged over his body, drinking in the spiked hair and the ponytail that settled between his shoulder blades. The weapons belt hung at his narrow waist, scabbard and sheath strapped to his thighs beneath his tight denim-clad butt.

Nothing about Adam was typical, even for a Warrior; from his choice of weapons to his sheer size—even his choice of footwear. Most Warriors wore the black armored boots. Only Erin and Adam veered from that path, but while Erin wore steel-toed hiking boots, Adam wore soft, brown suede boots that reached his knees and resembled moccasins in many ways. They couldn't offer much protection for his feet and legs in a fight, though by all accounts, Adam had little need for armor of any type. He was one of the few Warriors without battle scars—save those that Hunter gave him in trial for his offenses against Erin.

Adam moved suddenly, sliding the broadsword into its scabbard and turning toward her. For one timeless moment, she stared at his bare chest then the outline of his cock behind his jeans, achingly hungry for him. She met his startling blue eyes, and common sense kicked in.

Pretending she was reading was a lost cause. Jo vaulted to her feet and headed inside, making a beeline for her room and the safety it afforded at a near run.

"Jo?" His voice came from just behind her.

Forcing speech was beyond her. Instead, she slammed the bedroom door behind her and leaned against it.

Adam knocked lightly. "Jo? Please, tell me what's wrong."

"Nothing," she lied, grimacing that she'd sunk this low.

"If you're sure..."

"I am." Jo held her breath until she noted the sounds of him moving away.

She had to stay away from him. The longer she stayed with Adam, the more Jo wanted him. The kiss they'd shared, no matter how much an asshole he'd been afterward, had her glancing at his lips far too often and wanting more. She couldn't let this happen again, even if it meant hiding in her room as much as possible.

Worse even than playing the fool again was the fact that some part of herself was setting her up for the kill. The more time Jo spent with Adam, the more convinced she became that there was more to him than the loudmouthed, overbearing punk Erin had painted him, the more convinced she was that he was a sincere and caring man who wanted more than the simple release all Warriors thrived on.

If only she could believe he wasn't like every other Warrior beneath his exterior as he claimed...

What? I'll end up getting my heart broken again? That isn't an option.

****

Adam sighed, pressing his forehead to the door. Kissing her had been sublime, but then he'd opened his mouth and inserted his foot—as usual, it seemed. If he could just learn to keep his mouth shut and stop reacting without reason, he might have something good in his life. More than ever, he wanted that good thing to be Jo, for as long as it lasted.

He couldn't have explained exactly why he felt that way about her, but he did. What little he knew about Jo made him want to know more, but the cordless uplink didn't work away from major communication centers, and Kord hadn't approved the satellite uplink he'd requested yet. Without his computer, Adam felt like he was running blind. Jo knew much more than he

168

wanted her to know about him—and yet less than he did in all the areas that mattered most.

What did he know about her? She was passionate, intelligent, no-nonsense, tough and yet frightened of something he couldn't name, so frightened that she shied from him at every turn. But how much of that was her own demons, how much were the crap stories she'd been told about him, and how much was his big mouth shooting him down? Adam had to admit that he was often his own worst enemy.

The Warrior in him demanded he soothe any fears she had as he would for any protected, especially a *woman* under his care. The man in him wanted more than that.

Adam sighed. To have any chance with Jo, he'd have to avoid Foot In Mouth Disease for a while. and he'd have to shut her sarcastic mouth as well, or he wouldn't be able to stifle his knee-jerk reactions to her. If only they didn't talk to each other, he might be able to scale the walls Jo had in place.

Chapter Twelve

October 17th, 2024

Adam closed his hands on Jo's shoulders, kneading her muscles. At first she tensed, but she soon relaxed into his hands, allowing him to ease the ache she'd been rubbing at for the last ten minutes.

She stretched her back, her nipples straining against the fabric of her blouse. His mouth watered in anticipation of tasting them. He dropped to one knee behind her, forcing his ragged breaths to even, reminding himself of what he had to do. She was relaxed, and he intended to keep her that way as long as he could, but that meant avoiding conversation at any cost.

Jo turned her head to one side, moaning, and Adam used the opening to press his lips to her throat.

She bit her lip. "You shouldn't—"

"Shut up," he grumbled.

She looked at him warily. "What did you—"

Adam turned his head around hers, sealing his mouth to hers slowly, reverently. Jo backed off, her lips softening as he leaned with her.

Her hands traced his chest up to his shoulders, and she twisted toward him. Her lips parted beneath his, and she tasted inside his slightly parted lips, inviting him deeper.

He groaned, lifting her over the back of the chair and pulling her down over him on the floor.

Jo tangled with him, her legs wrapping around one of his, moaning as Adam played his thigh against her core, her mouth leaving his, her eyes closing and back arching. She was stunning.

"Jo," he began.

"Shut up," she ordered.

He didn't laugh, though he wanted to. "Gladly." As long as they were on the same page, he wasn't going to complain about it.

Her mouth returned to his, and she rocked her hips back and forth, riding the top of his thigh, the damp heat making him moan in need. It wasn't enough. Adam pulled her further up, pressing the ridge of his cock to her, seeking her agreement.

Jo arched away from his mouth again, grinding onto him with a gasp. "Adam," she pleaded.

"Shut up."

She nodded, pressing a kiss to his throat, her fingers working his shirt buttons open.

Adam turned her beneath him, pressing into her harder and returning the favor of opening her shirt. He dragged his off, watching hungrily as she did the same.

Then they were mouth to mouth again, the satiny material of her bra brushing his chest. She arched her back, and the satin started sliding away between their bodies.

He bit back a series of curses, the urge to pull her jeans down to her knees and take her hard and fast on the floor almost insurmountable. It wouldn't happen that way. He had far too much respect for Jo to fuck her on the floor when there was a bed twenty feet away. *Mine!* He did groan at that thought.

Adam lifted Jo from the floor and strolled toward the bed.

She laid her head back, rolling it to one side to watch the room passing by. "Where are we going?" she asked, then licked her lips slowly.

"Do you want me?" he asked, praying she wouldn't deny it.

"Oh, yeah," she breathed.

"Then—"

"I know. Shut up."

He sat on the bed, pulling her astride him. Jo pressed down on him, her nipples catching on the curls that lightly covered his chest.

Adam thumbed open the button on her jeans, smiling at her sharply indrawn breath. Her eyes closed again, and she shivered in the demure fashion she possessed as he eased the zipper down.

The sky blue underwear matched the bra they'd discarded in the living room. His gaze was riveted to her, and he cataloged every inch he would taste before he took her—all of it. If he could only decide where to start...

Her breasts!

Jo cried out softly as he leaned her back over his left arm and took a good portion of one breast into his mouth, sucking, licking, and stroking all at once. He slid the index and middle fingers of his right hand inside her loosened jeans, finding her clit through the sopping satin.

In no time, she was grinding against his circling fingers and holding his head to

172

whichever breast he chose to torment. It wasn't enough. He had to taste all of her before he sated himself inside her.

Adam settled her on her feet, steadying Jo as he stripped her jeans and panties off. On his knees, her scent taunted him, calling to him. He smiled. "Put your hands on my head," he ordered.

Jo hesitated for only a moment then ran her fingers through his hair. He extended his arms through the gap between her thighs and urged them wider. With his elbows hooked under her thighs, he grasped her waist and lifted. Her fists tightened in his hair, and she sucked in a startled breath. Women always reacted that way at his show of strength, but the results were worth it in the end.

Adam ignored the slight discomfort, positioning her sweet center in front of his mouth. He ran his tongue along her slit, millimeter by millimeter, biting back a groan as she wrapped her legs over his shoulders to pull him closer with her calf muscles.

He tasted all of her, inside and out, flicking his tongue over her, burying it inside her, and sucking at her clit. Jo's hands fisted in his hair again, and she leaned back in his hands, opening herself to him with a series of little cries of pleasure.

And then she plunged over, her legs and fingers tightening, her sheath contracting against his probing tongue, her honey coating his lips and chin, screaming his name. Still, he drove her on, determined to give her an experience she'd never forget.

Jo climaxed again, her cry choked as he thrust his tongue deeper, her hands shaking. "Adam," she managed, her weight sinking into his hands fully, nearly boneless.

He settled her on the bed, laying beside her. She was beautiful, her short hair mussed and her eyes closed, her nipples tightened to points and her thighs rubbing against each other restlessly. It was the most sensual look he'd ever seen on a woman. She arched her back, forcing her breasts toward him unconsciously.

Adam couldn't resist tasting them. Jo's hands wrapped in his hair again, dragging the leather tie away so that the black curtain surrounded his lower face and brushed over her breasts. Her body turned to his, her hands leaving his head, trailing down his chest and pulling his jeans open in silent demand.

He sensed her frantically, nearly cursing that she was nearing high cycle. Adam dragged his wallet out, pulled a condom free and ripped it open with his teeth.

"Adam?" she called in a surer voice. "You really shouldn't carry condoms in your pocket. The heat from your body, over time—"

She fell silent as he shot her a look of disbelief. *Of all the times to play doctor...*

He tossed the wallet away, pulled his jeans off, and then rolled the condom down his length, eager to feel her body gripping him. Jo didn't give him time to consider what position he wanted to take her in. She pushed him to his back and straddled him, encasing him in her heat smoothly.

He groaned, battling back release as she started moving over him. Adam met her motions, cycling faster and deeper until he felt the brush of her cervix at every pass, and still it wasn't enough.

Her eyes closed, and her head rocked back. She bit her lip, riding hard on him. Her body spasmed rhythmically around him, announcing how close she was to releasing for him again.

Adam forced himself not to come, desperate to feel her shatter around his cock instead of his tongue. She obliged him, a formless scream ripped from her lips as her inner muscles milked him toward his own climax.

He followed her over, growling harshly at his slipping control. He lay beneath her, sweat soaked and panting, shaken in a way sex had never shaken him before. Adam licked his lips, wondering at what this feeling meant. Was he printing on her? It was decidedly too early to know for certain. Did he want forever or did he just want her as long as they could keep their mouths otherwise occupied?

Jo collapsed to his chest with a sigh, and he wrapped his arms around her. A smile curved his lips, and he swallowed a laugh of relief.

"I've wanted to do that since the first day with you," he mused.

She went still, so still and quiet that it made him distinctly nervous.

"What is it?" he asked.

Jo shook her head, easing off of his cock and working her mouth down his body. Adam fought for a decent breath, his arousal immediate and undeniable. She peeled the condom off and tossed it into the waste basket beside his bed.

He groaned her name, needing to understand her actions, even as his mind struggled to function and his body responded to her attention. Her mouth closed around his length, and he cried out harshly at the ruthless efficiency with which she sucked him. His mind refused to cooperate. Whatever this strange mood was, he'd investigate it later. There was no way he was interrupting something so glorious just to insist that she open her mouth and end this cease-fire.

****

Jo studied Hunter's profile in the starlight, tracing every line with her gaze. He was everything she could imagine wanting in a man: responsible, funny, gorgeous, caring... Sure, he was almost a decade younger than she was, but Warriors matured younger than human men, coming to full adulthood at only fifteen. By that reckoning, they were contemporaries.

"Gorgeous night, isn't it?" Hunter asked.

"Definitely." She sighed, wishing he'd look at her instead of the night sky.

He turned onto his side, a playful smile on his lips. "What are you thinking?"

Jo could hardly believe her ears. It was obvious any move would have to be hers, and he'd given her the perfect opening. She pressed her body to his, stroking his length through his jeans and purring in satisfaction as he hardened.

"This is what I'm thinking."

She pulled the button on his jeans open and slid the zipper down, heartened by his sharply indrawn breath and piercing eyes. Jo tugged his shirt from his jeans and eased down his body, taking the head in her mouth and swirling her tongue around it slowly.

Hunter kicked his jeans away and dragged his shirt off, even unbuckling his weapons belt and letting it lay under him so he was nude head to knees. He paused as she took advantage of that fact and took him deep. He pulled at the clasp on her halter, releasing it.

"Gods, yes," he groaned, tipping his hips against her, sliding his length in and out of her mouth smoothly. "I've wanted this forever."

Yes! She'd hoped he was interested, that he simply hadn't pursued her for fear of taking advantage.

Jo pushed him on, determined to make him come, but Hunter had other ideas. He pulled her up his body and sealed his mouth to hers, parting her lips as he dragged her skirt up and her panties down over her bent knees and bare feet.

His hands were everywhere, kneading her breasts, stroking her clit then cupping her buttocks as he rolled her beneath him and thrust deep inside. Hunter didn't pause but took her in hard, fast strokes. His ferocity stunned and pleased her; she'd seen him fight beasts in a less involved manner.

The combination of the pure sensations and that thought sent her hurtling into a kinetic, breath-stealing orgasm. The stars seemed to spin around her; trails of light streaked across the sky.

Hunter filled her again and again, his cum flooding her with heat. He whispered his thanks to her and the gods, his body relaxing further than Jo had ever seen it before. He grumbled a curse, his mouth exploring her face, clearly still aroused and ready to experience a more subdued joining.

It was only three days later when her illusion of a future with Hunter was shattered.

She strode into the training house in Cross range, looking forward to seeing Hunter again. She found Erin instead.

"Where's your big brother hiding?" Jo called out.

Erin didn't look up from the ancient book in her hands. "Out at a bar, picking up a lay for the evening. You know those Warriors. Stab it, screw it, or marry it."

Jo's heart refused to hold a steady rhythm. Yes, that was precisely what Warriors were like. The problem was, she wasn't a "marry it". If she were, Hunter wouldn't be off screwing someone else. He'd be anticipating her return, eaten up by printing. She was just another "screw it" to him.

"Oh," she managed weakly, taking a shaky step back. "Thanks, Erin."

The girl's head snapped up, and she winced. "Oh, gods. No... I'll kill him, Jo. I swear I will."

"No. Don't do that. He doesn't... He didn't make any promises."

178

Hunter hadn't. She'd simply rationalized that he would when he was ready to, but Jo was honest enough to admit that she'd only been fantasizing—that, among other things. She'd read too much into his comments and his interest. Of course, Hunter wanted her. He was a young male Warrior, and she was a willing woman. His mentality only ran a few directions. Since she didn't actively need his protection that night, she was seen as material for simple release. It was nothing more than that.

Erin's voice brought her out of her self-recrimination. "Men are dogs, and Warriors worst of all! You know, men are genetically predisposed to being arrogant, thoughtless assholes. It comes from testosterone poisoning, and since Warriors have all the other traits of a high level of testosterone, I guess they just have to display that one, too."

Jo laughed though tears stung her eyes. It was hard to remember that Erin was only fifteen, sometimes. "Thanks. I needed that." She took another step toward the door. "I should go."

"Sure you won't stay?" Erin asked.

Her heart ached at the idea of seeing Hunter come in, that lazy post-coital smile on his face courtesy of another woman, smelling of her, tasting of her, thinking of her. She shook her head. "Not a good idea."

Erin sighed. "Of course not. Jo..."

"Yes?"

"What will you do now?" she asked, perhaps suspecting what Jo planned, the urge Jo had to run, to go someplace where she wouldn't have to

see Hunter, wouldn't have to treat him on the remote chance that he was injured, wouldn't have to deliver his baby from whatever woman he eventually chose.

"I don't know," she lied. In actuality, she was already planning a stop at the manor. Then she'd go home and pack. Piers wouldn't like her choice, but he would support it.

"Goodbye, Jo." Erin's voice was low and sad. There was little question that she knew this would be the last time they would see each other in Cross range.

Chapter Thirteen

October 18th, 2024

Jo snapped awake, staring at Adam miserably. She'd done it again. She'd had another meaningless fling with a Warrior.

Keep this up and you'll earn the title of blade chaser. She winced at that. As much as she'd like to deny it, one glance at Adam's bare chest had her salivating for another taste. Oh, yes. If he woke up now, she'd screw him in an instant.

Her mind protested that. She had more self-respect than that. Jo wouldn't be screwing him; she'd be making love to him.

Or, would she? Did both people have to want it to be more than bodies coming together for it to be making love? She bit back a groan at the fool she was. Why did her heart keep getting involved? It would be easier if she really were a blade chaser, out for nothing more than the quick thrill of bedding a Warrior.

What do I do now? She could leave again. Kord probably wouldn't argue it. It would mean she would be safely relocated in another range, and he wouldn't have to post a Warrior on her full-time and leave himself short in other areas.

And go where? Like it or not, I'm running out of options. If she went to Hunter range, she'd run into Hunter eventually—and Adam as well. She'd chosen Maher range in the first place, because Hunter didn't like visiting it. Well, that and the fact that she knew no Warriors in Maher range.

There's always Armen.

Until I screw an Armen. Jo bit back another groan, swallowing a sour lump in her throat. Todd Armen had come on to her before. How long would it be until she went for it and made this mess worse? It wasn't like she had a burning urge to relocate all the way to Europe, and... She sighed. Like it or not, she craved a Warrior, and she'd keep falling for them like an idiot until she ran out of ranges.

Unless I leave protection behind.

Her heart pounded at that thought. *Why not?* She hadn't been fed on; without her amulet, she was no more vulnerable than anyone else in the world.

Kord's warning echoed in her mind. Adam's plea joined it. What if they were telling the truth? What if the beasts would still target her?

Did it matter? No matter how close Kord kept a Warrior to her, there was a chance she could be killed—even with the amulet. In a world where purposely touching the beast to drive it away and praying for a Warrior's speed was your best hope, there was really no more protection in having it.

Jo eased out of the bed, pulling her clothes on silently. She would only have one shot at this. If Adam knew what she planned, he could stop her physically, demand she talk to him, convince her to have sex with him again, perhaps even convince her that sticking around as his toy would be enough for her.

It won't! She slipped out of his room and into her own. Luckily, she'd learned to live every moment as if she'd have to run. Her duffle was already packed and ready to go. Jo pulled on a jacket and shoes, hoisted it, and headed for the front door.

She paused at the peg board, her hand fisted around the amulet she wore, shaking. She had to do this. She took it off and hung it on the highest peg, taking down the MDX keys in the same movement.

Jo didn't look back. She couldn't; if she did, she'd talk herself out of leaving. She tossed her bag in the back seat, slid behind the wheel, moved the seat forward to accommodate her shorter legs, put her seatbelt on, started the engine, and gunned it down the gravel driveway—just as Adam launched through the cabin door.

His shout followed her, and she shivered, though she couldn't make out the words. She had to concentrate on her plan now. It would be Route 78 to 45, then south. She'd figure out the rest on the way. As long as she was headed nowhere near Ripley, she would be content.

****

Adam stood naked in the drive, staring at the departing SUV in amazement. *Not the vehicle!* He couldn't lie to himself about that. It wasn't losing his new MDX that made his heart ache. It was losing Jo.

He ambled back inside, stopping to stare at the amulet in sick resignation and confusion mixed. What had he done wrong? Why would she run from him?

Because we made love?

He snatched the amulet from the peg, his mind working at the problem. Had he convinced her to willingness? No. She'd been willing from the first kiss. He hadn't forced her in any way.

Had she thought he was just another skirt chaser? That was likely. He hadn't made his intentions clear, but he hadn't dumped her or treated her badly. Why would she leave before he'd made his intentions clear, before she was sure—and he was—what those intentions were?

Maybe he'd been too intent for her comfort. The sex between them had been explosive, a nonstop feast of sensation for half the night and a large slice of the morning. But they'd never talked. Every time one of them tried—mainly, Adam—the other would utter those two stupid words.

He winced at that. He'd never talked to Jo, though he knew she was upset about something, except to tell her to shut up and give him more sex. *Gods, what she must think of me!*

Adam strolled into the bedroom, lost in thought, and pulled on a fresh pair of jeans. He retrieved his cell phone with a sigh, hooking the headset over his ear, then grasped his boots and a clean pair of socks.

The only way to go after her was to call this fiasco in, but it was the last thing Adam wanted to do. If Kord or his father answered, Adam would have to endure "the discussion" about his self-control and interpersonal skills—or lack thereof, again. If Bryant or Curt answered, he'd have to put up with their shit. Neither option was particularly appealing, but every moment he wasted was another mile head start she had on him.

"Manor," he barked, resigning himself to hell on Earth to get what he needed to track her.

The phone emitted a sharp tone, and he stilled with one sock half on, swallowing a series of curses. They would just make the phone complain again.

"Manor," he stated slowly and calmly. Adam pulled on the sock, then the boot while the phone dialed, it rang twice and Bryant answered.

"Yeah?" he half-yawned.

"Get me a truck," Adam ordered without greeting him.

"Adam?" Bryant sounded only marginally more awake than he had a moment before.

"Who the hell else would it be?" he snapped.

"What is—"

"A truck. To the cabin. Now!" How much clearer would he have to make himself to wake his brother fully?

"What happened to yours?" At least he was conscious now, and the rustle of sheets on the other end proved he was moving.

"She took off on me, and I have to track her. Now, are you going to give me the means to do it or not?"

Bryant snickered. "The little lady doctor?"

"No, bonehead," he grumbled. "Cat woman. Bat Girl is hot in pursuit."

His brother's laughter deepened.

"Go soak your head," he offered Curt's usual response, at a loss for anything better. At the very least, the cold water might wake the little jerk up.

Adam yanked his other sock on, fuming. In truth, the three of them were too much alike. If he had answered this call from Bryant or Curt, Adam would have given them even more shit than he was being dealt. Still, that didn't mean he had to take it quietly.

"Poor Adam," Bryant drawled. "Women always running away from you. How'd you piss this one off?"

"A truck," he shouted. The last thing Adam needed was reminders of his failure with Erin right now. That would come from his father and Kord all too soon.

Just thinking of Erin filling Jo's head with all those old stories made him furious. It was no wonder that she'd run. She'd come into his life thinking of him as a complete creep. He'd never had an opportunity to prove he wasn't what she thought he was, and now the chance had slipped away.

"Cool your *Blutjagd*, brother. I just e-mailed Stan's Blackberry. He'll bring a vehicle to you within the hour. Is there anything else you need? A computer, maybe?"

"No. My main machine is in the MDX, but I have my tablet with me. Wait... I do need something. My wireless doesn't work out here. I won't be able to start a proper track until I reach town."

"And?"

"Pull Jo's file and read me the important parts."

There was silence save the tapping of keys on the other end then Bryant's muttering.

Adam paused, halfway to his feet to collect clean shirts. He forced himself to keep moving. "Bryant?"

"Wright. W-r-i-g-h-t?"

"That's her." He slid one arm into the shirt.

"No file."

"Joanne, with an e, Wright. She's a protected. We have a file."

"Correction, *mon frère*. *Crossbearer* has a file, and since I am not you, I am not going to hack into Cross to get it."

"What?" he demanded. "No one checked on this? I was sent off with a volatile protected and no—"

"It wasn't my job," Bryant protested.

"No. It wasn't." It was their father's job to make sure that the files came in with a new protected, and he'd dropped the ball. Adam was taking out his frustration on the wrong Warrior, but he could hardly vent on Lewis. If he tried it, the reply would be that if Adam hadn't screwed up in the first place, he wouldn't have needed the file.

His brother was abruptly serious. "You know what you have to do, don't you?"

Adam groaned.

"That's right, bro. You have to call Hunter."

"No. I have to call Crossbearer range." *Please, Gods! If you have any pity, don't let*

187

Hunter answer. Even the Lord König would be a blessing.

"Good luck, Adam." There was no taunt in that. Bryant knew better than anyone why he didn't want to make this call.

"Yeah. Thanks." He disconnected and pulled the headset off.

Adam took his time, pulling on his shirts, then the long leather duster he wore over them. He loaded up his weapons, taking special care with them. The Scorpion-style shurikens went in the inside pockets of the duster and the wushu in the padded sleeve down his back. He strapped on his full weapons belt, waist then thighs: his sacred weapon on his right hip, his broadsword on the left, and an arsenal of throwing daggers at his back.

Tyler Armen, the current weapons smith for the houses, had thought Adam was crazy to ask for sacred weapons in these specs, but the craftsman made them and they were consecrated in the Stone. Every Warrior deserved an indulgence for what he risked, and this was Adam's. At least it was an indulgence that aided in his duty, and he trained with them all.

At last, he had no excuse. Adam hooked the headset back onto his ear and slid the phone body into the Velcro pocket at his breast. "Crossbearer manor," he requested.

It was three long rings before someone picked up—and it was Hunter.

Adam bit back a harsh curse that his luck was as bad as always. "Hunter, I need information you have."

"What is it you want?" the young König demanded.

"Jo Wright. There's no file on her in Maher range. I need you to transmit it as soon as possible. In the meantime... Tell me about her."

"What's your interest? Why not wait for the file?"

Adam fisted the amulet, anticipating the shouting he was about to endure. "A track."

"A... What did you say?"

"A track. She took off on me."

"You? Kord trusted *you* with a woman? I thought he had more common sense than this. What did you do to piss this one off?" His voice promised another thorough ass-kicking at Hunter's earliest convenience, though any punishment would rightly come from Maher.

"Nothing! This is your fault. You and your sister. You're the ones who filled her head with all that Conan crap. That's ancient history, and I have paid my dues, Hunter. You, above all people, know what I paid for it, since you dished it out."

There was silence on the other end.

"Where would she go? Who does she have to run to?"

"No one." He seemed distracted.

"Everyone has someone, Hunter."

Again, there was no answer.

"I know her father is dead, but—"

"Her whole family, Adam. In front of her. We're all she has now. The Warriors are all she has left. Why did she run from you?"

"Why did she leave Crossbearer?" he countered, suddenly certain that they were connected somehow. Jo had never given him a straight answer about that. *Why would she leave the only family she has?*

"I don't know why she left. I never understood it, really." He seemed to consider every word. "Erin knows. I know she does, but she won't tell me. Maybe you should ask—"

Erin? His frustration spiked. How much harder could he make this situation? "I need to know this to track her—"

"Jo never shared her reasons for leaving," he snapped. "She just left without even a goodbye."

"Why would she leave the only family she has?" he demanded, no longer caring that this was the rival who would gladly slit his throat. "You have some idea. I know you do."

"Maybe..."

Adam held his breath, waiting for the one piece he needed to fall into place.

"Maybe, it was too hard to think of me as a brother once we were more."

He fisted the amulet in his hand. "You?" he growled. "You slept with her? But you had no intention of more, did you?" *How dare he! Hunter had to know that Jo wanted more. The Warriors were all she had, her family, but they weren't really her family. Not unless she became someone's mate. Whether she was in love with Hunter or not, she'd been spurned.*

"It's not what you think," Hunter protested.

"Look, just because she'd slept with Warriors before—"

"What the hell are you talking about?" he asked, seemingly horrified.

Confusion stole his fury. "What are you?"

"Jo never slept with Warriors. Sure, plenty of them showed an interest in her, but she never—"

"Shit." Adam's head spun, all the little things she said finally coming into focus for him.

"What is it?"

"Guess I'm back to the usual methods," he lied. "I better move."

"Find her, Adam."

Echoes of the last time Hunter spoke those words to him danced in his mind, though this time, it wasn't a threat.

"I will." He had to. But he still wasn't sure which extreme made her run.

****

Jo cursed solidly, a trait she'd picked up from the Warriors over the years, just one of their many bad habits she'd adopted, it seemed.

Somehow, she'd missed the exit she wanted—the second time so far—and found herself miles beyond Hattiesburg and low on gas. As much as she loathed the idea of pulling over in the middle of nowhere, she wouldn't make it back on the gas she had, and night was falling.

Getting gas would mean using her debit card, which would mean a trace for a Maher tracker, but at least she'd be doubling back afterward. Hopefully, Adam was headed to one of the other compass points, and she'd be long gone

191

before he got turned around and headed for the gas station.

It wasn't that she didn't have cash, but she couldn't be certain that the hundred in her pocket would fill the MDX *and* get her a hotel room. It was unlikely that she'd find an ATM out here, and she couldn't chance leaving a trail anywhere she'd be stopping for longer than a few minutes—at least until she'd made it clear that she didn't want to be found.

But how long would that take? She could take a thousand dollars out of her account at a time. It was a precaution the Warrior lords insisted on for their families. She smiled. It was a safe bet they hadn't counted on it being used against them. It was certain that they hadn't counted on her being able to use all of their own precautions against them.

Like most Warriors did, she kept a couple of emergency stashes in whatever range she lived in. In this case, she needed to reach Hattiesburg for the clothing and money she kept stashed in a bus locker. The bag hadn't been left there to facilitate running from the Warriors. It was her insurance policy in case she had to run from a beast and call in the Warriors, but she firmly believed in any advantage she had when it came down to the wire.

Her original plan was collecting the bag from the bus depot—if it was still there — staying overnight on the cash in her pocket, and hitting an ATM for the full thousand in the morning. If she withdrew a thousand at a time, moved on immediately every time she used the card and paid for everything she needed in cash, Jo could effectively drop off the face of the Earth for four or five days at a time, changing direction whenever she felt the need. It would be Mobile or Gulfport tomorrow...or maybe Baton Rouge or New Orleans.

She scowled. *Unless they get the police looking for the MDX.* The Warriors didn't usually get more than a few trusted protected with the police involved in any situation, but she *was* driving a stolen Maher vehicle.

It wasn't as if she had much choice in the matter. Going for her own vehicle, even if she could count on it being at the house in Ripley, would mean walking into Adam's hands—or at least the hands of one of his relatives. Renting one meant the Mahers could hack the agency's computer to retrieve the beacon code and track her, mile by mile, with the GPS signal. Knowing what she did of Adam's cyber-tracking skills, that would happen within moments of the deposit for the vehicle posting on her card.

If you could count on one thing with a Warrior, it was that he didn't like anyone having the ability to track him as he tracked others. That meant any vehicle a Warrior purchased had the locator beacon removed within hours. Stolen or not, the MDX was the least traceable option she had.

Jo turned into the Exxon station, pulling up to the pump. She slid from the vehicle, stretching her back.

"Help you, Ma'am?" the attendant asked.

"Yes. Fill it, please." She handed her card over, forcing her fingers to release it when she wanted to snatch it back. She didn't have to do this. She could sleep one night in the MDX.

Jo shivered, glancing at the sunset. She certainly wouldn't sleep if she tried it. Though she knew that four walls and a door wouldn't stop a beast, the relative exposure was incomprehensible to her.

"Problem, Ma'am?"

"No. Nothing. I—just need the ladies' room."

"Around the back."

****

Adam sighed at the insistent beeping from the tablet plugged into the cigarette lighter in the F150. She'd used one of her cards. *Finally*, he could find out whether or not he'd spent half the day heading in the wrong direction.

One keystroke brought up the information he'd been searching for. Adam thanked Dobler that he'd been rational enough to anticipate that she'd head 180 degrees from where he'd been ordered to take her.

Jo was close. If she took time to eat at this stop, he'd have her before she traveled another mile.

Normally, he'd feel a sense of accomplishment at a track passing so well. He couldn't seem to sort how he felt about finding Jo. He was relieved, nervous, hopeful and... *Damn it!* She left the bed they'd shared and run from him. Why the hell was he aroused?

194

Just the memory of Jo in his arms had him rock hard. It was damned uncomfortable and more than a little disconcerting. He wasn't a trainee or a first night. He should be able to control his drives better than this, unless...

"Stupid for a woman," he breathed, for once allowing himself to seriously consider what he wanted instead of denying that it was possible. Kord had been much younger than he was when he printed, and Corwyn Lord Hunter had been about the same age. Though it was early for printing, it wasn't impossible.

No. He wouldn't consider the possibility that he was printing now. After he'd found Jo and they talked this out, he'd entertain the possibility that she was the one he wanted to spend the rest of his life with.

The pain in his gut stole his breath, and he noted the direction, roaring in frustration, his heart aching and monstrous visions nearly stealing his sanity. The feeding was close, too close, and in the direction he was tracking. "Not Jo," he begged. *If you have any mercy at all, let it not be Jo.*

****

"Sir?" Jo called out, wishing that she'd looked at the attendant's name before she left the MDX. She stopped at the pump, signing the slip and pocketing her card. "Sir?"

He was nowhere in sight. She considered her options. The attendant was probably in the men's room or the shop. She could leave the

195

dollar-fifty for the Pepsi with the receipt and get back on the road.

A movement at the corner of the building drew her attention. Jo waved the dollar bill, offering him a weary smile. "There you are. I was just about to..."

He stepped into the light, but it wasn't the attendant. Jo's stomach churned, and she backed toward the MDX, the plastic twenty-ounce bottle slipping from her fingertips and splitting on the pavement with an ominous hiss of escaping carbonation.

The blood on his mouth and chin was proof enough of what he was. Jo fished the keys from her front pocket, jumping as he smiled a fang-heavy smile, his shimmering red eyes crinkling in amusement.

She reached her hand back, making several failed attempts to slide the key into the lock, unwilling to take her eyes off of him even that long. A hand closed on her wrist, and she screamed, wrenching away and running. The last functioning brain cells she possessed argued that she had nowhere to run, no protection, no cover, no escape.

A broad chest blocked her way. Jo saw it too late, crashing into the wall-hard body even as she tried to turn. Pain ripped through her arms as hands grasped at her.

Jo looked around fearfully, counting the pairs of eyes closing on her. *Four. Oh, God.* She was as good as dead.

The one she saw first reached her side, chuckling as he wiped the blood from his face with a torn shirt in the Exxon blue. He dropped the fabric at her feet and reached for her.

She backed away—then to the side as she encountered one male body after another. Jo sobbed. There really was nowhere left to go.

"Shhh," the beast taunted. "No need for that. We'll make it quick, Dr. Joanne. Just a few little pinches, and it will all be over."

Chapter Fourteen

Fury burned in him, and he let the shuriken fly, striding toward the group as the beast leaning over her fell and the others looked at the metal star protruding from his chest in dull surprise. They looked up, searching, red-eyed and with their fangs extended.

Jo was faster on the uptake. Her gaze swung in his direction, locking on him even in his ghosted state, because she knew who she'd see and correctly postulated where she would see him. Though she might not consciously acknowledge it, Jo knew no other Warrior would be coming for her, and she sought him out personally as a result.

The scent of human blood and beast played havoc with his senses. Though he didn't see blood on Jo, he couldn't be certain that she hadn't been fed on yet, and the uncertainty made him crazy for revenge.

She sobbed, her mouth forming his name silently. It was the final straw. Jo was his, and no beast would touch her.

Adam drew his sword in his right hand and sacred weapon in his left. He unghosted, knowing he wouldn't need stealth with this level of *Blutjagd*. Moreover, he knew the sight of him in this state struck terror in all but the highest level beasts.

As he expected, they shied away from their intended prey. *Jo!* Two of them distanced themselves from her, but the final one stepped forward again and grasped her by the throat, dragging her around like a shield. He noted that, vowing silently that the beast would die painfully for it.

The other two were dead in short order. Adam bolted between them, spearing the one on the left through the heart with his sacred weapon and beheading the other with the sword, taking his heart as he fell for good measure. He sidestepped the spray of foul blood smoothly. He turned to the final one as Jo choked, trying to claw the hand around her throat looser.

It was obviously a low level; otherwise, it would have fled while he was occupied with the others. Adam considered his options carefully. Whatever he did, it would have to be quick and fatal.

"Weapons down or I kill her," it ordered, relaxing its hold just enough to allow Jo a deep breath.

Adam nodded, a plan taking shape.

"No," Jo pleaded, gasping slightly as the grip tightened in warning.

"Shut up," Adam growled, meeting her eyes fully, praying she'd see what he intended her to. He placed the dagger on the ground then the broadsword, snatching an amulet from his belt and throwing it at her.

The beast ducked behind her, probably believing the object was another shuriken. Adam was already back on his feet, broadsword in hand before she caught it, looping a second amulet around his left wrist in case he needed it.

The blast knocked the beast backward and Jo onto her stomach. The air left her lungs in a blast, but she managed to keep her grip on the amulet. That was Adam's cue.

He leapt over her, landing astride her body. "Get it on," he shouted, throwing one of his daggers to take out the beast. Adam noted more closing on them in annoyance. When would beasts learn not to fuck with him when he was pissed off?

Jo got the amulet around her neck, her hands shaking, then tucked it beneath her shirt.

Adam collected his scattered weapons in a rush. There was no way he was going to make the same mistake Talon Lord König had in battle. He kept his weapons close so they couldn't be used against an amulet.

He turned, dragging Jo up by her upper arm, turning his back to her. He closed her fist on his leather duster. "At my back," he reminded her.

She nodded, pressing her body flush to his. Before the beasts discovered the use of null weapons, this had served two purposes. In addition to keeping a protected out of the way of a Warrior's blades, it utilized the amulet to protect the Warrior's back from beasts. Now, it just meant that Jo couldn't wander into the way of a shuriken or hand-held weapon.

The one down side to having Jo pressed to his back was the fact that he couldn't concentrate on anything past her shaking and sobbing, his mad urge to protect the woman he wanted as his mate, and the insistent ache of his cock her proximity caused. He was undeniably stupid for her.

The beasts gave him little time to suffer in his discomfort, materializing and attacking three to one. Adam took them out, one after another, efficient shots that would ensure terror from their brethren in battles to come as their knowledge of his prowess grew.

When all three lay dead, he dragged Jo along to the MDX and liberated the keys from her fisted hand. He pushed her into the passenger seat and slammed the door behind her. Adam circled the vehicle, slid in, and settled the sword between her thighs, half in preparation and half in warning not to run from him again. He started out, thankful that his tablet was in his pocket and the F150 was far enough away not to be suspicious to the police who would investigate the mass murder at the Exxon station.

Miles passed in silence. At last, Jo said his name in a shaky, questioning voice.

The urge to pull over and paddle her backside for scaring him this way warred with his duty. He needed time to collect his control again. "If you know what's good for you, you'll keep your mouth shut," he snapped.

She winced, silent tears coursing down her cheeks. Adam glanced at her several times, fighting the need to pull over and kiss away her tears, the urge to strip her naked and search for injuries. If he gave in to that, he'd make love to her right on the side of the road, oblivious to any dangers coming for them.

He pulled out the headset for his cell, hooking it on left-handed. "Manor," he managed in a voice that the damned bit of electronics recognized. To his surprise, there was an answer on the first ring.

"Adam," Kord barked. "I take it that massacre was your work."

"I got her back alive and unharmed, and she's accepted our protection again."

"Accept— You didn't tell your brother that she left her amulet behind."

"Didn't I? Must have slipped my mind." He knew he hadn't, and he knew he was lying outright to a house lord, but he wasn't about to admit it. Protected professional or not, he might have been ordered not to go after a protected who'd refused the amulet. That hadn't been an option.

"Should I send Bryant to relieve you?"

He fisted the steering wheel, images of his randy brother pursuing Jo cutting deep. "That won't be necessary," he managed through gritted teeth.

"If you're sure..."

"I am. If that changes, I'll let you know." *If she refuses me, I will have to ask for a replacement when I battle the madness.*

"Good. Do we need to change plans?"

"No. She ran the opposite direction. I knew she would." Adam glanced her way.

Jo darkened, perhaps at how easily he'd anticipated her, but she didn't voice a protest about it.

Kord sighed. "Good. Then I'll leave you to it."

202

Adam grunted a reply and disconnected. Jo offered no comment, and neither did he. They had a lot to discuss, not the least of which was his printing. He prayed to Ani that Jo was what he believed she was.

****

"What did you think you were doing?" Adam demanded, towering over her in the cabin. "You listen to a Warrior. You obey."

The ride back had done little to calm his anger. He still bounced back and forth between the thought of smacking her bare bottom pink—the image of which typically launched him to the other extreme—sliding his cock into her from behind, hearing her gasp of delight as he slammed home inside her... He shook his head, knocking the fantasy loose. They had to settle this first.

Jo flinched, nodding silently, no longer crying, thankfully.

"I have half a mind to strip your amulet for this." He couldn't really do it. All he could do was suggest to Kord that they strip it. The Council of Lords would have to make the final decision for all the houses.

She paled, fisting the disc in her hand. "You wouldn't really, would you?"

He ground his teeth, itching to tell her he would just to scare some sense into her. He couldn't bear to make her fear him. "No," he admitted. "You know I won't."

"How?" she breathed. "How do I know you won't?"

"I gave my vow."

She shook her head, fresh tears pooling. "No. Piers Cross gave his vow."

"Which I uphold," he assured her.

Jo nodded, her grip on the amulet loosening slightly.

Adam reached out and stroked a wave of hair above her ear, laying his forehead to hers. "They have to strike where they can hurt us most," he reminded her. "That means taking out our doctors. In other words—"

"Me," she finished for him.

He cupped her head. "I won't allow it." Adam worked the amulet from her hand, staring at the seal. "I gave you my seal," he whispered. If only she knew what he meant by it.

"Kord can't spare you forever," she reasoned, "and if I relocated to Texas, the whole eastern range would be without medical coverage."

Adam shivered at the idea taking shape. His grandfather would let Adam stay forever if he were printed. It would be a simple matter of moving Bryant to the southwest and Adam east, a trade of resources, and they'd done that for less.

The beasts were courting war by attacking their doctors, but no beast since Veriel had been stupid enough to target a Warrior mate. By the virtue of that association alone, she should be safe. But would Jo want that?

"Adam." She wasn't questioning him. Jo's voice was not quite an invitation though more than a greeting.

"Do you want me to stay forever?" he asked. "I will, you know."

"But Kord—"

He tilted his head to one side and kissed her, muting her response. Jo sank back to the wall as if seeking its support.

Adam pulled back, meeting her eyes. "Do you want me to stay forever?" he asked again, praying to Ani that she knew what he wanted.

"You really mean...forever, don't you?"

He nodded, keeping rigid control on himself. If Jo refused him, he'd have to request to leave her. Adam consoled himself in that Kord would send Lewis to her. Considering the circumstances, he wouldn't send one of the unmated men. If he sent Bryant or Curt, and Jo chose one of his brothers, he wouldn't survive it. Even the thought of one of them bedding her had his *Blutjagd* burning merrily.

Jo drew his mouth down to hers and kissed him again, a kiss that held the promise of more. Adam's bloodlust receded several notches. She turned, guiding him toward the bed they'd shared, issuing a silent invitation.

Adam stopped her, shaking his head. "Not without an answer."

"Adam?"

"Do you know what *Endspiel* is?" He was close. He hadn't questioned that since he'd felt the feeding.

Her eyes widened. "Why did you stay so long?" There was a hint of desperation in the question.

His throat constricted in near-panic. She wasn't going to agree. Adam started to back away, controlling the urge to roar out his loss stoically. "I have to..." he choked out.

Jo clasped her hands around his jaw, turning his eyes back to hers. "Why didn't you tell me?"

He shook his head, unable to put his many reasons into words.

"Do you know why I ran from you?" she asked.

Adam shrugged hopelessly. "Because I was so intent, I guess." *Face it. You're not Hunter. Why did you expect she'd want you the same way she wanted him? If she even wanted him to take her as mate.* There was so much that was still uncertain.

"No, Adam. Not at all."

He waited patiently for her explanation.

"I—" Jo dropped her gaze to his chest.

"Jo?"

"If I'd known you were printing, I wouldn't have run," she managed. Jo glanced at him then away again, a deep blush coloring her cheeks. "I swear I wouldn't have."

"I don't think I understand that." He hoped he did, but he didn't want to misunderstand her now. It was too important to get this right.

"Think about it," she grumbled.

"Jo," he warned. Adam was having trouble reigning in his frustration. He had to know where she stood, and half answers weren't getting him that.

"You're printing."

"Hell, yes, I am."

"What if I'd really been a blade chaser? What if I'd only wanted a one-night stand and you wanted forever?" Her eyes were over-bright with unshed tears.

Adam pulled her to his chest, uttering a series of curses under his breath. He'd thought that of her once, and he hadn't liked it any better than she had. Worse, he'd been afraid that was what she thought of him. If only he'd taken the time he should have, she would have known better and not run.

"I told you I'm not like the other Warriors you've met," he reminded her.

Jo sighed against his chest. "Yes. You did tell me that, and I didn't listen."

"I want forever, Jo. I'm saying it. I can't promise that I'm perfect, but you'll have the best I can give. You know what forever means to me. Are you still running?"

She didn't hesitate. "If you really want forever, I'm not going anywhere."

****

Jo held her breath, waiting for Adam's response. His chest hitched. Then his hands were tipping her head back. For a moment, he didn't do more than stare into her eyes.

"I love you. You do know that, don't you?" he whispered. Adam didn't give her a chance to answer. He claimed her mouth urgently.

She met him head on, winding her arms around his neck as Adam lifted her by the waist. Before Jo quite knew what was happening, he set her on her feet again, the mattress to her thighs.

Adam stripped off her jacket and shirt, letting them fall. He groaned, cupping one bare breast in his hand. "You love torturing me," he accused.

"No. Torture will be when I tell you I'm not wearing one."

"If you do, you won't last long," he promised.

"Meaning?" Jo asked, gasping as he tweaked her nipple lightly.

The look he shot her was a mixture of pure male sexual drive and amusement. "I can ghost with the best of 'em, darlin'. A quiet corner is all I need to—investigate the claim."

Her breathing hitched at that. Jo watched in stunned fascination as Adam stripped the rest of her clothes and shoes off, on one knee before her as if he were proposing like a human man would. He parted her legs gently, kissing at her lower abdomen and sending shivers of pleasure through her.

His fingertips stroked up her perineum and over her sex, picking up moisture that he used to lubricate her clit for his touch. "Oh, yeah. You're thinking about it. You're thinking about wearing a tight little skirt and having me take you in public, ghosted so no one can see us." His fingers circled slowly.

Jo's head spun lightly, visions of that situation stealing her sanity. He'd do it, and she'd like it. "And if your ghosting fails?" she asked. How much self-control could he boast when he came?

Adam chuckled. "Guess we'll have to find out." He rose, looking between their bodies as his fingers returned to her slit, then slid inside.

She grasped at his arm, wrapping both hands around his taut muscles, seeking strength to hold off until he made it inside her.

He closed his eyes as if the sensation were too much for him. "By Ani, if you don't undress me soon, I'm going to come in my jeans just watching you."

She pulled at his shirt frantically, all but ripping the buttons off in her haste. Adam shouldered the shirt off, his hand leaving her body. Jo reached for his jeans, but he took a step back, shaking his head.

"On the bed," he requested.

Jo eased onto the mattress, his hungry eyes following every move. She laid down, trailing her fingers from her breast to her pubic curls slowly. His gaze stayed locked on it right down to the clit he'd abandoned. He dragged off one boot and then the other, watching her circling fingers the whole time. When she couldn't stand the pleasure anymore, she moaned, needing him inside her.

Adam's hands moved to his weapons belt, unbuckling the thigh straps, then the waist. Jo wouldn't have believed how quickly he could undress. It almost seemed Adam went from half-dressed to nude in the blink of an eye.

That's it, she mused to herself. *You didn't blink the entire time.*

He reached into his jeans pocket and drew out his wallet, liberating another condom though there were surely still some in the nightstand drawer from when he raided the bathroom for a box. Jo watched him tear it open, the latex nestling to the engorged head of his cock and sliding down. Her mouth watered at the glide of his hand, the urge to taste him beating at her.

As if he read her mind, Adam smiled. He knelt on the bed, his gaze locked on hers as Jo spread for him, her heart hammering at the intensity in his eyes. Maybe it was the knowledge that this man was sealing his soul to hers, or maybe it was the idea of offering herself to him with that understanding, but she knew this time would be different for them.

Adam planted his elbows at her shoulders, holding his body just above hers, his cock pressed just between her labia. "Forever," he promised.

Jo nodded, her entire body aching for more. She grasped his hips, guiding him into her with a gasp. He filled her, a hot, insistent thrust that seemed to stake his claim on her without question. Jo wrapped her legs around his hips, her hands skating up to his shoulders.

"Gods, I won't last," he groaned, his body pistoning into hers again and again as if he were helpless to control himself.

She rose to meet his body, already at the precipice. "We have forever," she reminded him. *And forever of this will be Heaven.*

As if her statement was the final straw for him, Adam seated himself in her fully and cried out. The wash of heat, at first contained, burst free and flowed into her.

Jo gasped in surprise. The realization that the condom broke, eclipsed by the sensation of his cum inside her, sent her hurtling over into orgasm. She screamed, her legs tightening around him reflexively, holding him in. She pulled his face down to hers, seeking his lips.

Adam shook in her arms, pulling back slowly, his eyes wide. He stroked his hand along her cheek. "I'm sorry. Please, believe me that I never intended—"

She rolled her hips, tightening her vaginal muscles against his softening cock, smiling at his groan of pleasure. Still, he shot her a look of misery. Adam slid out of her body and removed the tattered condom with a curse.

"You couldn't know it would break," she assured him.

He tossed it in the general direction of the waste basket. "You warned me, and I didn't listen. Gods, my grandfather is going to kill me, and I—"

"I won't be lodging a complaint with Kord about it. If that's what you're worried about."

"Oh, no. I deserve that. You have the right to do it, and you should do it. I shouldn't have put you in this situation without your permission. I had no right to take that chance with you. You didn't give me permission. If you conceive—"

Jo laughed heartily at his speech. "Are you telling me you don't want a baby? I thought you Warriors were predisposed to wanting a few dozen."

The fierce hunger was back on his face, his misery forgotten for a moment. "Are you giving me permission?" His voice went gruff.

She considered that for a moment. She'd always said she'd start a family before she reached thirty, and she was only a year off of that mark.

But this was one subject you didn't flirt around with when you were dealing with a Warrior. If she said 'no', he'd try his best not to make another mistake, though it might be too late, Warrior potency considered. If she did conceive, thanks to the broken condom, he'd feel guilty for breaking the Rules of Sanction and might go so far as to turn himself over to Kord for punishment, even if she didn't want him to.

On the other hand, if she said 'yes', he would do his best to make sure she conceived before she left her fertile window. Warrior mentality being what it was, he would be constantly aroused as long as she was fertile, if he had permission. Every other concern, save her safety, would take second place to his drive to produce the heir she'd agree to carry.

"I know what this means to you," she began.

His cock hardened in anticipation, but he held himself in check. "Yes?" he prompted her.

"Oh, yes."

Adam's tension melted into a look of fascination then into pure bliss. He turned over her then entered her smoothly, sighing at her moan.

"Of course, I did warn you that carrying condoms in your pockets weakened—"

"Jo?" he interrupted her.

"Yes?"

"Shut up and kiss me."

Section Three:

Bryant
and
Shana

Opposites
Attract

A Lesson in Temperance

About the card...

Temperance

Shana could be said to exemplify the heart of the word temperance. She avoids excess, takes the safe route, and believes in avoiding extremes. Though she doesn't realize it, in her quest to live to this ideal, she is extreme in her own way.

That is where the deeper meaning of the card comes in to play. Because Shana and Bryant are polar opposites on most subjects, they have to achieve a middle ground, recognize their strengths, and use them as needed, work together, and finally—find a way to be safe and secure with each other.

Other possible meanings of this card are renewing your energy stores and healing—which Bryant does a bit of in this story—and joining forces.

Chapter Fifteen

April 20th, 2030
Somewhere in the foothills of Arkansas

The child came from nowhere. Shana would have sworn under oath that the road was deserted. Then she yawned, and the little boy appeared in her path, barefoot and wearing a muddy pair of pajamas.

"Oh, no," she breathed, dragging the wheel to the left and slamming on the brakes.

Shana realized her mistake immediately. The road was a mess of heavy clay-based mud, and the move sent her into a sidelong skid. Shana fought the wheel, releasing the brakes and trying to steer her way out of the skid, but all four wheels were hydroplaning over the slick surface, and there was no hope of controlling the motion.

The car tipped as the right two wheels slid into the drainage ditch. Shana squeezed her eyes shut, every muscle tensing in anticipation of the crash to come.

It wasn't so much a crash as a jarring stop. There was a sickening sucking sound, as the car sank into the thick layer of mud at the bottom of the ditch. She cursed aloud as the side airbags deployed, then burst.

She sat in the aftermath for a moment, her breathing labored. "Some help you are," she grumbled at the deflated airbag that brushed her hip. Well, there was no sense in sitting here all night. At the very least, she needed to make sure the child in the road was all right.

Shana planted her feet on the slight hump between the front seats and fumbled for the seatbelt release. The road was dark, without streetlights or house lights to aid her in her escape. She cursed her luck. She'd followed the directions the gas station attendant gave her precisely, but this deserted stretch of road couldn't possibly be the right way to the conference in Little Rock. Either Shana misheard him or he'd been playing some prank, a prank that had her trapped in a ditch on a muddy road.

She pushed up at the car door, but it was too heavy to heft straight up from her precarious perch. Shana gave up and started unrolling the window. It would be a tight fit with the extra thirty pounds of padding she carried on her five-foot-nine frame, but she couldn't sit in the car, waiting for help that might never come.

The handle was wrenched from her hand as the door moved. Shana lost her footing. She grasped at the seatbelt, using the locking mechanism in her favor to stop her sudden drop. Then she pulled her foot from the cold mud with a grimace of disgust.

Hands circled her arms and dragged Shana up through the now-open door, depositing her on her feet. She slipped, gripping her car to keep from landing in a mud puddle.

"You okay?" a man asked.

Shana nodded, scanning her gaze around for the child. Had she missed him? How far did the car slide? "Is the little boy all right?" she asked urgently.

The man chuckled. "Jes fine, Miss. Jes fine."

She looked to him in the deeper darkness outside the limited globe of light from her headlights, trying to gauge his humor. What was so funny in her nearly running down a child? And what was a child that young doing in the road at this time of night? He couldn't have been more than six.

Her questions stuck in her throat. Two eyes glowed a flickering red in the darkness. Shana shook her head. "I'm unconscious," she reasoned. "I hit my head when I crashed. Or, I fell asleep at the wheel and this is all a dream." *Yes. Those are the only plausible explanations.*

"Tha's right, Miss. This is all a dream."

But the grip he had on her arm was no dream. Shana couldn't recall ever feeling touch in a dream. The mud in her shoe and the firm but not painful grip on her arm couldn't be a dream, could they?

The smell of unwashed body assaulted her. She definitely didn't smell in dreams. Shana recoiled, pulling at his hold.

It didn't loosen. She looked to those eyes in rising panic. *This isn't real,* she pleaded. *Things like this don't happen in real life.*

"Jes settle." The man's voice was soothing—if he was a man.

For a moment, Shana calmed. Then common-sense kicked in, and her situation became very clear to her. He could kill her. He probably *would* kill her. "Let me go." Shana wrenched her arm back then rebounded against him when he didn't move.

"Calm down, Miss." His voice was impatient, seemingly annoyed with her refusal to follow his orders.

She punched him across the face, her breath catching on a cry of alarm at the pains shooting up her arm. True, Shana rarely had cause to hit anyone in her life, but she remembered that they didn't typically feel like a hot brick wall when she did.

"No," another male voice barked.

Shana spun in the first man's grip, her heart racing at the sight of another pair of glowing eyes. She shook her head, shocked beyond coherent speech. Why had she come here? She'd been safe at home, and Shana had always preferred to be safe. Had she really thought this out-of-state conference would be an adventure? This was more adventure than she wanted.

The second man closed his hands over her shoulders, and the first man released her and moved a pace back. Shana stiffened, then relaxed in his arms, her entire body warm and comfortable. Even her foot didn't seem cold anymore.

"Like this," the second man crooned. "Remember that the kinder emotions are harder come by. Make them love you, not fear you. Master Jörg taught me that."

Shana nodded, though his speech hadn't been intended for her. She licked her lip in a fierce hunger. The fact that she was intended as an object lesson in teaching the younger man about physical love was arousing. Even more arousing, the older would touch her as a means of teaching. Shana knew he would. She wanted him to touch her.

Her nipples tightened against the cotton bra cups, and her panties were abruptly damp against her aching core. She shifted against him, seeking pressure to ease that ache.

"That's right," he urged her. "Come to me."

Shana needed no more encouragement than that. She tipped her head back, moaning as his lips closed over hers. The kiss was hot and hard, whispering of all the experiences he intended to grant her. His mouth left hers, exploring her face then her throat. Shana arched her spine and laid her head back, offering herself to him.

"Touch her," he instructed his young charge. "Slowly. Draw out the moment."

The smaller male body nestled behind her, and Shana gasped at the erect lengths pressing into her, front and back. One pair of hands kneaded her breasts, teasing at the already-hard nipples. The other pushed her skirt up her thighs, an unhurried glide that told her it was the man in front of her whose hand sought out the damp strip of panties between her thighs. Shana spread her legs for him, and he rewarded her with another kiss.

"Now," the younger man demanded. His breath teased at her throat. His tongue darted out, licking along the sensitive skin.

Shana shuddered at that, then groaned in acceptance. It felt incredibly erotic, and she couldn't imagine why she had considered stopping him a moment before.

"Better," the man in front of her complimented his student. "But no. I will taste her first, at the height of her pleasure. Then we will both have her."

Her body rioted in pleasure, demanding that. The thought of both of their bodies piercing hers at once nearly sent her over without any help from the men gifting her this experience. A whisper in her mind swayed her from that, promising greater pleasures if she held off for them.

"You want to touch me, woman." He didn't question that she did.

She nodded, her fingers trailing over smooth skin. Had he been nude when he came to her? There was a faint memory of clothing, but it hardly seemed important. Not when her hand had just circled his cock and elicited a growl of male satisfaction from him. Pleasing him was a much more intriguing concept than unimportant things like a naked man walking around in the middle of the night, just waiting for her to come along.

"Yes, you," he breathed.

Shana stroked him, and the fingers caressing her found the nub of flesh, making her legs shake in near climax. His mouth returned to her throat, nipping at her skin, stroking at her flesh in a way that made her head spin.

****

Bryant scowled at the lewd scene laid out before him. He'd been investigating this band of beasts for almost a month, and this was the perfect chance to cripple them. Without their high-level master, the low levels would have much more difficulty taking prey and would be easier to pick off. Without whatever elder turned them to instruct them, the learning was slow and painful. For that, Bryant would be eternally grateful to gods he thanked for little else.

But this form of 'teaching' turned his stomach. The high level was using coercion to force the woman to serve them. Presumably, the flashes of coercion from the low level meant the beast was learning how to control humans by sharing in this experience.

The high level had used some sort of illusion to drive the victim's car off the road—an animal or maybe a child. Those were the most popular ruses employed. The illusion had alerted Bryant, and the coercion had served as a beacon to bring him the rest of the way. Luckily, he had been close to their ambush spot this time.

He moved toward them, as the high level pulled back, his fangs descending fully for a feed. The low level pulled at his foul, tattered jeans, freeing his cock for the violation to come. Bryant sneered at that. It must have been some time since they'd taken prey of a size to clothe the younger beast.

Bryant took the high level's heart first, swinging around the mass of entwined bodies to take the low level's before the shock of his slain master could spur him to motion. The stomach-wrenching sense of a beast feeding made Bryant turn back in dismay. He dragged the creature off of his prey and slit his throat in a spike of pure fury, as much at himself as at the beast.

Never turn your back on a dying beast, even one with a mortal wound. How many times had Kord and Adam all but beaten that into him? He'd had to take out both beasts, but he'd lingered too long. He should have been faster.

It had been a half-baked attempt and weakly executed, but the high level had marked her for his brethren. Now they could all track her. *Damn them!*

The woman weaved on her feet, one hand going to the track of blood running down her throat and the other dragging her skirt down her thighs. She sobbed. He grimaced at that. The coercion had broken with the death of the high level. The woman was left in confusion, pain, most likely horror at what had happened to her.

Bryant cleaned his blade and sheathed it, offering his hand. "You're safe now. Come with me, and I'll protect you." He had to offer his protection. She'd been fed on. He'd failed her.

She backed away, tripping over the body of the low level and righting herself by a grip on her car. She shook, looking from one body to the other, then to Bryant.

It wasn't unexpected. She didn't know whether or not to trust a man who appeared out of nowhere and killed two other beings. It was what he'd expected her to do. His duty required that Bryant not traumatize her any further if he could help it, but there were more beasts closing on them, and he had to do everything he could for her unless she told him rationally that she didn't want his protection, even if that meant forcing her to accompany him.

But first he'd try to convince her. "Please, trust me. There are more nearby. We have to leave here." All low levels that he knew of, but there might be another high level. Even in these lean times, a high level rarely took on more than seven or eight low levels for his own. It was too time and energy consuming to be worth the protective layer they offered. The number of low levels closing seemed to indicate at least one more high level somewhere nearby.

"Who are you?" Her voice was tremulous and weak.

"My name is Bryant Maher, and I only want to help." He turned his head, grinding his teeth at the unmistakable sound of ripping metal.

The woman was abruptly at his back, where he would have ordered her in battle anyway. "What is that?"

Bryant grumbled a curse. "My car. The damn beasts have destroyed my car." Repairing the Stingray would be expensive. Worse, Bryant would have to convince Adam to let him spend the money. After this screw-up, that wouldn't be easy.

This isn't the right time to think about that, he chided himself. The band of beasts had just pinned Bryant in the middle of nowhere with a traumatized victim and were closing in on them in overwhelming numbers. As much as Bryant hated to admit it, the Stingray wasn't nearly his biggest problem.

He grasped the woman's hand and started leading her away from the road to the woods beneath. She pulled away, turning to run from him. Bryant hefted her over his shoulder, ignoring her blows and stilling her legs so she couldn't kick. He didn't give her a chance to complain. The beasts were nearly on top of them, and she was obviously not in the mood to follow his commands in battle.

"Let me down," she demanded, but her voice hitched.

"Look Miss—"

"Parsons. Shana Parsons. Now let—" She grunted, as Bryant jumped over a stone then slid, wrenching himself upright.

"Do you want to face more of the beasts?" Bryant grimaced at the fact that she was acting like a searchlight, leading them in. The beasts had turned cross-country after them, but they were too close to stop and protect her now. Even if he tried, Shana wouldn't be likely to accept his protection yet.

"What are those—beast things?"

"This really isn't the time—"

Shana laid a punch on his spine.

Bryant jumped in response. "That hurt, you know."

"Good. Now let me down or answer me."

"Beasts are roughly what you'd call vampires," he answered, half-sliding down a muddy incline.

She hit him again.

A wild urge to drop Shana and leave her to her fate gripped him, but his duty wouldn't permit that. Bryant tightened his hold on her. "Knock it off," he growled. Why couldn't they simply accept his help and be grateful for it for once?

"Vampires don't exist," she informed him.

"You're right. Vampires don't exist, but beasts do," he countered as patiently as he could.

"And what are you? Abraham Van Helsing? You look good for your age," she offered sarcastically.

Bryant chuckled at that. Shana was down but not out. "A whole lot better, baby."

She started to protest but stopped with a squawk as Bryant skidded to a halt. He cursed fluently at the group of beasts surrounding them. Usually, low levels wouldn't attack a trained Warrior without being ordered to do so by an elder, but they were obviously counting on their numbers to save most of them, and they were most likely right about that. Bryant's sacred weapon was drawn again and the first beast dead before the ring was complete.

A beast stepped forward, clapping, a measured sound that conveyed his disregard for who and what Bryant was. Bryant grumbled a curse at that. It was a second high level, just as he'd feared. No wonder the low levels were so willing to take this chance.

"Most impressive," the beast stated in a bored voice. "Your brother would be pleased."

"Hardly," Bryant snapped at him. No. Adam would not be amused by his current situation in the least. In fact, if this got back to the new Lord Maher, chances were that Bryant would be the proud owner of a few new scars in trial for this one. How the hell did he let himself get trapped this way?

The beasts had stopped him only twenty yards from the river. While it wasn't true that beasts couldn't cross water, only the high level would be able to keep track of them once the strong current dragged them a few miles downstream, and by the time they did catch up, Shana would be protected. They would have no reason to come then. There was always easier prey than a protected human.

"Name yourself," Bryant commanded him. *Might as well observe the formalities on the way. Might be the last time I get the chance to ask the question. Think! How do I get out of this one?*

The high level smiled a fang-heavy smile. "Kirrel. At your service, Warrior."

Hardly. "Let's get this over with." Bryant scanned his gaze over the area, evaluating the possible moves he could make and their probable outcomes. The nearest riverbank was a small cliff away, but it was likely that Bryant would break his ankle in the jump. Even Warriors took a week or so to recover from a broken bone, and in the meantime, they would never reach safety.

"Bryant," Shana began, no doubt about to suggest he put her down.

"Quiet," he grumbled. *I need to think. There has to be a better choice.*

"This is simple," Kirrel reasoned. "Even you can't fight fifteen beasts at once. You're not a König, after all."

Nice try, but I am not jealous of Curt for that. "You're not suggesting I give up?" Bryant asked in mock disbelief.

"I'm suggesting a simple trade."

His stomach tightened at that. Warriors didn't make deals with beasts. "I'm listening."

"Give us the woman, and you may walk away to fight another day."

Shana tightened her grip on his jacket, shifting against Bryant's shoulder, as if counting the beasts around them.

"She is a bit of a pain," Bryant admitted, stalling for time.

The bridge was too far, and it would be too easy to chase them down that way. Warrior genetics or not, Bryant would eventually get tired of carrying Shana. Worse, fighting out that direction would leave the high level at his back, the last place Bryant wanted him.

"You wouldn't dare," Shana gasped.

No, Bryant wouldn't, but he had to come up with a better plan than taking on fifteen beasts at once with a woman slung over his shoulder. "You haven't exactly asked for my protection, have you?"

"I'm asking," she pleaded.

Bryant charged the high level. With any luck, the move would cause the low levels to scatter in confusion. If he wasn't quite that lucky—*this doesn't seem to be the night for it*—he might at least take out his most dangerous adversary and cause the weakest left to scatter. That would even the odds up some.

Kirrel obviously expected the move. His claws slashed out, and Bryant was slowed in response by Shana's added weight. He took the beast's heart but felt the tearing of claws as he streaked past the parting line of startled beasts.

He slid and tumbled down the slope to the bank of the river. Bryant dropped Shana in the water and dragged off his jacket. He'd had practice swimming in his boots, but the long, leather jacket would only drag him down. Besides that, it was torn and stained in beast blood, so it would have to be discarded at some point. He retrieved his phone from his belt with the thought of keeping the delicate device above water then dropped it atop the jacket in disgust. It was broken, pierced by one of the claws that wounded Bryant.

"That's it. We're stuck here." Bryant dove into the river after Shana.

Chapter Sixteen

April 21st, 2030

"We can't sleep here," Shana complained. She surveyed the ramshackle barn in the gray light of the rising sun.

"There is nowhere else to sleep," Bryant pointed out to her. "The house collapsed more than ten years ago. Be glad there is any shelter at all. The next farm is five miles away."

"But— But there are probably rats in there."

"No. Field mice but not rats." He strode into the barn, his still-wet black hair swinging around his shoulders.

Shana pressed a hand to the squirming in her stomach. She shook her head. Bryant was admittedly gorgeous, despite that mop he called hair, but she'd never felt this sexually attracted to a man before.

Except those beast things. Her stomach rolled at that, the butterflies morphing into angry snakes. How could she? It had to be some sort of trick. After all, Bryant said the stories about vampires were loosely based on these beasts. Maybe they had the legendary mental powers.

"Are you coming or not?" Bryant called out.

"Yes." Shana followed him into the dim interior, hoping the structure wasn't going to collapse around them.

Bryant took her arm, guiding Shana to a work table that looked to be only slightly more sturdy than the barn itself. "Sit here."

She pulled herself up gingerly, half-expecting it to crumble under her weight. Bryant pulled a plastic bag from his sodden jeans and opened it. The smell of isopropyl alcohol was powerful.

"What are you doing?" she asked.

He pulled out a gauze pad. "Cleaning the bite. It's not as deep as it might have been. Good thing. I am not equipped to put stitches in you. All of the heavy first aid gear was in my car." He cleaned his hands first, taking the last of the foul black stuff that she assumed was beast blood off of skin that was irritated beneath. Bryant set the pad aside and pulled out another. "He only got one fang in, and he missed the artery entirely, so you didn't bleed severely."

Shana winced as he stroked the alcohol-soaked pad over the cut gently. His hands on her skin were disconcerting, making the low burn of arousal for him all the worse. "Is this really necessary?"

His mouth quirked up in a half-smile. "You said you like safe. You dunked it in the river, and you have no idea where else that beast had his mouth."

She shuddered, her arousal abruptly forgotten.

His smile disappeared. "Sorry."

"Have you ever been bitten?" she asked quietly.

"Gods, no!"

"Then why do you do this? Did they kill someone you cared about?"

Bryant didn't answer. He cleaned the cut thoroughly then collected up the other gauze pads and tossed them all aside.

"That's littering," she reminded him.

He waved his arm at the rotted walls surrounding them. "In this junk heap?"

"It's still littering."

Bryant scooped the pads up and tucked them into his back pocket. "Happy?" he asked, looking more than a little annoyed at her concern.

"It's a step in the right direction." *Better would be getting me home.*

He rolled his deep blue eyes.

"Shouldn't you clean out your own injury?" she asked, trying not to wince at the deep gashes in his side.

Bryant fingered the ugly-looking one at his waist and shrugged. "My body takes care of itself. In three or four days, it will be fine."

"That? You're dreaming. It needs stitches and—" Shana swallowed the rest of her argument as Bryant shot her a look of warning.

She nodded. "Okay. You don't need to clean it," she conceded carefully. "Why do you do this? You never answered. Did they kill someone you care about?"

"Sure. Lots of people, but that's not why I do this." Bryant didn't meet her eyes, and he played with the red-stoned ring on the pinky of his left hand. If that stone was a ruby, it was worth a fortune.

"Why do you?" she asked for the third time.

He cracked a smile. "It's the family business. I was born to it, trained for it from the day I turned fifteen."

Well, that was a scary thought. "Who did these—beasts kill?"

"My father. My grandfather. Every dead man in my family as far back as anyone remembers. They'll kill me too—someday, when I get sloppy or old and slow." He twisted the ring on his finger idly, rolling it beneath the pad of his thumb.

Shana found forming a response difficult. "Are you at war with them or something?"

Bryant sighed. "Yes. I'm afraid we are."

****

Shana's green eyes widened in surprise, and she hooked a lock of the honey brown hair that escaped the bun behind her head over her ear. "What do I have to do with this?"

Bryant rocked the ring back and forth on his finger, trying to ignore her question. Kord had been a fan of leather pants and silk shirts, especially on nights out with his mate. Adam liked exotic weapons. Every Warrior deserved an expensive passion for what they risked. His car could be destroyed, but a beast would have to kill him to take Bryant's ring.

It was worth as much as the car, without a doubt. The heavy brushed titanium band housed a nine karat blood-red ruby, acid etched with the Maher seal: balance scales surrounded by a garland of laurel. Half the cost of the ring was the fact that two stones had been damaged before the etching was perfected.

"Bryant?" Shana called out nervously. "Why me?"

He shrugged. "You're food and entertainment. It's a lot easier to kill you than to kill me." It was the harsh, unvarnished truth, but maybe that would make her more likely to accept his protection.

She choked at that. "How do I get out of here?"

"We walk. Two days to the closest phone."

"Two days?" Her voice went shrill in near panic. "But the convention center has to be closer than that."

He met her earnest expression dead-on, his ring momentarily forgotten. She was off by more than sixty miles. A niggling of unease settled in his stomach. Bryant had wondered how the band kept getting people into this hellhole, but this was the first chance he'd had to ask. The high levels always erased that memory first.

"Who told you that?" he asked, praying that there hadn't been time to erase Shana's memories of how she got here.

"The attendant at the gas station on State Road six-thirty-two. I stopped there for directions. He directed me this way, but—" A pained expression clouded her face. "He set me up. Didn't he?"

Bryant nodded stiffly. *But he won't set anyone else up. A bought human who facilitates deaths is fair prey, and he's my prey.* "What did he look like? The greasy blonde?" He'd refueled there several times. There were only three attendants that worked the afternoon and evening.

She scrunched up her nose in a look of distaste that announced she'd avoided that particular attendant. Bryant reminded himself that the man probably looked rather threatening to Shana.

"No. The clean-cut redhead."

Of course. His looks would inspire trust, especially from women traveling alone, and he was probably well-paid with the valuables of victims. He could afford the look he carried off.

"What are you going to do to him?"

Bryant smiled at that, his bloodlust already burning, but just an edge. "Don't worry. It won't be very painful." *He won't live long enough for it to be painful.*

"But that's—that's—"

He shook his head. "He set you up to be raped, fed on, and probably murdered. He's done it before, and he'll do it again, unless I stop him."

"So that makes it all right?" she asked in seeming exasperation.

"Let me guess. You don't believe in capital punishment, even in the most extreme cases."

"Two wrongs don't make a right," she replied stubbornly.

"What do you suggest? I let him get more people raped and killed?"

She faltered. "Well... No, of course not. Prison—"

"Excuse me, officer? This clean cut, all-American boy next door is in league with the vampires hunting these hills, and I just wondered if you would be so kind—"

"Very funny," she snapped.

"No. It's not funny. That's what you have to get through your head. This is a war, and Mr. Clean Cut is killing people. It's not an accident. He's setting them up in cold blood. The police will think we're insane. I am the only thing standing between you and a lot of other innocents and death. That's not funny."

"Well, you saved me. Thank you very much. Now, get me out of here and you can go back to your little war, while I get out of Oz."

Bryant grimaced. "It's a little more complex than that."

Her face darkened, most probably in rising frustration. "Why?"

"You've been fed on."

Shana pressed a hand to her neck, swallowing hard. Too late, Bryant remembered that she had no idea what that really meant. It had been months since he'd had to explain this to someone; and subtlety, as Erin was so fond of pointing out, had never been Bryant's strong suit.

"You're not becoming one of them," he assured her. Damn the movies *Blade* and *The Forsaken* for making that part of the mythos! At least Bram Stoker's *Dracula* had that part right.

"Then why does it matter?"

"They can track you now. That's how they followed us last night. That's how they will follow you again tonight, if I'm not protecting you."

"Anywhere?"

"Anywhere you go, they can and will follow unless you're under my protection."

"And what am I supposed to do about that? There has to be a way to end it."

"Accept my protection. A beast very rarely preys on someone who's protected. It's too much of a risk for too little return."

"You hanging over my shoulder for the rest of my life?" she replied hotly. "I don't think so."

"Afraid I'd embarrass you with your prim and proper friends?" he countered. *And why would I care if she was?* "Well, don't concern yourself, princess. I give you an amulet and a little kiss, and then you're free to go. As soon as we get to a phone, anyway." *The sooner, the better.*

"A—a— You are seriously deranged. You know that, don't you?"

"Oh, am I? I suppose you don't believe the beasts really exist, now? You just ran yourself off the road and decided to have sex with a couple of rednecks?"

"Of course not," she grumbled. "They tricked me somehow." Shana rubbed a hand over her forehead, looking weary. "Somehow," she repeated.

Bryant's anger faded somewhat. "Yes. They did. I guarantee that I won't disrupt your life unless a beast is stupid enough to try and attack the amulet."

Shana laughed weakly. "You? I find it hard to believe that you can do anything that isn't completely flamboyant."

He sighed. She'd pegged him with that statement. "I can be unobtrusive when I need to."

Invisible, if I want to. "I can blend anywhere I have to."

She scanned her eyes over him with a scowl, her gaze settling at his shoulders.

Bryant shifted uncomfortably under her inspection, then forced himself to relax, pushing his hair back over his shoulder. "What?" he demanded in a sudden flash of understanding. "Lots of men wear a ponytail with a tux these days." He even owned a tux. Not that he'd ever used it, but he owned one.

"Sure. Mr.—what are you? Six foot two?"

"Three," he grumbled.

"Figures. Mr. Six foot three and looks like an escapee from a horror film hall of fame. Even trading in your current attire for a tux— Bet you'd still wear that ring, wouldn't you?"

He bristled at that. Damn right, he'd wear his ring. What was wrong with that? "So?"

"That's a real ruby, isn't it?"

"Yeah. So? I have a little money. People excuse eccentricity when they think you're rich."

Shana rolled her eyes at that pronouncement. "What do you drive, Mr. Unobtrusive? Let me guess. A Beamer twenty-thirty LM with the two-thirteen remake, overbored for performance."

He searched her face. He'd studied that car, considered buying it until the Stingray caught his eye. Adam had been relieved that he'd chosen the Stingray. By all accounts, the Beamer had barely passed minimum safety testing, but safety wasn't his concern. "Nah. Highly overrated. The handling for the horsepower isn't up to spec for me. I prefer the twenty-twenty Retro Stingray. But cars can be changed. You can rent staid cars, you know. I don't have to drive the Stingray." *I prefer it, but I don't have to.*

"You made my point," she grumbled.

"Which is?"

"You don't know how to blend."

"You don't think I could drive a safe little Mazda like you?"

"By the traffic laws?" she hinted.

Bryant didn't answer that. Again, she'd pegged him, but with his response time and ghosting abilities, who cared about that? It wasn't like his life was a safe one, no matter how he drove, and sometimes people's lives depended on how fast he got to the scene of an attack.

"Thought so."

"I never said I led a *safe* life. I just said I could blend if I needed to—for as long as I have to."

"Sure you can," she replied sarcastically.

"So, now I'm being condemned for the car I drive?" he asked.

Shana shrugged.

"Fine. Let's take a look at you, Ms. Stuck-Up."

She opened her mouth as if to protest.

"Gorgeous hair pulled into a bun so tight you look like a 1950s spinster. Sensible shoes with a knee-length skirt. The safest mid-priced car on the market. Reading glasses, because you don't want to risk sticking something in your eyes. Sensible cotton panties and bra. A safe condo in a safe neighborhood and a non-threatening job in early childhood education. You even drive rather than fly."

"How could you—" she gasped.

"You just proved my point," he taunted, repeating her words back to her with great satisfaction.

"Which is?" Her voice was gaining strength again.

"For all your lip service at playing it safe, you have absolutely no survival instincts." Bryant plowed on, determined to prove her inattentiveness to her. "I got a good look at your bra and panties last night, between the wet blouse and..." He waved his hand at that, unwilling to delve too deeply into the beast playing at her body.

She paled at the reminder.

"You're headed to the convention center. A decent Warrior knows all the major events that draw people into his area."

Shana groaned. "Early childhood," she grumbled. "You saw my car, shoes, and hair."

"And, you complained about leaving *your* car behind while we were walking last night. It's not a rental. So, you drove here rather than fly."

"What about the reading glasses?"

Bryant smiled. "You squinted when you were trying to make out the design on my ring. If you don't wear glasses, you should."

"And the condo?"

His smile felt more strained. "Fifty-fifty shot. Women like you either live in an old family home or an apartment. You struck me as the minimalist type, and the neighbors are closer, in case you scream."

Her eyes flashed in anger.

"So, are you going to accept my protection or not?"

Shana blushed deeply. She glanced to his lips, then away. Bryant raised an eyebrow at that. So, she wanted a kiss, did she? This could get very interesting.

****

"So, are you going to let me protect you?" Bryant asked.

"You? You are danger personified. I don't want you anywhere near me." Shana almost grimaced at the lie. She wanted Bryant close, closer than was prudent.

"You don't want the beasts near you either. Right?" he reasoned.

"Well... No. Not really," she admitted.

"Then the only safe thing for you to do is accept this amulet." He held the necklace between them.

"And," she hesitated, feeling her cheeks darken in a deep blush, "you have to kiss me to do this, right?"

His smile made her heart skip a beat. "Would one kiss be so dangerous?" His voice was dark and seductive.

Oh yes. One kiss from Bryant is likely to be fatal. But what a way to go!

Bryant closed on her position as if she'd agreed, and Shana felt her heart rate accelerate.

He was going to do it. That rogue was going to kiss her.

The amulet settled over her shoulders, the disc coming to rest over her breasts. Shana didn't look at it. The intent set to Bryant's eyes held her full attention.

His fingers worked at the bun in her hair, and the damp strands curled around her face. He smiled his approval at that, making her feel pretty and wanted. His hands settled on her cheeks.

"Do you want my protection?" he whispered.

Shana nodded, unwilling to trust her voice wouldn't squeak.

He lowered his face until the foreign words he murmured teased her lips with heat. Her nipples hardened in response, and her whole body sensitized in anticipation of his touch. She closed her eyes as he fell silent, and—

Bryant kissed her forehead and moved away abruptly.

Shana opened her eyes, hurt and confusion warring in her breast. "What... Why?" she managed.

He raised an eyebrow, a mocking smile turning up one edge of his mouth. "What did you think? That I'd be flamboyant?" Bryant closed on her again, raking a hot look over her body. "Do you want me to be flamboyant?" he offered. His body pressed to hers, his hands gripping the table on either side of her hips. "I can be as outrageous as you want me to be."

Shana ground her teeth in frustration. He was taunting her. "Certainly not," she snapped, pushing back at his shoulder.

Bryant shrugged and ambled away, seemingly unaffected by her refusal. "Your choice," he called back, "but you don't know what you're missing."

She didn't answer that. In truth, Shana couldn't concoct an answer that wouldn't make her appear the child in a midst of a tantrum she was hiding inside.

"Just one thought, Shana."

"Yes?" she managed evenly.

"Safe isn't much fun. My life may not top sixty-four years, but it won't be boring while I am alive to enjoy it." Then he was gone, disappearing into the darkness past the tack room.

****

Bryant stretched out on the musty hay, his cock aching. He grumbled a curse at that.

Stopping had been stupid. Making fun of her had been worse. She had been willing to let him take release, though she had wanted to play it off on the fantasy of being swept off her feet by a rake. Bryant had played his share of sex games, and he'd bedded his share of blade chasers. So, why the hell hadn't he just finished what he'd started back there?

"You're losing your touch, Bryant," he berated himself, pulling the alcohol swipes from his back pocket. "Not littering. Not taking women. Next thing you know, you'll be driving a

Mazda by the traffic laws and giving up your ring."

He shook away a vision of a baby seat in that Mazda. "Not me. Not ever," he vowed.

Despite his lineage, Bryant had never flirted with printing. Not even Ms. Strait-Laced was going to change his mind about that. If he took release with her, it would be hot, mindless, and over the minute they reached a phone.

Chapter Seventeen

Shana stared at Bryant, memorizing every line of his body as he walked. The man was sin incarnate, a body created for carnal adventure, coupled with the attitude to revel in those pursuits. She licked her lips, watching the way his jeans caressed his butt, wishing that she could run her hands over it just to see if his body was as hard as it looked.

She had given up trying to decipher this arousal not long after his aborted kiss. It wasn't just that Bryant was gorgeous. His words taunted her, replaying in her mind until the damned things actually made some sick sort of sense to her.

So Bryant isn't Prince Charming. Big deal! Most women don't wait until the wedding night to have sex with a man, and this is definitely not a chance that's likely to come twice in life. Didn't Grandmother always tell me that a woman should have one secret that she held close to her heart?

Shana glanced at Bryant's sculpted backside again. *What a glorious secret a night with him would be!*

"You all right back there?" he asked.

"Just fine," she lied. Shana was getting blisters from the leather shoes drying on her feet, but admitting it would be akin to admitting her inability to meet this challenge.

"Up for a climb?"

She stumbled in surprise, taking the opportunity to grasp at his shoulder for balance.

In a lightning-fast move, Bryant was facing her, catching Shana against his chest as his motion threw her further off balance.

For a moment, she didn't speak. She didn't feel capable of coherent speech, of saying anything that wouldn't make her sound like an idiot. "Uh... Thanks." She managed what she hoped passed for a nonchalant tone. "Wasn't watching my feet, I guess."

Bryant nodded, setting her back on her feet but not removing his hands. "No problem. It's part of my job description." He released her, tracing his hands slowly along her hips as if testing her balance before he turned and strolled away.

Her knees were rubbery, her stomach fluttering in response to his touch. Oh, yes. A night with Bryant could easily be the highlight of her life.

He stopped a few yards from her, cursing wildly.

Shana forced herself forward. "What is it?" she asked.

"The rains have destroyed the trail."

"And this means..."

"Going around means another day, at least."

Shana considered that. Another day of staring at Bryant's body was enticing, but they hadn't found much in the way of food. Her complaining stomach made the decision for her. She stepped out onto the steep incline.

Bryant grasped her by the arms. "What are you doing?" he asked.

She smiled. "Weren't you the one who said safe wasn't fun?"

"You really want to chance this?" His voice sounded of disbelief.

"Chicken?" she challenged, pushing away the memory of how many times she'd turned away from that taunt over the years.

Bryant snorted in laughter. "You're on."

****

She's actually going to do it. Bryant forced himself to watch the hazardous trail instead of the woman preceding him down the slope. He had been certain that she would choose the extra day of travel. It was safe, sure, exactly what he would expect her to do.

Bryant grimaced at her slight limp. She no doubt had blisters, thanks to her dunk in the river.

Saying Shana had been displeased when he dragged her out of the water would be like calling his sacred weapon a butter knife. He smiled at the memory of her sputtering, slapping him around the head and face, and calling him a jerk for even pretending to hand her over to the beasts.

He glanced at her white cotton shirt, a rumble of hunger unrelated to appetite bringing his errant cock up fast. Bryant breathed a curse at that, arguing that he was stronger than his curse.

He wasn't the typical Maher Warrior. Bryant was thirty-two years old and had never had a brush with printing. He took his release often, not because he lost control if he didn't, but because he *liked* sex. There was nothing wrong with liking sex. He wasn't his brothers, his father, or his grandfather. Bryant was as normal as a Warrior could be.

If Shana had sex with him— *Shit!* That thought made him harder. *If* she had sex with him, he'd make it the best sex she ever had. Bryant prided himself in making sure both he and his partner had a great time in bed. But they wouldn't have sex because he couldn't control himself. It wouldn't be because he had no choice.

Curt couldn't say for certain how much of his lack of control with Erin had been the Maher genes and how much had been the interfering Stone. He couldn't even rule out that both of them being Warriors hadn't worked against them.

Bryant was lucky; he didn't share the Maher weakness.

His eyes strayed to Shana, and his cock pulsed, as if arguing that point.

He pushed away the rebuttal. It had simply been too long since he'd taken release, but there were any number of blade chasers who would gladly give him another go, once he got Shana back to civilization and kissed— He ground his teeth. And said his goodbyes.

He forced his mind back to the subject at hand. He *didn't* share the family weakness for release and printing, and there wasn't an interfering Stone taunting him. Erin held the Stone's power now. Even if she hated Bryant enough to use the Stone's power against him, Erin had too much honor to force anyone to print.

Bryant tensed, his mind numbly noting Shana's abrupt disappearance. Her scream shook him, propelling him forward. He crashed through the bushes, grasping the stalks as his feet slid from under him on the same mud slick that she'd discovered.

A hand grasped his ankle, and Bryant reached for her blindly with his free hand, dragging Shana toward him. The sound of tearing fabric was loud even in comparison to his ragged breathing and pounding heart in his ears. He sent up a fervent prayer that he hadn't torn skin with her clothing. She was human, and her healing wasn't even a quarter as fast as his was.

Her hands fisted in his shirt, and Bryant wrapped his arm around her, trying to calm his thundering heart and rapid breathing. He noted his trembling hands in a wry sort of amusement. He was scared, and he wasn't really sure why he was.

"Are you okay?" he asked.

She nodded, looking at the inhospitable drop below them with a sigh of relief. Shana laid her cheek to his chest, closing her eyes.

A smile pulled up at his lips. "Enough excitement for you?" he teased.

She growled what sounded like an unladylike curse. "Just get me off this hillside, please."

"As the lady wishes."

Chapter Eighteen

Shana stared at Bryant across the small fire he'd built outside yet another abandoned farm. "There are a lot of them, aren't there?" she noted.

His forehead creased in confusion. "A lot of what?"

"Abandoned farms."

"Ah. Yeah. In my grandfather's day, they were all running. Then the river shifted, and there were periodic floods. It was too poor a region for the government to care. The farmers changed crops to try and counter the increased ground water, but it was new and they played out the soil pretty quickly." He waved a hand around them. "Half of this is swamp for four months a year now."

"That's sad. All of those families forced off like that."

Bryant played with his ring, nodding silently.

Shana adjusted his shirt on her shoulders. His had a small tear, but after he pulled her from the bushes, hers had been no cover at all. She shivered in the memory of his gaze traveling the length of her body. He'd swallowed hard and looked away, pulling off his shirt and turning his back to give her privacy to change into it. He still had the skin-tight black t-shirt beneath, so she hadn't argued taking the button-down shirt that reached to her mid-thighs.

She bit her lip as Bryant stripped off his t-shirt and laid back, using it as a pillow while he stared at the stars. Her eyes wandered over his

251

half-naked form, settling over the cut at his hip. She moved toward him, hardly able to believe her eyes, but getting closer didn't change what she saw.

"You're almost healed," she exclaimed.

Bryant touched the spot. "Yeah. It'll scar, but a few more days will make it look like an old scar."

She touched the deep pink line of knitting tissue gingerly. "This was what you meant. You said you didn't need to clean the wound."

He sighed. "I have accelerated healing. It's a family trait."

"You're connected to those beasts somehow, aren't you?"

His fingers brushed over hers, then retreated. "The original beasts who spawned the rest were related to my kind several millennia ago. These beasts are just infected. They aren't like me at all."

"You don't drink blood or anything, do you?"

He snorted in laughter. "If I did, I wouldn't be starving right now." He pulled his lips back, baring his teeth as if to assure her that he didn't have fangs.

Shana moved her hand to another scar. "You've been hurt a lot in your life."

"No more than any other Warrior," he dismissed her.

"You've never wanted anything else?"

Bryant met her eyes. "Like what?"

"A different life... Or something?"

"We call it a curse. Even if we want something different, we couldn't be happy not hunting. I don't think we could function that way. We'd go nuts."

"But have you ever wanted anything different?"

He shrugged. "I suppose all Warriors do—at some point, before they give up dreams of the impossible."

"What did you want to be?"

Bryant smiled. "A cop."

She rolled her eyes. "Always something dangerous."

"Always someone who protects others," he countered.

"Protecting people is important to you, isn't it?"

His smile faltered. "Yes. It is."

"What is it?"

"It is our most sacred trust. We always protect the innocent." Something in his manner was guarded.

"You didn't once," Shana guessed, uncertain what gave her that idea.

He looked toward the fire. "Yeah. I forgot how important it was once."

"What happened?"

A stiff smile returned to his lips. He traced a scar above his left nipple. "See this?" He moved his hand to another scar at his right shoulder without waiting for her answer, lingered only a moment, then moved on to another, closer to his neck. "And these?"

"Yes? What are they?"

"Reminders. The first was a gift from my grandfather. The other two were gifts from my

253

father. They didn't let Curt take a blade to me, and they left me standing for him, beaten to a pulp already... He broke three of my ribs and knocked me unconscious. That was my lesson never to shirk my duty to protect an innocent again." He shook his head. "I learned it well."

Shana shuddered at the barbarism inherent in their justice system. She wanted to soothe away his hurt. "Curt is your brother?" she asked, hoping to lead him to safer, happier ground.

"The younger one. Adam is the oldest."

She stroked her hands over his chest, and Bryant closed his eyes.

"It was Curt and Erin I should have been protecting," he murmured.

Shana laid a kiss to a scar a hand-width above the one the beast gave him, and he groaned.

"Erin gave me that one."

A stab of jealousy lit in her breast. Shana was touching him, and all Bryant could think about was this Erin person. "Your girlfriend?" she asked acidly, cursing the fact that she cared. Or maybe cursing him, just in case he did have a girlfriend. Yes, that was it.

Bryant barked in laughter. "No. I tried, though. I tried to get her to marry me. That's why she scarred me."

Her heart ached at that. "You must have loved her very much."

His eyes opened, and Bryant searched her face, abruptly serious. "No," he admitted. "I didn't love her. I just wanted her. A lot of men *wanted* Erin."

"What happened to her?"

"She married Curt. He does love her."

Shana stared at him in disbelief. Bryant had a way of surprising her. She never knew what to expect next where he was concerned.

He stood, kicking dirt over the fire. "We should get some sleep. It's still another five hours or so to the cabin in the morning." He walked away without looking back.

She sighed. Again, he'd thrown her a curve ball. Just when she thought he was opening up to her, he shut her out again.

****

April 22nd, 2030

Shana bit her lip, staring at Bryant in the pale morning light. They would reach the cabin and a phone today. If she intended to seduce him, now was the time.

She turned toward him, stroking her fingers along the ridge in his jeans. Bryant groaned in his sleep, bucking his hips against her as if asking for more. Encouraged, she traced the lengthening rod as it stiffened. She pressed her lips to his chin, cupping his sac in her hand.

The soft stubble on his chin scraped her lips. Then his mouth covered hers, his tongue seeking access and sparring with hers when she granted it.

Bryant broke off the kiss, his entire body taut and his breathing as ragged as hers was. "Be sure you want this," he warned.

Shana nodded, barely able to catch her breath, let alone talk. She'd been kissed before, but never by someone who seemed to put his entire body and soul into the act. She nodded again. She wanted this more than she'd wanted just about anything in her life.

He hummed a low note that made the ache between her thighs throb in time with her heart. His eyes locked on hers, pinning Shana in his gaze. Her body responded fiercely, her nipples coming to points that brushed his chest when she breathed and her core hot and wet.

"You're sure," he whispered, as if it surprised him. "You're never going to forget this." It was a solemn vow full of dark sensuality.

"No, I won't," she agreed.

Bryant's hands traced the tips of her breasts. "I won't be stopping."

She shook her head. Shana didn't want him to stop. It felt too good to stop now.

He traced his hands down her ribs and around her waist to cup her buttocks. Bryant pulled her hard to his erect length, smiling at her moan of surrender.

"No one will ever fuck you like I will, baby." His mouth closed on hers again, capturing her answer.

Yes. This was what she wanted. This would be her personal secret, and no safe man would ever fuck her like this. Women dreamed of a mad encounter with a man like Bryant for their first time. Shana would have that dream in the flesh.

****

Bryant pushed her skirt up her legs, smiling as she tipped her hips to facilitate the move. Her hands cupped his face, and her mouth returned to his. Their kisses were hot and hard. Bryant knew there was a wild side to Shana somewhere; he was just glad it was her sexual side.

Shana wiggled her bottom out of the plain, beige cotton panties she wore then pulled at his jeans frantically. When Bryant took over, her hands returned to his face, slipping back to wind in his hair. He shuddered at that; for all that she complained about the length of his hair, he noted that her eyes focused there often. Almost as often as they focused on his ass or his cock, when she thought he wasn't watching. He'd dreamed of her burying her hands in his hair as he buried himself in her.

He slipped the head of his cock between her thighs, teasing Shana with thrusts that drew the fluids dripping from her swollen slit to her clit. Her kiss became more fevered, and she moved with him. He groaned at her increased wetness. He was working her into a froth, and he wouldn't take her until Shana begged for him.

She tried to guide Bryant over her, but he held back. If he took her now, it would be over all too quickly. Shana would never forget this encounter. If he was lucky, she might let him take her again.

"Bryant," she pleaded.

Maybe if he brought her to climax more than once... He didn't hesitate. He pulled back then rolled her beneath him, using the rigid base of his cock to stimulate the sensitive spot at her pelvic bone.

Shana wriggled against him, her plea for more lost in another heated kiss. Bryant thrust two fingers into her, stilling in surprise.

It wasn't her climax that stopped him, though the force of it might well have done so anyway. Her cry was pure and heartfelt, and he didn't doubt that her reaction was completely honest. Virgins rarely played games with faking a response, and the scrap of skin at his fingertips attested to the very big mistake he'd almost made with her.

He looked around at the rundown barn, guilt eating at him. This was wrong. He couldn't do this.

Bryant ground his teeth at his insistent arousal. He'd never worried about the women he'd bedded before, even the virgins, but he'd never bedded a woman in such rough circumstances before. He pushed away memories of sex on hiking trails. *It wasn't the same. I've never taken a woman like this before, and I won't start now.* He eased his hand from her slowly, laying a kiss on her cheek.

Shana bit her lower lip, her expressive green eyes announcing her confusion. "I offered," she choked. "Why didn't you—"

"Shh. Not like this." Bryant shook his head, trying to find the words to explain himself. "It's your first time."

Her face darkened to a pale crimson blush. "I offered myself to you, and you're turning me away? *You?*" Anger and hurt warred in her voice.

He fought back irritation at that, reminding himself that she had laid herself open to hurt with him, and he had fumbled it again. She probably didn't believe that he had no honor, only that he had done something unexpected and tactless, from her point of view.

"I'm not a complete rogue, Shana. Do you want to remember your first time this way? In a bed of moldy hay and dust? Do you?" He touched her cheek. "Please, let me make it better than this." *Anywhere but here.*

For a moment she seemed incapable of answering. She pushed at his shoulder, and Bryant rolled away to his back. He dragged his jeans up, watching Shana out of the corner of his eye as he fastened the buttons over his still rock-hard length.

She didn't look at him. She smoothed her skirt over her thighs and grasped her underwear in shaking fingers. Shana pushed to her feet and all but bolted into the morning light.

"Don't go far," Bryant instructed her. He rubbed a hand over his face. He hadn't meant to hurt her, but he had. "I am not Curt," he grumbled. "I won't take Shana the way Curt took Erin."

He groaned at that. If only Shana was really his to touch. If only she wanted him like Erin had wanted his brother.

Bryant shook away the thought impatiently. "No. I don't want that. I just want sex. I am not the typical Maher."

****

Shana bit back a sob. Of all the brainless moves she'd made in her life, that one had to be the worst of the lot! What had she been thinking? Had she been thinking at all? Just a meaningless fling with the vampire hunter?

She couldn't even do that right. Just when she thought she had Bryant pegged as a self-serving ladies' man who'd screw her and walk away, leaving her with nothing but hot memories of one truly wild moment in her dull life, the man had to go off half-cocked and... She groaned at the unintentional pun. He had to go and get noble on her.

"Face it, Shana. You can't even lose your virginity in an interesting fashion." She did sob at that. Well, there was nothing to do but go on from here. She started working the panties back up her legs. "Yeah. You'll end up marrying an accountant or a college history professor." She grimaced at that. Every college history professor she'd ever had was capable of putting dust motes to sleep. She sighed. "And, you'll be a virgin on your wedding night," she grumbled.

Shana peeked around the edge of the barn, watching Bryant stroll out of the cover. He'd donned his weapons belt and boots, but his t-shirt was dangling from his back pocket, leaving his chest deliciously bare. He relieved himself against an overgrown wood pile, seemingly oblivious to any propriety at all.

She backed away, pressing her back to the rough wooden walls, her hand fisted over her womb. Just the sight of his cock made her ache for him. Memories of him teasing her with the tip made her wet and hot all over again.

"Not good," she decided. It would be better to go to her wedding night as a virgin than to torture herself with memories of Bryant for the rest of her life. Wouldn't it?

Chapter Nineteen

Shana looked around the cabin in surprise. It was comfortable and well kept, with only a light dust settled on the surfaces. It was also much larger than she would have expected for a cabin: at least two...possibly three bedrooms and spacious common areas. He'd stopped on the way in and started a generator that looked as if it was meticulously maintained and was obviously stocked with enough gas for an extended stay.

"This way."

Bryant led her deeper into the structure, past the kitchen and two closed doors, into what appeared to be a master bedroom. She stared at the bed, her body staging a revolt that demanded she pull him down on it. He took her hand and drew her past it and toward a small alcove.

"Not yet," he answered her unspoken plea.

Her head spun at that. Despite hours of arguing that this was a bad idea, she couldn't deny that she wanted this, that she'd let him take her to that bed and have sex with her when he asked. She shivered at the thought that Bryant wouldn't be asking. When he was ready, he would simply flip her libido on like a switch and take her to ecstasy on the rush of it.

Bryant opened a front-loading washer and flipped open a lidded garbage can next to it. He pulled off his t-shirt and tossed it in the garbage. His eyes traveled down her body, and Shana nodded in understanding.

She kicked her shoes away and unbuttoned her skirt, pushing it over her hips. Her underwear followed. Shana let them fall to her ankles, raising her eyes to Bryant at last.

He wasn't watching her, as she'd hoped...or maybe feared. He'd removed his armored boots and belt, setting them atop the dryer, then moved on to his jeans. She watched, transfixed, as he yanked the muddy fabric off his feet, taking his socks with them. He pitched his clothes into the washing machine and looked to Shana.

His half-erect cock hardened. He stepped toward her and fisted his hands in the hem of the shirt she wore. His shirt. Bryant stripped it off and pitched it over his shoulder into the garbage can. He worked at the catch on her bra, and the fabric slid away in his hands. It landed, unheeded by either of them, in the washer.

Shana shivered, her gaze locked with his, not daring to glance down his body again, knowing he was as hard as a man could get and intent on her.

Bryant sank to his knees, urging her back a pace. He scooped up her clothes, his face so close that his breathing teased at her stomach. He stood slowly, depositing the rank clothing in the washer. He added detergent, then started the cycle.

He took her hand again and guided her through the bedroom and into a bathroom. It was shockingly large, considering for the size of the cabin...and clean. Bryant didn't speak. He started the shower, a multi-head setup with a wide bench in the center.

There was no need for words between them. He stepped into the spray, and Shana followed. He motioned to the bench, and she sat, closing her eyes and sighing as the hot water washed away the days of mud and grime.

She gasped, meeting Bryant's eyes as he started bathing her. Shana didn't watch the mud washing away. She could barely keep her eyes open and focused as Bryant soaped his hands again and again. His fingers traced every inch of her body, circling her nipples, following her ribs, cupping her calves and thighs, and finally playing at her throbbing core.

He rose up on his knees, leaning into her; but just when she felt certain he would push her thighs further apart and take her, he massaged a fragrant shampoo into her hair then leaned her head back and rinsed it, his fingers combing through and tugging gently as they worked knots out.

Shana moaned in longing. He eased her head forward, and she opened her eyes, abruptly dizzy and disoriented. Her vision sharpened, locking on the individual water droplets that fell from his long dark hair, that ran down his cheeks and beaded on his eyelashes and lips.

Bryant nodded and turned off the water, collecting a stack of towels. The torture began again. He dried her body and hair slowly, leaving her breathless.

She grasped one of the towels, drying his hair. He settled the towel in his hand across her lap and leaned forward, giving her a better vantage point to dry it—while he took one of her breasts in his mouth. She stroked the towel over him, unconsciously matching his ministrations, drying all of him that she could reach.

He explored her body with his mouth, up to her shoulders, then throat, ducking away when she would have kissed him. She fisted the towel as he returned to her breasts: one, then the other, before trailing down her body to press a kiss in her curls, his whiskers combing them as his fingers had the hair on her head.

Bryant pulled the towel from her lap, letting it fall to the floor, then lifted her knees over his shoulders and eased her to the edge of the bench. His breath teased at her body. Shana let her head drop back as his tongue flicked over her clit. He stroked his tongue lower, sensitizing every inch of her before delving inside.

Shana dropped the towel, winding her hands in his hair and pulling him closer. Her breathing came in strangled gasps, and her whole body trembled. His tongue continued its plunder. He sucked at her, licked at her, even nipped at her tender flesh. It was exquisite. Shana reveled in the pleasure he gave her even as she begged him to end it.

He didn't push her over this time. Bryant knelt up abruptly, catching her knees and lowering her feet to the floor as his mouth closed over hers. The sweet taste in his mouth incited the ache in her to a riot.

Bryant broke of the kiss. "Here or the bed?" he asked, his voice gruff.

She wrapped her legs around his hips and urged him closer. She needed him. Now.

"Be sure. I can give you a bed." His eyes called him a liar. The stark hunger in them announced that he would pay a dear price for that, if he could bring himself to wait that long at all.

She shook her head. This was supposed to be a crazy chance. It wasn't supposed to be sane and predictable. It wasn't supposed to be respectable.

Bryant grasped her hips and slid deep in a single thrust. Shana arched back over the bench, crying out as much in pleasure as in pain. Bryant's groan rumbled through her body. He guided her face back to his, his kiss at once urgent and reverent. Just when it felt that kiss might get out of control, he executed a single slide out and back in, as if testing her readiness.

"Now," he rasped.

She expected him to take her on a frantic ride, but his thrusts were slow and solemn. His mouth mated with hers, again and again, soothing words surrounding her as the pain receded and pleasure washed over her body in warm waves that seemed to intensify with every stroke.

"You're close," he whispered.

Close didn't begin to describe her state. Shana rode the crest of pleasure, closing her eyes as the waves finally swamped her. She was all but numb to his continuing thrusts, whimpering as her entire body came alive with starbursts of sensation, firing every nerve seemingly at random.

His heat swirled through her, a maelstrom within the storm still raging in her. His harsh cry sounded of surprise mixed with the expected enjoyment. Bryant muttered a curse, going still inside her as his erupting cock buffeted her with pulse after pulse of his heat. That final sensation forced her past endurance and ripped a scream of surrender and longing from her, longing for this moment never to end and surrender to whatever Bryant wanted from her to have it.

Shana came to realization slowly, her cheek pressed to his chest, her hands still grasping handfuls of his hair, his hands tracing her back, as if memorizing every line of her body, and his cock still buried deep inside her. He dipped his head, nuzzling his lips to hers, his whiskers making hot spots on her chin and cheeks.

He's marking me. Her body made urgent demands at that. Yes. She wanted to be marked as his, but that wasn't something that was likely to happen.

At last, he eased out of her body. Bryant lifted her into his arms and turned toward the hall, his stride purposeful.

"Where are we going?" she asked, confused by his silence.

He didn't smile. Bryant didn't even meet her eyes, though his voice was gentle and sounded somewhat of bemusement. "To the bed, Shana. Once could never be enough with you."

Chapter Twenty

April 23rd, 2030

Bryant stroked his fingertip along her lower lip, watching Shana sleep much as he had watched her sleep for the last few nights. She sighed and turned to him, seemingly seeking him in her most unguarded moments.

He shook his head, confused by the ache within him. Bryant had never slept with a woman he'd had sex with before, never stayed past a few moments after he screwed her into a deep slumber. Curt and Adam had spent whole nights with women they took release with before they printed, but Bryant never had. He'd never felt the urge to, yet more proof that he wasn't the typical Warrior of Maher.

It wasn't just that Shana was under his protection. Bryant felt certain that he would have stayed with her, even if he'd picked her up in a bar for the night, though he couldn't have said definitively why he would do something so out of character. Release was release. This was something else.

"Why are you so different?" he whispered, halfway wishing she would answer his question in that sexy voice that manifested only when he was buried to the hilt in her.

Bryant had deflowered virgins before. He'd slept with scores of women. Hundreds in the seventeen years he'd been cursed. Never before had he felt the need to take one so tenderly.

"Release is release." He repeated the words he'd said so often when Curt and Adam tried to tell him how life-altering the sex that sealed printing was. This time, he said it with much less conviction.

Release had always been rough and fast for Bryant. Even with virgins, he had worked them to a frenzy and given them a wild night of memories to treasure.

But not with Shana. He'd worked her up gently, feeding her arousal to a more potent edge than he'd ever bothered to build before. Then he'd taken her slowly, reverently. The sex was akin to a prayer, a communion.

A promise.

"A promise of what?" he questioned, his heart pounding. Bryant shook his head. "Not printing," he begged. "Please, not that."

When a Warrior of Maher fell, he fell hard and fast. For all that he taunted the other men in his family for their weakness in matters of love, he always knew he wasn't immune, somewhere deep in his heart. That's why Bryant never stayed the night. It was his attempt at escaping, his quest to prove he was stronger than the urge to tie himself to a woman and produce his two-point-five young Warriors.

"I *am* stronger," he decided.

Bryant pushed from the bed, his stride purposeful. He pulled the spare cell phone from the charger and opened the line, knowing it was at full power with a four-hour charge.

It was simple. He'd call Adam and have a car delivered. *As soon as possible.* Shana would go

269

back to her safe life without him. There was little chance that he'd ever see her again. The beasts were dwindling, and there was much easier prey around than a protected woman. Why would they attack her?

"Simple," he assured himself, breathing a sigh of relief.

He opened the connection, but he didn't press the buttons. Bryant closed his eyes, unable to still the shaking in his hands as his fingertip wavered over the 'one' button to start dialing. The dial tone sounded much too loud, and a cold sweat coated his brow. He hadn't even left her. He hadn't even called for the car to leave her, and he wanted to scream in frustration, in the torture of losing a lost love.

It wouldn't be simple. Bryant would face printing madness. He'd be a veritable madman for days or weeks, until he conquered his nature. Then he'd be free to go on with his life.

Or would he? He ambled back to the bedroom doorway, shutting the connection on the phone to avoid waking her. He stood, staring at Shana, his heart struggling to hold a steady rhythm. Could even the madness erase this need to have her in his bed? No, not just in his bed! *In my life!* Did he want it to take that away from him?

"No."

He jumped. Bryant hadn't meant to say it aloud. He hadn't wanted to admit it at all.

"It's true."

He conceded defeat gracefully. If Shana turned from him, he'd face the madness and give her the freedom she wanted. He wouldn't leave her while there was any chance that she'd accept him. He couldn't.

Bryant turned the power off on the phone and dropped it on top of the robe thrown over the dresser. He returned to the bed, taking Shana in his arms and burying his face in her fragrant curls.

"Please, choose me."

****

Shana burrowed her face in the warmth beside her, stilling as arms circled her. She bit her lip, her mind supplying the truth.

What had I expected? That Bryant would leave me in the night?

She squeezed her eyes shut. She *had* expected it on some level. It would have been easier if he had left. Facing him after what they'd shared, knowing it was just another night of sex to him, would be pure torture.

He stroked his hands down her buttocks, and his knee urged her thighs apart. His breathing was ragged, as if he was restraining himself, and his erect cock brushed over her seam.

Shana realized she was wet, already throbbing—a slow, steady beat not unlike his thrusts in the shower. She pushed down on him with a sigh of relief. He met her movement, filling her with his body, completing her, even as he made her long for more.

271

Bryant threaded his fingers through hers, drawing her hands above her head as he turned her beneath him. His kisses were deep and drugging. She wrapped her legs around him, levering herself further onto him; and Bryant moaned in delight.

She opened her eyes and found herself pinned in his gaze. His expression shifted continuously: fierce, tender, driven, uncertain. It was as if she were being gifted with a rare glimpse inside his soul.

Her orgasm rolled over her without warning, and Bryant joined her, their cries mingling much as their bodies did. They panted in the aftermath, his sweat-slicked body teasing at hers. For a moment, neither of them spoke.

Shana looked away from the intensity in his eyes, her mind rioting. She couldn't keep doing this. She wanted more than this, and taking more would only make her want it more acutely.

"What is it?" Bryant asked.

"I don't—" She couldn't say it. As catastrophic as his leaving would be, Shana couldn't ask him to stay with her. Not now. If he refused her, she'd never live down the hurt.

"Usually do this?" he finished for her, just a touch of humor in his tone.

Shana nodded. It was as good an excuse as any, she supposed.

Bryant chuckled. "Virgins rarely do have practical experience."

She darkened at that.

"Do you regret that it was me?" he asked, abruptly serious.

"Never." She shook herself mentally. "I just—
" She faltered.

He released her hands, tracing a finger along her lips, his eyes soft and dreamy. "Just what?"

"I never thought I'd do this."

"Make love with a man?" he asked, no trace of a smile curving his lips. Bryant looked hungry and distracted.

"Of course not. I mean... I knew I would someday, but..."

"But?" he prompted her, laying a kiss on her chin and inhaling deeply.

"I guess I thought I was the type to wait until the wedding night," she stammered, feeling her face go a shade darker at offering the admission while he lay buried in her, still hard and occasionally pulsing.

He seemed to consider that carefully. Bryant brushed his lips over hers, and she gasped at the feeling of a final eruption within her, her mind numbly supplying that he had to feel really good to have aftershocks that notable. His tongue teased at her upper lip, stroking just inside her parted lips and flicking across the surface as he retreated.

"As far as I'm concerned, you have." His voice caressed her face.

Her heart stuttered at that. Did she dare hope that she'd heard him right? "What do you mean?" she asked.

"I'm asking you to marry me." He grimaced. "Oh, gods. I'm doing this all wrong. I don't have a ring. I should be on my knees. I should—"

She kissed him, unable to bear his self-recrimination any further. Bryant was fevered, a hair off of desperate.

"You're doing it just right," she assured him.

Bryant smiled, his hand cupping her cheek. "Only if you say 'yes'."

Shana took his hand in hers, removing his pinky ring and placing it on the middle finger of her left hand. Even at that, it was a bit loose on her. She touched the metal disc over her chest. "I'm wearing your amulet and your ring."

He nodded, his eyes locked on that ring in longing that she prayed was for her and not the piece of jewelry. "Is that a 'yes'?" he asked.

"I don't suppose you'll ever drive the speed limit," she mused.

He sighed. "Probably not, but I'll switch cars if you like."

"Only with me."

He nodded urgently. "Yes?" It was obvious that he was having trouble controlling his nerves.

"Can I keep the ring?" she teased, winding her hands in his hair, fully expecting him to balk—or to offer to get her a ring of her own.

"Yes. Anything. Except my hair. I am not cutting my hair."

Shana smiled, pulling his mouth down to hers. "Yes, and I don't want you to cut your hair."

Chapter Twenty-One

April 24ᵗʰ, 2030

Adam fisted his hand on the steering wheel of the rental, scanning the dark, dirt track ahead. When he found Bryant, he'd kill the thoughtless pup himself, unless he was at Death's door.

Being out of contact wasn't unusual in itself. The fact that Adam had felt a feeding, then several kills in his range, was typical enough, though he cringed that some poor soul had been fed on. Bryant wasn't a first night in the habit of reporting every kill. Adam had assumed all was well, though he was prepared to see a full file on the new protected show up in his in-box the next morning.

Then the call came in. Adam shuddered at the memory. A state trooper had contacted him in his search for Bryant. That was when Adam had known something was wrong.

His younger brother doted on his car. The 2020 Retro Stingray was Bryant's life. Even if beasts had torn it apart, piece by piece, he would have had the pieces collected, replaced, and reconstructed into his high-gloss black baby with leather interior. He absolutely *would not* have willingly abandoned the car, no matter the circumstances.

Adam had flown out immediately. It hadn't taken him long to find where the car had lain. It had taken only hours longer for him to find the shattered phone and torn jacket, covered in dried blood—human and beast. He'd lost the trail there, at the bottom of a muddy slide into the river.

Bryant had been running but struggling. The tracks were clear on that fact. That bothered Adam. He would have felt it if his brother died. He wouldn't have felt even a serious injury if Bryant ghosted to hide himself from tracking beasts. Visions of his brother, running injured and maintaining ghosting to save himself, taunted Adam. Was he unable to reach a safe haven?

This was his last hope. He was on his way to the closest cabin. There were no protected in this area. It was the only plausible place for Bryant to head in an emergency, if he was on foot. If he wasn't there, Adam would backtrack toward the river. There were several abandoned farms between the cabin and the river that Bryant might have sought cover in. It would mean criss-crossing back roads, but Adam had a half-ton truck and all the time in the world, if it meant his brother's life.

He stared at the cell phone miserably, forcing himself not to try calling again. Every time the other phone rang without answer until the voice mail picked up, a part of him died. He was Lord Maher, and the family was his responsibility. If Bryant died... He forced that thought away, peering through the windshield.

He stared at the cabin, praying he wasn't hallucinating. Adam let out a breath he hadn't realized he'd been holding. There were lights on at the cabin.

His mind sorted through the possibilities. Maybe Bryant wasn't badly hurt but was recovering, hoping not to worry Adam. Or anger him with his carelessness. Maybe the phone was damaged; he couldn't remember how long it had been since the last time it had been checked. Maybe...

Adam ground his teeth in frustration. There was no way to know until he saw Bryant.

"If the pup isn't dying, I will kill him," he promised again.

He parked the truck and let himself into the cabin with his key. He passed through the first few rooms, stopping in the master bedroom doorway in surprise.

By the amulet laid between the woman's breasts and the jagged cut healing on her throat, Adam deduced the reason for his brother's staggering gait in the mud. He'd obviously been carrying the woman.

He looked to the cell phone, forcing back his *Blutjagd*. Bryant had never shown self-control sexually, but turning off the phone and leaving Adam to worry went past even his usual disregard for others' feelings. Adam considered the beating he'd give Bryant—as soon as he woke him to administer it.

The woman moved her hand, and the light glinted off the ring on her middle finger. Adam went still, his mind putting together the other small clues. It was Bryant's signet ring she wore, the Maher seal etched into a blood-red ruby. If there was one possession more precious to Bryant than the Stingray, it was his ring; and now this woman was wearing it.

Adam bit back a laugh. *So, Bryant isn't immune to the Maher urge to take a mate after all.* He leaned against the doorframe, watching them sleep. Adam considered walking away and leaving them in peace, but he did owe his brother some repayment for all this worry, for making him leave his wife and children for no good reason. He cleared his throat as loudly as he could.

The woman sat up abruptly, dragging the quilt to her chest, her eyes wide in terror.

Bryant came up with his sacred weapon, his *Blutjagd* like a bonfire surrounding him, his body placed to protect his mate. He stared at Adam in disbelief for a moment, then lowered his blade with a series of curses, rubbing a hand over the new beard on his chin, then over his neck.

"Bryant," the woman called, her voice shaking. "Who is that?"

"It's all right," he soothed her. "This is my brother's idea of a joke."

"It's not very funny," she complained, tucking the quilt under her arms, her face and chest flushed crimson in embarrassment.

"I agree. Adam, do you mind?" he hinted.

Adam smiled. "You think this is my revenge? Not in the least. Wait until Curt and Erin hear about you—"

"Adam! And Erin probably damned well knows everything," he grumbled. "Now, will you kindly—"

"I think I'll stick around for a few minutes. After all, I want to meet my sister-in-law." He scooped up the phone. "At least, I hope she's my sister-in-law. If you pulled a stunt like this and she's not, I may have to kill you myself for it."

The woman grasped at Bryant's shoulder, paling at that. "I am," she offered quickly.

Adam watched her reactions in confusion. Did she really believe he'd kill his own brother?

Bryant scowled at him, running a hand over hers in comfort. "Quit scaring my mate," he growled, his *Blutjagd* warning Adam off.

Adam cleared his throat, looking to the woman pointedly.

He nodded, calming somewhat, accepting that Adam's teasing was through. "Adam, this is my mate, Shana. Shana, this tactless oaf is my older brother, Adam. We call him Conan. You can guess why."

A smile pulled up at the edges of her lips. "Ah. I see. It's a family trait."

Adam laughed heartily at that. "Yes. I'm afraid it is."

Shana sighed. "It's going to be a long, hard road." She scowled at Adam. "Let me guess... You don't drive the speed limit either."

Before Adam could question what she meant, Bryant was howling in laughter.

Section Four:

Gabriel
and
Reggie

Twice
Printed

Chapter Twenty-Two

July 26th, 2046

Adam sighed, then rubbed a hand over his eyes. He'd found her. It might be the one thing that would make Gabe snap out of it and fight.

Who knew a Warrior of seventeen was capable of printing? It hadn't happened in millennia. Even Mahers hadn't gone earlier than their twenties. But his younger son had.

Worse, Gabe had called it wrong.

You can't know that. Adam had been wrong about Jo, after all.

No, he hadn't been wrong about Jo. He hadn't known what to think then. Luckily, his mate had wanted him. Would that Gabe had been so lucky.

Adam studied Regina Carter carefully, using his ghosting to his fullest advantage. As long as she didn't know he was watching her, there would be no posturing, no fake face, and no lies.

The young woman looked miserable, but there was no telling why she was. Regina stared into space, her knees drawn to her chest, her stained tennis shoes peeking from beneath the trench coat she wore over faded jeans.

The loud speaker announced the bus departing for Raleigh and points beyond, echoing in the near-empty space. Regina stared at her ticket, her free hand straying to the empty space where her amulet once hung. She sat there, forcing hitching breaths to even, letting her bus leave without her.

Adam allowed his ghosting to fade away. Her gaze slid to the edge of his black leather duster and jeans, but there was no other reaction to his appearance. Regina didn't even raise her eyes to see which Warrior stood over her. Of course, his soft brown boots would have told her that as well as seeing his face. If she'd bothered to look that direction, but she hadn't.

"Why did you let the bus leave?" he asked. Adam prayed she'd say she didn't really want to break things off with Gabe. It might be the only thing that turned his son from his race to oblivion.

Regina shrugged. "There's light here."

That was it? The only reason she hadn't run further tonight was fear of meeting a beast on a dark bus? "No other reason?" he snapped.

"Does it matter?"

Her voice was devoid of emotion, much as Gabe's had been when he'd surrendered his sacred weapon for a cabin key. What the hell was wrong with her?

"It does to my son." That being the case, it mattered to Adam.

She winced, going a sickly shade of gray. Her hand fisted around the bus ticket, crumpling it. "I can't be what Gabe needs." There was a touch of desperation in her answer.

Adam wondered at that. Why desperation? Did Regina wish she *could* be what Gabe needed? Was there some misunderstanding? Was there something a heartfelt talk would clear up between them?

He crouched to her eye level, but Regina looked away, her eyes wide. She trembled and wrapped her arms closer around her legs. Why couldn't she look at him?

"Why did you run?"

She shrugged, seemingly at a loss for words. Or perhaps she was unsure of her own reasons for acting.

"Were you afraid of Gabe?" Women had found the intensity of a printing Warrior frightening before.

A silent shake of her head was his only answer.

"Of me?" He'd scared more than his share of protected, though he'd never done so purposely.

Her gaze met his for a moment. Then it slid away, and she offered another negative response.

That was clear enough. She hadn't run because she feared him, but she did fear him.

Adam felt his patience fraying. With his son's sanity and life in the balance, he was dealt an apathetic young woman who wasn't able to explain herself. What had he done to piss off the gods this badly?

Regina stroked the empty space where her amulet should lay again.

"Why did you leave your amulet behind?" That fact alone had nearly driven Gabe over the edge of madness. The idea of the woman he was fixated on being unprotected was too much for him.

284

She opened her mouth, but only a sigh escaped. She hunched her shoulders and dropped her ticket. While it fluttered to the floor, she started rubbing her eyes.

"Explain yourself, damn it," he ground out from between clenched teeth.

"I can't keep it. I'm not..."

"Not what?"

"Worthy to wear it." Her voice was so low, Adam almost didn't hear her.

His anger flared. "We don't give women amulets to get mates."

Regina didn't answer him. She curled further into the plastic chair.

"We give amulets to those marked by beasts. It's a duty to protect you. Nothing more. You're as worthy as any other protected to wear it."

She shook her head, wiping away tears with the back of her hand.

"Do you want to be hunted by them?" he asked, gentling his voice.

If he couldn't report that Regina wanted to be Gabe's mate, the only hope he had to give his son was that she still wore his amulet. Knowing that she'd refused that too would be the final straw for Gabe.

"No," she managed in a tremulous voice. "I don't want that."

Adam grasped her hand, then turned it palm up. He deposited the amulet in the center of her palm and then folded her fingers around it.

Regina stared at it.

"Put it on, Regina. Then I'll drive you home."

She closed her hand tighter around it. Her breathing went ragged; she took a deep breath, then nodded.

"Gabe made you an offer. You don't have to accept it. No one will pressure you to." He'd like to, but he wouldn't be doing Gabe any favors by it. Not to mention it was dishonorable and against the Rules of Sanction.

"Right," she whispered.

Adam settled into the chair next to her. "If there's any chance, Gabe will want to work this out with you."

Regina shook her head. "I can't be what he needs."

His heart sank. "If he does this... If Gabe breaks printing with you, there's no turning back."

She seemed to stop breathing. Her stillness was near absolute. A tear slid down her cheek.

"Do you understand me, Regina?"

"Yeah. I—I understand."

"Is this what you want?"

Another tear spilled down her cheek. Then a third.

Adam forced himself not to snap at her again. "Regina?"

"I can't," she repeated. "I just can't."

Adam tapped down his fury. "Then it's over."

She nodded her agreement.

****

Adam strode into cabin six, praying Gabe would listen to reason.

His son lay, curled on the bed, clad only his jeans, pale, thinner already than he'd been two days earlier. Gabe didn't react to his presence. He stared into space, much as Regina had.

"Did you find her?" It was a good sign that Gabe addressed him. It meant he wasn't completely unaware.

"I did. She's wearing the amulet again." Adam didn't say 'your amulet'; it wouldn't be right to give Gabe hope now.

His son's eyes closed in seeming exhaustion. "Good. She's safe."

"Yes. She is. You have my vow." Adam pulled Gabe's sheathed weapon from the back of his belt, extending it toward his son. "Take this." *For the love of all the gods, do this one thing for me. Show me you still have fight.*

Gabe opened his eyes, stared at the sacred weapon for a moment, then turned his back on it.

"Damn it! Fight, Gabe." If a beast found him in this state, he was as good as dead.

"There's no reason to. Either the madness wins or I do. That's the way it is."

Adam's *Blutjagd* blazed merrily. Gabe was slipping away from him, and there was nothing Adam could do about it.

Chapter Twenty-Three

April 15th, 2051

"Good evening, Regina."

The hair at the back of Reggie's neck went up in warning. No one but the government called her Regina. *The government, Adam Maher, and beasts.* The former two being highly unlikely and impossible—respectively, that meant there was a beast stalking her.

Her blood ran cold at memories of the beast who'd taken her blood. It had whispered that loathsome name as it pulled at her clothes to bare her throat.

"Such poor manners," the voice chided.

Reggie whirled around, gasping at the sight of—not one, but rather—four pairs of glowing red eyes and fang tips.

I'm dead.

She didn't question it. Given enough time, one beast could kill her with a null weapon or amulet bruises. If they were here in force, they meant to kill her.

But why? Reggie wasn't a medical professional. She didn't supply support for the Warriors. She was just a simple protected. Killing her would hurt morale, but it wouldn't slow the Warriors down or hinder them in any way.

"Much better," the leader purred.

He took a step toward her, and Reggie backed away. It was hopeless, of course.

The beast moved faster than she could see, coming face-to-face with Reggie. He stopped a whisper from touching her. Then his hand closed on the collar of her button-down shirt, setting off the amulet.

The punch of the amulet's power sent her tumbling backward, over the couch and to the hard wood floor behind it. The rip of fabric and sound of splintering wood made it clear the amulet had done its job of throwing the beast as well.

Let's just hope it does the rest of the job before one of the Warriors has to make burial arrangements for me.

"Ahhh... That is a *much* nicer view," the beast taunted.

Reggie pulled the ripped shirt closed over her bra. She maneuvered to her knees. The beast smiled, and she backed away.

The next touch came from behind her, knocking her to her stomach. Reggie rolled away, then back to her knees. She struggled to her feet.

They were everywhere, encircling her body. There were six. No, seven. One touched her shoulder, sending her reeling into another...then another...and another, like a living pinball ball trapped between the bumpers.

They retreated a few steps in unison and let her fall. Reggie lay, curled in a ball, gasping for breath. She ached from dozens of bruises rising on her skin.

"Give her a minute to recover," the leader instructed. "Then we will begin again."

"Why?" Reggie asked. Why didn't they just kill her? There were plenty of null weapons in her home they could have already bashed her head in with.

"What does an amulet do when one of my kind touches you, Regina?" His voice was oily; it made her skin crawl.

"Hurts like hell," she grumbled.

"Yes, it does, but what else does it do?" he prompted her.

Reggie stuttered in shock. The beasts wanted to call a Warrior in? She looked from face to face, her stomach churning. *This is an ambush. I'm the bait.*

"Very good," he murmured, as if she'd spoken the words aloud. "You draw in the one we want, and we kill him."

"Oh, God, no. Not that."

"There is only one close. He will come for you, and he will come alone...to us."

Her stomach threatened to empty, and a cold sweat coated her body. Reggie swallowed down the urge to vomit, her mind spinning. She couldn't stop them. They were stronger than she was, faster, and there were seven of them.

"You don't want to know which Warrior is going to die for you tonight?"

A vision of Gabe flashed into her mind. Reggie shook it away. She didn't want to know, especially if it was Gabe.

"This man will die for you. You should know his name, Regina."

Reggie trembled hard. "No. Don't."

"The death of a young Warrior may well kill his father. The untouchable Adam Lord Maher—"

She sobbed. *Joseph or Gabe?* Adam only had two sons.

"—falls when his son falls."

Her breathing went strangled. She didn't want to hear it, but she had to know. "Which...which one?" she managed to gasp out.

The beast smiled as if at a favored child. "His younger, of course. It is always more crushing to a Warrior to lose a—"

Reggie vaulted to her feet and ran. She made it only two steps toward the door.

A beast appeared in her path. He pushed her back into the bumper ring. Reggie cried out in frustration more than in pain. She couldn't escape them, which meant she was going to be their bait, one way or the other.

When it was over, she lay on the floor, tears rolling down her face, sobs ripped from her throat.

The leader of the beasts squatted beside her. He cocked his head, giving the impression of an oversized raptor waiting to dive on prey. "Gabriel of Maher," he crooned. "Remember the name, Regina. This is the man who will die for you."

She closed her eyes and vented an anguished scream. *Remember it? How can I forget it?*

****

Gabe groaned into the phone, knowing what was coming next. "And what did Brandon Lord

Hunter say?" he offered with just a note of irreverent challenge.

"Gabriel Allan Maher," his father snapped, sounding more like Gabe's mother than the unbeatable Adam Lord Maher. "Do not go there with me."

He sighed. "I was set up," he protested. "They didn't tell me she was David's—"

"And you just had to find out how good she was. Didn't you?"

"Hey! Mahers are known for their drives."

"You more than most," his father grumbled.

Gabe winced at the reminder. "Ancient history."

"Not for anyone else. Brandon suggested I leash you. He said... Now what was that?"

"You have a nearly eidetic memory, Dad. Just spit it out." Whatever the Lord Hunter had said was sure to be spectacular.

"Never mind."

"Might as well tell me before Daniel does."

Adam paused. "He said it was what he would have expected of you five years ago."

"Thanks," Gabe grumbled. Some people never let a man's history die.

"You can't be that hopeless seventeen year old forever, Gabe."

"I'm not! I just make bad choices, from time to time. You're not unknown for that yourself...Conan." He grinned, anticipating his father's reaction.

"Trial. As soon as you get back here, pup."

Gabe chuckled. "Looking forward to your—" The rest died away on a wave of awareness. "An amulet. It's close." He swung his head around, locking the direction he needed into his memory.

Adam was abruptly all business. "Have no mercy."

"I never do. I'll call you." He disconnected without waiting for an answer, then slid into his truck. Gabe headed in the direction he'd marked, scanning the road for signs of a house or movement in the trees.

The series of attacks took him by surprise, and Gabe swerved. His *Blutjagd* flared, and several others answered. Gabe wrapped his ghosting tight.

Either there was more than one beast attacking the amulet or the protected was going to get one hell of a lecture for pummeling a beast. Either way, the barrage of sensation meant two things: he had a more precise sense of direction and distance, and the situation had gotten much more dangerous.

No. There's one more fact. Whoever the protected was, he or she was likely going to be in a lot of pain.

The amulet went silent, and Gabe forced himself to breathe. The stillness didn't tell him anything. The beast might have fled, abandoned the game. The protected might be injured.

Or dead.

No. He couldn't think like that. It would drive him insane if he thought he'd failed a protected so horribly.

Any closer and the beasts will hear my engine. Time to go in.

Gabe pulled the truck off the road and started through the woods, silently, quickly, determined to reach the protected. The next barrage of amulet strikes nearly sent him to his knees, and the combined *Blutjagd* of every Warrior in range of it was scorching.

It ended as abruptly as it started, and his heart stuttered. Still, a small, isolated house was in sight. The door stood wide open, as if in invitation.

Gabe's skin crawled. This was a trap, a deadly one, the sick game of a diseased, damned beast.

Sobbing from inside steeled his resolve. Trap or not, a protected needed him. Her scream shook him.

What the hell are they doing? Taking her apart, piece by piece? He shuddered. Lorian had used a sword against Erin, when she was a child. They could do something like that again.

No. Keep your mind in the game.

He stepped through the door and followed the sound of sobbing to a comfortable living room.

He did a head count. *There are four beasts.*

That I can see. If his father taught him one thing, it was that there were almost always more beasts you couldn't see.

Gabe couldn't see more than the jeans and tennis shoes of the person laying on the floor. She shook in the force of her sobs. She was his highest priority. The beasts were too close to risk confronting them outright. That meant taking out at least two beasts before he moved again.

The one crouched next to her was the first one he'd like to take out, but he'd situated himself so that the couch blocked most of his body. The ones standing across from him would have to do.

Gabe slid two of his shurikens out and prepared to move.

The crouched beast spoke. "Come now. One would think you don't want to get up and play with us again, Regina."

Gabe faltered in disbelief. It wasn't possible. Was it? Her voice disabused him of that hope.

"Go to hell." It was simple, inelegant, a choked whisper of sound from a woman with more strength than any four others he'd met.

Gabe's hands shook. The need to kill every beast who'd touched Reggie rose up with a vengeance. Without delay, he threw the first two shurikens. He swept a third out of his pocket and sent it away before the first two hit.

The first two struck home, right on target. The third embedded in the wall with a sickening crunch, passing through the mist of a beast. Gabe moved to the right, noting a strained whisper from the last beast.

"One word, and I kill you too."

Gabe jerked his head around at the sound of Dubrae's voice, just in time to see the beast stand and disappear.

A rapid movement of Reggie's hand caught his eye. *ASL.* She'd tried to convince the Warriors that sign language could aid them in battle.

He searched out the sign in his memories. Thumb to ring finger. *Seven. Seven what? Seven total? Seven left?* Gabe prayed it wasn't the latter. If it was, they were both as good as dead. Five wasn't a much better number, but seven high levels on one was a death sentence for most Warriors. *For anyone who isn't König born, König trained, or my father.* Reggie jerked, tumbled to her stomach by the push of the amulet. Gabe launched toward her, pulling his sacred weapon. He sliced it in the direction he knew the beast to be. There was a satisfying cut into tissue, but it wasn't a death wound. Then the beast was gone.

A gust of air against his cheek warned Gabe of an incoming attack. He ducked. Invisible claws gouged into the mantle, and Gabe thrust upward, behind the ribs and to the heart. The beast started to crumple, and Gabe moved aside, watching the body appear before him.

Three down. One severely injured. Out of seven? He kept moving. The last thing he wanted was to give his enemies a stationary target.

This was different than the usual battle. This form of fighting depended on silent stealth, a deadly game of hide and seek. *With Reggie as the prize.*

The squeak of wood to his right was all it took for Gabe to throw a small blade that direction. Gabe was in motion just afterward. Once the weapons left his hands, they were visible. That meant his position was pinpointed. He couldn't allow that for long.

The one he'd injured fled; he was obviously heading to ground to heal. The latest fatality was already dead on the floor.

Five down. Two left. Or four. If Reggie's numbers are accurate. Maybe she didn't see them all either.

Stop it. Deal with the known. Anticipate the unknown.

Reggie moved abruptly, scrambling to the side, her eyes wide and wild. She focused at a spot over her left shoulder. Gabe took the hint. He threw one blade and drew another, already on the run. The beast flickered, and the next blade flew. *A heart shot for the kill.*

The beast fell, and Reggie flipped to her hands and knees, skittering onto the cold stone hearth with a sob. Her shirt gaped open, torn, her lush breasts, encased in lace, fully visible.

Gabe snapped his gaze away. Now was not the time for a hard-on...or for trips down memory lane.

Assuming Dubrae was the only one left, he'd target Reggie to draw Gabe into his claws. Why not beat the bastard to the punch?

For a moment, there was no sign of attack. The only sound in the room was Reggie's hitching breaths and half-swallowed sobs.

Dubrae needed a null weapon, and he chose the poker for the fire. The iron came up, and the beast became visible. It wasn't that he relaxed his ghosting, but rather that Gabe knew what he'd see and where, breaking the power's ability to shield the beast.

Gabe grasped the beast by the wrist, stopping the swing halfway to his target. Reggie's scream was ear-splitting, but neither of them paid it any attention. Dubrae met Gabe's gaze a split second before he pierced the beast's side with his sacred weapon and ripped it free to bleed him. Gabe flipped the weapon around, preparing to drive it up into the heart. The beast dematerialized, streaking away into the night.

Reggie made it to her feet, pressing to his back, trembling, gasping for breath.

Gabe's mind kicked into gear. Dubrae had been the leader. Even if there were others, his loss would have them in disarray for a short period of time. *But not for long.* It was time to move. He turned partway and scooped Reggie to his chest by one arm. Then he took off at a run.

In his truck, speeding toward the closest Maher cabin, he took the time to sneak peeks at her in the faint dashboard light.

Reggie's dark hair was shorter than it had been five years earlier, a full two-fingerwidths above the shoulders it used to cascade over. She had the same ample body, full and lush from her breasts to her hips and thighs.

But now that body was curled into a semi-fetal position on his passenger seat. Bruises were starting to come up. Her clothing was ripped. Her eyes were closed, and she was quaking hard. Gabe closed his hands into fists around the steering wheel. Why was he always too late for her?

Chapter Twenty-Four

Gabe punched the code into the cabin lock with shaking fingers, then pressed his thumb to the isometric scanner, Reggie cradled to his chest. Though he could punch the access code to any cabin from memory, her shivering probably wasn't helping matters.

If his memory served him as well as it usually did, she was shivering worse than she had the last time he'd saved her. That was bad news, considering the fact that she'd needed a dozen stitches that time.

He calmed himself as the door popped open. Gabe didn't smell human blood. He didn't feel any growing tacky spots on her clothing.

She might have broken bones or internal injuries. There was no way he could know that until he got her inside. That would determine what he did next.

Gabe pushed the door open with his knee, marched through, then kicked it shut behind him. He elbowed the rocker switch on the wall to turn on the floor lamps. Bypassing the couch, Gabe settled Reggie on the futon set before the empty hearth. It was closer to the lamps and gave him more room to examine her for injuries.

There were many more bruises than he'd initially seen, and he expected more were yet to rise, but none of them were severe. Realization came quickly. "He was toying with you to draw a Warrior in." Hadn't he already reasoned the beasts were playing a game when the door was left wide open?

"Yes. He was. He said..." She stopped speaking on a gasp, as he stroked his fingertips over the old scar on her side.

Gabe turned her slightly, looking for a new injury. There didn't seem to be one. "Said what?" he prompted her. Truth be told, he wanted more than information. Gabe wanted to hear her voice. It had been too long since he'd enjoyed that simple pleasure.

"I was bait for you. Not any Warrior, but *you* in particular, and you..." The same gasp emerged when he touched the scar tissue again.

She shouldn't have *a scar.* Gabe hadn't anticipated her reaction to his battle the first time; she'd taken a claw tear as a result. But it was more than that. He'd offered her reconstructive surgery for the scar. She'd refused it. Reggie had claimed she had no place accepting it, since she'd refused him.

Her voice shocked him out of his bittersweet memories with a jolt.

"You were supposed to strike at your father the only way they figured Adam could be hurt."

Gabe nodded solemnly. "Kill the son to hurt the father." It was an old game. It had been tried many times before, with varying degrees of success.

Adam Lord Maher had made more than his share of enemies. He was the quintessential armored knight of the Warrior world, a modern-day Lancelot, undeafeated in battle. *Save for the*

Königs. His wife and sons were Adam's only weak spots. Luckily, they weren't easy to kill either.

Reggie's hand cupped his cheek, bringing Gabe's attention back to her face. His heart stuttered on inventory. Tears dotted her eyelashes, and tracks of them had made her cheeks raw. There was a pleading note to her expression, accentuated by her red-rimmed, tired eyes.

Without conscious plan, Gabe trailed his fingertips along the scar again. Reggie arched her back, her breathing going ragged. She squirmed closer to him.

His mind took a holiday as his body responded. Gabe sank over her, enjoying the fit of their bodies he'd missed for so long. If he was going to be completely honest with himself, no other woman had taken the edge off his fond memories of Reggie. He didn't doubt none would.

Reggie wrapped her arms around his neck and raised her head, tipping it to one side.

The right. She always tips right for me.

Their kiss was slow and deep, a sweet reminder of how well they meshed sexually. There was no question that they weren't going to stop with a simple kiss.

Who am I kidding? This is anything but simple. Reggie had never been simple. *I wanted to die when she left me last time.*

The combination of that realization and his trilling cell phone broke the spell. Gabe ripped his mouth from hers. He backed away, drawing her hands from his body, shaking his head in disbelief.

What the hell am I doing? Didn't I learn anything five years ago? Isn't being burned once enough for me? How many bad choices am I going to make.

Probably one more.

The phone trilled again, and Gabe fumbled it up, his hands trembling more severely than they were at the door.

"Gabe—"

"I have to take this," he interrupted her. Gabe settled the phone to his ear, opening the connection while he tried to ignore his aching cock. "Here," he managed in a steady voice.

"The determination is?" his father asked. His tone was a clear indication that he'd been waiting for Gabe to call since the network showed the keypad entry to open the door.

"It's minor. They were playing cat and mouse with her to get the drop on me."

From miles away, Adam's *Blutjagd* spiked. "You, specifically?"

"Yes. The beast told her he was drawing me in, that they knew they were bringing *me* in."

"What beast is marked for this?" He didn't need to be more specific. A beast who targeted a Warrior or his family became public enemy number one in the Warrior world. Every house would have his file within the hour, and they would run him down like the dog he was.

"Dubrae was running the show."

His father was silent, but Adam's *Blutjagd* stepped up another few notches.

Gabe winced in response. No doubt, his father had guessed what the true aim of this attack was. Neither one of them spoke for a long moment.

"The damned beast wanted to hurt me," Adam surmised.

"Yeah. That was the plan."

His father's *Blutjagd* rose to a scorching conflagration, then tapered slowly. Adam muttered several curses. "I'm... I am *so* glad they failed."

Gabe smiled in spite of himself. "So am I. It wasn't a sure thing."

"You fought well. I counted five down. How many escaped?"

"Two. I was trained by the best."

"I have scars that disprove that, but... How's your victim?"

Gabe looked at Reggie out of the corner of his eye, his heart stuttering and his lessening cock surging up again. She was rumpled, beaten, in torn clothes. She also had kiss-swollen lips. How was she?

Beautiful. Sensual. Ready. Gods, her scent was intoxicating!

"Gabriel," Adam warned.

"Good. She's...good." He snapped his head around, trying to squelch an errant thought that she was good enough to eat. "Lots of bruises. She's going to be sore as hell for a week or two, but nothing worse."

"We'll have to move her." His father was obviously distracted with the particulars.

"Yes, we will." There was no way Gabe was chancing a repeat of tonight.

"Which protected is it?"

It took clearing his throat and a healthy dose of self-recrimination for his cowardice to force his voice to function. "Regina Carter."

Adam groaned. "I'll send someone to take over for you."

Gabe swallowed down his protest. It was better to let someone else do this. Despite breaking printing, he lacked common sense around Reggie. *Stupid for a woman. That's what Dad calls it. That's what every Maher man since at least Kord has called it.*

Her hand closed on his arm, squeezing lightly. Gabe met her gaze. She was pained. She was questioning him. Reggie offered a shaky smile, reminiscent of the one she'd shot him as they'd sewn up the tear in her side.

"I'll get Joseph. He's only a few hours away."

"No." His voice hardly seemed his own. He wasn't leaving her. Not until he knew her mind.

"Not your brother, then. A mated Warrior would be better. You're right. I'll have Bryant fly—"

"No. I'll do this. I...want to do this." His cock seconded with gusto.

"Gabe?" The tension in his father's voice warned that he was close to being ordered away.

"There's no reason not to—"

"There's *every* reason not to! She ground you up the last time. You handed me your blade, Gabriel."

And that had scared his father as he hadn't been scared since his mother had been threatened before Joseph had been conceived at their seal.

Reggie winced. She withdrew her hand, seemingly crushed by Adam's heated response, though she couldn't have heard all of it.

"No," Gabe replied calmly. "There is no reason. I've broken printing. I'm just a Warrior to Reggie now. Nothing more."

She pulled her hands back to her chest, averting her gaze. Her throat worked on what was probably a sob.

Liar! He felt *something*, and he knew it. Gabe cupped Reggie's chin up, reassuring her silently. His heart rate eased as her expression did the same. He knew he was lying to his father. Now she knew it, too.

"Unless Reggie wants you to replace me," he finished.

Her face went a sickly pale. "No. There's no reason to. Is there?"

"None. You have my vow." No matter what it was between them, Gabe wouldn't be a threat to Reggie. He wouldn't allow himself to be.

Adam sighed. "Why are you determined to do this?"

There seemed no safe answer to that. "Because I'm a Warrior. I offered my protection, and I'm going to live to it."

"If that changes—"

"I'll call," he promised.

"The Stone protect you." It was their most solemn prayer.

"She will." But looking in Reggie's eyes, he wasn't so sure.

****

Reggie's heart thundered in her chest, making her lightheaded. Gabe's words were cold and cutting, but his eyes told a different story. She wasn't sure which to trust, but her gut said the eyes won.

But what if she was wrong? What if he'd told the truth? What if he really was just a Warrior to her now? What if she was just a duty to him?

Just duty and a convenient piece of ass.

His kiss was nothing like what she remembered. At seventeen, he'd been fire unleashed, passionate, a demanding lover. He'd been printing then.

Had the years changed him so much? Or was this just sex for him? Just release with a woman he no longer had feelings for? What if he *couldn't* have feelings for her?

That possibility had tortured her when she'd refused him, but she'd been right to refuse Gabe. At eighteen, she hadn't been ready to commit to him in the way he'd needed. The price of failing him once he'd sealed would have been his death. She couldn't do that to him. So, she'd run like hell; it was the single most painful thing she'd done in her life, and she'd regretted it every day since.

The stream of hot breath against her lips was the first indication she had that he'd hung up and returned to her. He parted her lips, pressing Reggie into the futon as he caressed her, inside and out.

His hand settled over her breast, and he broke away from the kiss again. His midnight blue eyes opened as hers did. "You're not scared of me, are you?" he asked softly.

"No." Never that, but the situation scared the bejesus out of her. If he didn't love her... If he wasn't *capable* of printing again, she'd blown it, just as she'd always feared she had.

Gabe nodded. "I want this, but if you don't..."

"I do." Reggie just hoped this wasn't all there was in store for them.

He stood, lifting Reggie into his arms.

She grasped at the edge of his jacket. "What are you doing?"

"Taking you to the bed. If we stay on the futon, I'll feel compelled to build a fire. I don't intend to wait that long."

Reggie smiled. That sounded like the Gabe she remembered.

But it wasn't. There was no mad rush to undress, no groping hands...and no rolling around on the mattress in a clutch. Instead, he lowered her to her feet beside the bed and went to work.

Gabe slid his jacket off, then his shirts, boots...his jeans and socks together. He turned his attention to Reggie, peeling the shirt down her shoulders, his breath fanning her forehead and temple. Her bra went next, his nimble fingers flicking open the front closure. She hardly breathed as he trailed it down her arms and peeled it and her shirt off her hands together.

Reggie waited to see what he would do next, her mouth watering in anticipation, drugged by his touch. It wasn't the Gabe she remembered. This was a hundred times better.

He cupped her breasts, bringing the already-pebbled nipples to aching points that he stroked harder.

"You're trembling," he noted.

"Yes." Her voice emerged as a gasp, and she weaved against him.

Gabe didn't answer. He lifted her onto the mattress, settled beside her, and sucked her breast into his mouth. Reggie closed her hands in his hair, arching up, faint in pleasure.

Still, he took his time, moving from breast to breast, driving her toward climax when he'd barely touched her. It was maddening, and she couldn't take it anymore.

His hands covered hers, stilling her when she had her zipper halfway down. Gabe shushed her complaint, then stroked his parted lips down Reggie's stomach to the open button. He laid a kiss in the opening, sending a shiver down her spine.

Gabe shushed her again. He released her hands and eased the zipper down. Her jeans and panties retreated down her hips, inch by inch. His mouth explored in the wake.

The kiss on her newly uncovered curls freed her tongue. "Gabe. Please don't tease me."

Her clothing slid another few inches away, baring her to the cool room air and the heat of his breath. "I'm not teasing. I'm worshipping you."

Reggie bit her lip, stopping herself from joking that he had enough goddesses to worship in his pantheon. A religious discussion wasn't what she wanted.

"I'm going to worship you until you're exhausted." He pulled her jeans and panties to her knees. "Let you sleep." He removed one tennis shoe and then the other. Gabe tossed them over his shoulder. "Then worship you until you beg me to stop."

She groaned, closing her eyes as the last of her clothing left her body.

"Starting now."

Gabe pushed her legs wide and dined between them. He didn't start with her clit, but rather went straight to flicking his tongue inside her.

Reggie's body exploded in pleasure. She clawed at his shoulders with her short nails, sobbing out his name.

He retreated, laying a kiss on the outer lips. "I want to know so much," he whispered.

Like why I left you. Please not now.

"Do you still like a man sucking your clit while he fingers you?"

The memory of him doing it made her head swim. "You know I do."

He was silent for a potent heartbeat. "Sadly, I don't know it."

She opened her eyes, aghast at the realization of what she'd just said to him. "Oh, God. I—"

"But I'm damned well going to find out."

His mouth latched onto her aching nub, and two fingers thrust inside her. Reggie choked on a scream, too shocked to do more than arch up for more as she climaxed.

Gabe stroked his tongue up the length of her slit, and he eased his fingers out slowly. "You *do* like that." His voice sounded of awe.

Answering him was a physical impossibility at that moment. Aftershocks wracked her body, nerves cross-firing in wild abandon. Phantom sensations of Gabe sliding home inside her as he often had before intensified the aftershocks.

Gabe pushed up the bed until he'd settled next to her. He gathered Reggie into his arms, adding the alluring scent of his aroused body to the sensory overload.

As the aftershocks slowed, warmth seeped into her muscles. She breathed deeply, drinking in his scent. *The smell of safety. The scent of love.* She hoped.

A quilt settled over them.

Reggie forced her eyes to focus. "What are you doing?"

Gabe chuckled, his chest vibrating under her cheek. "You think I don't know when you're about to fall asleep on me?"

He was right. The night had left her nearly exhausted. But still... "We need to talk," she mumbled.

"Shhh." Gabe wound one of the loose curls at the ends of her hair around his finger. "Sleep first. Talk later."

She wanted to answer, but sleep beckoned, and Gabe's arms were too comforting to resist.

****

Gabe sighed, staring at Reggie as if to reassure himself that he wasn't dreaming. No. She was real enough. The taste of her making his mouth water was proof of that.

But what do I do now?

Common sense said that he should call his father and get the hell out as soon as possible. The situation was a powder keg. Breaking printing with Reggie last time had nearly destroyed him.

There's no saying I can print on her again.

"Yeah, right," he growled.

Of course it was happening. Gabe had felt the burn from the moment he'd learned what protected lay, shivering and sobbing, on the floor. He'd wanted to tear every one of the beasts who'd touched her apart, piece by piece, painfully, slowly, with *extreme* precision.

And now... He was laying in bed with her, feeling all too nurturing and protective. *Possessive, damn it!*

Honesty being a virtue Warriors valued, it was only right to admit that he'd have his cock buried inside her already, if she hadn't been so worn and frayed by what she'd endured tonight.

And when she wakes?

Gabe bit back a groan. He'd be battling the madness again if he let it go much further and then found she wasn't serious.

I have to protect myself. That meant learning what went wrong last time and finding out where they stood this time. Most of all, it meant not making love to her until he accomplished it.

Assuming, of course, that the rest was favorable. The odds were definitely against him.

I should just call my father in and leave now. But he knew he wouldn't. Warriors didn't abandon printing unless they had no other choice.

Chapter Twenty-Five

April 16th, 2051

Gabe groaned, throwing an arm over his face to block the sunlight filtering into the room from around the blinds. He wasn't sure what had roused him in the first place, but he was tired, and a cranky Warrior was no one's idea of fun.

There was a faint tickling along the length of his morning erection.

"What the—?"

The mouth engulfing him stole his ability to form coherent thoughts. Realization came in an instant, regardless.

"Reggie!" *Oh gods, what is she doing?*

But Gabe knew very well what she was doing. *And if she doesn't stop doing it soon, she's going to get a mouthful...plus some.*

Despite his grand plan, Gabe wanted precisely that. He thrust his hips up, seeking it. At his reaction, Reggie doubled down her efforts, reducing him to a groaning, panting mass of nerves. He tilted his hips back and forth, sliding deeper into her heat.

It didn't take long to push him over the edge. Reggie drank him down. She laid soft licks and kisses along his length as he shuddered, spent nearly to a stupor.

She pressed her lips to his lower abdomen. "Now we can talk," she breathed.

Talk? After that, she wants me to form words?

****

Reggie waited for him to say something. Any old thing would do.

No, it won't. I want him to tell me he lied to Adam, that I'm not just a protected to him. I want him to tell me he needs me, just like last time.

When he remained silent, her worst fears were confirmed. Reggie blinked back tears and edged away from him.

Gabe's hands closed on her arms, and he dragged her to his chest. "You want to talk?" His voice was low and gruff.

She swallowed back a wave of fear. Gabe was entitled to his anger at her. She'd more than earned it. "I think we should."

He nodded slowly. "What do you want from me, Reggie?"

Everything. But she'd already abused that trust. As terrible as it sounded, Reggie couldn't come up with a single thing she wanted...except him.

"You don't know. Do you?" He uttered something in German. It was probably a curse.

"I...I know what I want."

"Then why can't you *say* it?" His frustration was impossible to miss.

And I caused it. "I've hurt you once, Gabe." She had lived with that for the last five years. It was time she said it aloud.

He stared at her, seemingly waiting for more information. But where did you start with something so complex?

314

With the truth. "We were so young, Gabe." *Too young.*

"Age doesn't matter when a Warrior prints."

"A seventeen-year-old Warrior is a man," she conceded. "An eighteen-year-old human is still a kid. A...a scared kid."

Gabe opened his mouth as if to speak, then closed it again. When he managed to force something out, his voice was uncertain. "You weren't ready, and I rushed you? If I would have given you space and time—"

"I don't think you could have given me that much time. You were printing, coming to *Endspiel.* I needed time to mature, to...to be sure of myself."

"Sure of yourself?"

Reggie nodded.

"What the hell does that mean?" There was no heat in the demand. He sounded honestly perplexed.

"Warriors have no uncertainties about marriage. You print, and it's forever." She paused, collecting her thoughts.

"Go on." There was an edge of urgency in the request.

"I've seen a marriage go bad."

"A *human* marriage."

"I'm human, Gabe. You Warriors seem to forget that there is a human involved in your mating. Well, most of your matings."

He paused, then nodded.

"How many times did I hear my mother say it?" She swallowed hard, her stomach churning at the memories.

He stroked a hand along her cheek, cupping it to urge her gaze up to his again. "What did you hear?" His voice was a whisper, but it was encouraging.

"'We married too young. We should have waited. We weren't ready.' They hated each other, because they rushed to getting married, and they rushed to having me, and..." Tears pooled in her eyes. One spilled over, clearing her vision somewhat.

Gabe brushed it away. "And?" he prodded her.

"What if I'd been rushing, too? What if I'd ended up hating you like my mother hated my father? It wouldn't just be a messy divorce with you." Reggie took a deep breath. "It would have killed you, Gabe. Can't you see that? If I rushed... If I was wrong, I'd have killed you, and it would have been all my fault."

He seemed to have trouble forming words. "Why did you run from me?"

She sobbed, her heart aching at the memory. "Because I couldn't force myself to look you in the eye and say 'no'. Because I knew... I knew, if I stayed, I'd rush into the whole wife and mother thing, no matter the risk to you if I was wrong."

****

Gabe gaped at her, shocked. "You left me because you were afraid of...?" He couldn't form the words. Reggie had feared failing him as a mate.

316

She burst into tears. "I didn't know what else to do."

Oh, gods. She really didn't. She didn't feel she could look me in the face and say that then. Gabe hugged her to him, waiting for her tears to taper off. He considered her reasoning.

Her parents' divorce had been bitter and ugly. They had married young, the week her mother turned eighteen. The whole thing made sense, from her point of view.

She continued, halting words spoken half into his chest. "I never wanted to hurt you, but I couldn't...couldn't be what you needed. Not then. I just...couldn't..."

"Kill me. Or even chance it." The thought was oddly comforting. He'd believed she ran because she didn't love him. Gabe had never dreamed she ran because she loved him that much.

At a loss for words, Gabe guided her face up. Her lips trembled against his.

Reggie eased away, gasping for breath. "I'm sorry. I never—"

"If I asked you now? Have you matured, Reggie? Are you sure of yourself?"

She stammered out his name.

"Reggie?" If she couldn't give him an honest answer...and a favorable one, he'd have to get the hell out of Dodge. He couldn't play this same scene twice.

"Is that something you're likely to say?" she managed.

Gabe examined her expression. She didn't seem frightened by the possibility. He'd assume she was shocked that he was capable of printing on her again.

Better to let her know the state of things than to let her believe a no-strings affair was possible. "I think it's highly likely I'll end up saying it."

Her arms circled his neck, and she snuggled closer to him.

His body argued his mind's refusal to take her up on such a blatant offer. He had to protect himself. "Are you still a scared kid, Reggie?"

"No. Not anymore."

****

Reggie held her breath, praying he'd believe her. Gabe had no reason to trust her sincerity.

If he's printing again...

She couldn't count on that. Adam had made it more than clear that she'd screwed up that possibility when he'd tracked her down after she'd run. Once he broke printing, he couldn't print on her again, could he? Adam had said Gabe couldn't, but Gabe said he could.

Adam had been furious at her for making Gabe break printing. So furious that it had amazed her when he'd let her keep the amulet. *Not only let me keep it but returned it to me himself.*

"I am glad to hear that," Gabe whispered.

He didn't look glad. Reggie couldn't identify his expression. It wasn't any of the biggies: anger, joy, fear, or sadness. If anything, he appeared lost in thought.

Just when she felt her heart might burst from pounding in the midst of a massive anxiety attack, he moved. Gabe captured her lips in a slow but searing kiss. He pressed his hands to her hips, bringing her closer to him.

His renewed erection slid between her thighs, teasing at her outer labia. Reggie tried to force herself down on him, but Gabe gripped her hips, stopping her when only the head breached her. He tipped his head back, licking his lips.

"Gabe, please. I've missed you so much."

A wicked smile curved his lips. "Say it again."

"I've missed you. Every day."

"Not that. Say my name."

"Gabe?" She'd said his name several times since he saved her from the beasts the night before. What was so special about—

Reggie's thoughts scattered, as Gabe pushed her to her back on the bed and thrust inside her. He didn't smile at her cry of shocked surprise and pleasure. His expression was something fierce, an unspoken possession.

Gabe slid back slowly, then returned, deeper than the first time. He kept eye contact, driving her to a kinetic climax in a handful of thrusts, then he followed her over with a groan.

They lay together, Gabe buried inside her, his heat radiating through her body. His cock bucked against her inner walls, and Reggie closed her eyes, tipping her hips up to meet his.

"Enough," Gabe grumbled. "If you keep that up, we won't get out of bed today."

Reggie laughed, relaxed as she hadn't been in at least five years. "Would that be so bad?"

319

He didn't waste time considering his answer. "You know it wouldn't be."

****

Gabe slipped out of his truck, pushing his sunglasses up his nose, smiling widely.

It had taken him half the day to force himself to leave Reggie. In the end, it was a practical matter than convinced him it had to happen.

Reggie had only the clothing she'd worn the night before, which meant she had no spares to wear while she washed those. Not to mention that she had no shirt to that set of clothing. Of course, Gabe smiled at the idea that he had absolutely nothing against the idea of Reggie without clothes.

He went still, his hand on the doorknob. Without question, he pulled his sacred weapon. There was something. A slight sound, perhaps. Movement somewhere in the house. Gabe followed the faint sounds, ghosting lightly, moving silently.

It was dim enough in the house that a high level could be there, though he suspected a minion was more likely. It would be too easy for Gabe to tear down a drape or something similar, driving a beast away.

Though it was equally unlikely that a beast had left human minions behind to challenge him, there was no car. What other options did that leave?

A thief? His *Blutjagd* flared slightly at the thought of someone stealing from Reggie.

Maybe it was the local sheriff. He considered fully ghosting, just in case. After all, there were five dead beast bodies somewhere around. They'd been removed from the living room, but from the smell, he guessed they were still burning.

"Ah, there you are," Joseph greeted him, breezing out of a bedroom with a box in hand. "I saw your truck pull up." He stopped short and stared at the weapon in Gabe's hand.

Gabe sheathed it with a shrug and released his ghosting. "Didn't know who was here." He looked around his older brother's shoulder. "Reggie's room?"

Joseph darkened, his gaze wandering to a blank spot on the wall. "Yeah. Uh...look..."

"Good. She needs clothes." Gabe elbowed him aside and strode into the peach and eggshell warmth of Reggie's bedroom.

He didn't waste time. The suitcases were in the bottom of her closet, as they had been at her old apartment. He tossed them on the mattress and flipped them open. He went back for several pair of shoes and sandals and placed them in the larger suitcase.

Her drawers were arranged roughly the same as he remembered, as well. Gabe started pulling out necessities and placing them in the suitcases.

Joseph stood in the doorway, one arm braced on the frame. His expression said he was highly disturbed by something. "I can do that," he offered.

Gabe raised an eyebrow, then tucked a stack of bras into the smaller piece of luggage. "No need to. I know what she likes."

The sight of Joseph going from pink to crimson had Gabe biting back a blast of laughter. He added underwear and socks to the smaller suitcase, then jeans, shirts, and light summer dresses to the larger.

Finally, Joseph found his voice again. "This must be murder on you, little brother." His tone made unwarranted apologies.

"Surprisingly, not at all. Doing this isn't the least bit painful." Gabe paused in the process of pulling out pajamas. He lifted out a black silk nightie. "This is new," he mused.

Joseph was across the room in the blink of an eye. He yanked the nightie from Gabe's hands and tossed it at the suitcase.

Gabe blinked in surprise, the vision of Reggie in the sheer confection fading fast. "What the hell are you doing?"

His brother placed his hands on Gabe's shoulders. "Don't do this to yourself, man. Just don't. Let me pack for her. Tell me what to pack, if you insist."

"Don't do *what* to myself?"

"Don't obsess over it. Don't think about what guy she might have worn that for." He jerked his head toward the suitcase.

Gabe scowled. He shook off Joseph's hands, grabbed a stack of pajamas without looking at them, then headed for the suitcase. "It doesn't bother me." He hadn't even considered it until Joseph said it. Once the pajamas were in the suitcase, he grabbed the overnight bag and headed for the bathroom to collect up her toiletries.

Joseph followed in his wake. "It doesn't bother you? Seriously?"

It did...a bit, now that he allowed himself to think about it. *But not much,* he conceded. "I haven't been celibate for the last five years, either," he reasoned himself out of his frustration, while he packed her toiletries inside the bag. "She wasn't mine, Joseph. Why should I let it bother me?"

He motioned his brother out of his way, then deposited the overnight bag on the bed with the other suitcases. That accomplished, Gabe started zipping up the cases. He made sure to fold the silk nightie into the larger one before he closed it.

Joseph groaned. "You really should get out while you can."

Gabe ignored him, zipping the final suitcase closed. "I'm fine, Joseph. Quit worrying about me."

"Right. Sure. Not another worry," he grumbled. Joseph had never been a good liar. The years hadn't changed that.

Gabe led the way to the driveway, the suitcases in hand, and the overnight bag slung over his shoulder. He stopped short, his initial unease returning with a rush. "Joseph, how did you get here?" None of the Maher vehicles were here.

"With Dad. He helped me get rid of the bodies, then left me to start the preps for the move. He'll be back to get the first load soon."

"Back from where?"

****

Reggie smiled at the sound of the front door opening. She didn't even want to calculate how fast Gabe was driving, if he was back already. "If I've told you once," she shouted out, "I've told you a hundred times." She headed for the living room. "You won't die in battle, if you wrap your truck around a—"

The rest died in her throat, and she gripped the doorjamb tight. Reggie smoothed the Warrior's button-down shirt over her thighs. She was acutely aware of her nudity beneath.

Adam Lord Maher's gaze was hard and assessing. She reminded herself that the man never missed a thing. His jaw tightened down a notch, and his body was a mountain of muscle, tensed to fight.

"Regina," he rumbled out.

She took a step back into the bedroom, the hair at the back of her neck standing on edge. "Lord Maher."

He scanned his gaze down her body.

She pulled down at the shirt again, self-conscious. "My clothes are...um...washing, and Gabe went to—" Reggie backed off another few steps, as he advanced on her. She ran aground on the dresser and reached back to steady herself.

His gaze locked with hers, then traveled to the rumpled bed. Her cheeks heated at the fact that his heightened Warrior senses were taking in everything.

"Fucking hell! I knew I shouldn't have left him with *you*."

Reggie's face flamed, and she straightened her spine. She met his gaze head on, when he whirled back to glare down at her.

"This isn't happening again," he stated. "I'm not going to let you—"

"It's not what you think," she defended herself.

"Less than a day, and you're already in bed with him again."

"I can't deny that part," she admitted.

"I'll bet you can't. How long did it take you...precisely?" he challenged.

"He kissed me first, if you must know."

His eyes narrowed, and he growled a series of curses in Spanish and French.

"But I'm not going to leave him. Gabe—"

"You're not going to have the chance," he decreed.

Her heart pounded in fear. "What?"

"He's not coming back."

Reggie gripped the dresser, feeling faint. Warrior rules made a sickening march through her head. He was house lord; Adam could follow through on that.

"He's my son, and I control his movements," he confirmed for her.

"But..." What could she say? He did control that.

Adam was in her face faster than she could track his movement. "Do you have any concept what your last little stunt did to him?"

"He had to break—"

"Gabe handed me his weapon," he roared. "My son wanted to die. He wanted to die because of you!"

Reggie blinked back tears. "I never meant to—"

"I don't *care* what you meant. Once was understandable. You didn't know what fire you were playing with then. Now you do. I'm not going to let you kill my son by yo-yoing him again."

"I don't intend to." But something told her Adam wouldn't believe her.

"Intentions aren't good enough. You had good intentions last time, and look what happened. I told you five years ago, if you made Gabe break printing, if you forced him through that hell, there was no turning back." He paused, seemingly waiting for an answer, though he hadn't asked a question.

Reggie nodded, her throat closing up on her in her misery. In Adam's mind, there was no turning back, because he was acting as roadblock to any attempts to do so. You didn't get around a roadblock as large as Adam Lord Maher. Any attempt would get her heart ripped out...figuratively and literally.

He motioned toward the bed. "Whatever happened here, Gabe is just confused. That's why I'm sending him away." He backed off a step, visibly calming himself. "There is no turning back."

She didn't answer. What was the point when she wasn't being given options and her opinion wasn't welcome?

He took another step away. "I'll send Joseph to protect you."

"Don't," she managed. The last thing she needed was another disapproving member of Gabe's family hovering over her, another bitter reminder that she'd blown her only chance with Gabe.

Adam stared at her, seemingly considering it. "Dale—"

"No. Don't send anyone."

"Dubrae—"

"He'll have to track me. Besides, if you won't let Gabe near me, he has no reason to follow me. He wants Gabe...and you. Not me."

"What if—"

"What does it matter?" she cut him off. Reggie headed for the bathroom. "Just go away." She closed the door behind her and leaned against it, waiting for his explosion at being dismissed. After a few tense moments, she heard the front door slam shut.

Reggie sank to the floor, trying to decide what to do next. The Warriors would be preparing for a move. Maybe she should just ask to be moved to one of the other ranges. Adam wanted her gone, and he wasn't going to allow her to be with Gabe. That a given, being as far away from the lot of them she could get was probably the best move she had available to her.

If only she could convince her aching heart of that, she might not want to break down into hysterics at the thought of doing it.

****

Gabe could tell by his father's expression that the coming scene wasn't going to be pretty. He'd refused to answer his cell phone on the way back; if Adam couldn't order him away before he got to the cabin, he had a chance of working this out with his father.

He slid from the truck and dragged Reggie's suitcases out after him. Gabe headed for the cabin door, intent on going straight through Adam if necessary.

"Stand down," Adam ordered.

"I don't see a fight. Unless you're saying you intend to start one, of course." If his father did, Gabe was going to do his level best to send his father away defeated.

Adam stepped across the base of the porch stairs, his arms crossed over his broad chest. That brought Gabe to a momentary halt. For a long moment, they glared at each other.

"Don't force my hand, Gabe. Don't be stupid."

Stupid for a woman. "It's my choice. The Rules of Sanction say—"

"Your movements are at my whim," he countered.

Gabe ground his teeth in frustration. "Fine, but I'm taking my woman with me." His father didn't control that.

"Your— You are not *seriously* telling me that you've—"

"Head over fucking heels, not that it's any of your business. Who a Warrior prints on or takes as a mate is no one's business."

"Put the luggage down."

Gabe complied. "I'm not leaving without her. Nothing in the Rules of Sanction allows you to force me to." He wasn't above convening a Council of Lords on the matter if he had to, but he hoped Adam wouldn't force him to do it.

"Then I'll appeal to you as a father to a son."

"Won't work. You've done stupid things in pursuit of Mom. Every man in the family seems to have, *including* Uncle Curt. Hell, he's lucky not to have been beheaded for his. It would be more than a little hypocritical for any of you to tell me not to take a chance on printing, don't you think?"

His father's *Blutjagd* spiked a notch. "And if I decide to beat this insanity out of you?"

Gabe hiked his jacket off and dropped it over the larger suitcase. Then he started limbering his shoulders and loosening his muscles. "Won't work, but feel free to try it."

A pained expression settled on Adam's face. "You're going to do this, no matter what I do to stop it. Aren't you?" His voice was hoarse, broken.

"Break my bones. Give me shit duty. Throw all your power as Lord Maher and all Uncle Curt's power as Lord *König* at me. I've screwed this up once, and I'm not doing that a second time, no matter what it costs me."

329

"*You* didn't screw it up the first time."

Gabe sighed, pushing a hand through his hair. "Yes and no. To some extent, it wasn't ideal, which is no one's fault. I think Reggie was right to refuse me. Her reasons were sound."

"She didn't give you reasons."

"She has now. Like I said, she was right to refuse me. I was in a hurry last time. I didn't take the time to put Reggie at ease. I wanted an answer she wasn't ready to give me."

His father stared at him, seemingly stunned. "You're not serious. It was a matter of *time*?"

"Deadly. I didn't have the time to give her, and that's the one thing she needed from me. Now, are you going to kick the shit out of me or just let me go inside?"

"I won't take your weapon again. I can't do that twice."

"You won't have to," he vowed.

Adam's scowl said he would take it out of Reggie's hide if he had to, illegal or not. He sighed, moved aside, then motioned Gabe toward the door.

Gabe nodded his thanks. He hefted the suitcases and his jacket, then strode to the door, feeling satisfied with his success. That lasted until he saw Reggie.

She sat, curled on the couch, wearing her still-damp and rumpled clothes with one of his t-shirts. Her face was tear-streaked, and she fingered her amulet as if she was considering leaving it behind again. She stared into the cold hearth.

"You're not planning something stupid, are you?" he asked.

Her hand fisted around the amulet.

"It won't be my father tracking you this time, Reggie. I'm not letting you go twice. I think I made that clear."

"He said—" She took a calming breath. "He said you weren't coming back."

Gabe placed her suitcases on the floor. Then he reached down and tugged Reggie to her feet, feathering his lips across hers.

She sobbed. "He said, when I left you—"

"Shhh. There's no need for this," he soothed her.

"I could have killed you." That came out a wail, and Gabe considered going outside and hitting his father for good measure.

"But you didn't." Gabe tucked her head beneath his chin. "And you won't. Will you?"

The moments until she answered were the longest of Gabe's life.

"You know I won't."

"Then I suggest we unpack and get you out of these wet clothes."

"Probably a good idea. Looks like you brought me a bunch more."

"Who said I intended for us to be dressed today?" *Unless she wants to model that silk nightie for me.*

Chapter Twenty-Six

April 24th, 2051

Reggie looked up at the sound of the front door opening, then went back to the email she was writing. Gabe took a shower and started a load of wash before he joined her.

Perfect timing. She hit 'send' on the email and closed the mail pane.

Gabe stretched out on the bed next to her. "Emailing your dad?"

"No. Dad is somewhere in Eastern Europe, being Dad." In other words, he was busy living the life he'd claimed Reggie and her mother had robbed him of. *Complete with a girlfriend nearly as young as I am.*

"Mom? I know you usually talk on the phone, but—" He went silent, probably reading the pain in her expression.

"Just work," she changed the subject.

"I'm sorry, Reggie. I didn't know. When did she—"

"Two years ago. Car accident on a snowy interstate." She made a show of closing her *Airbook.* "She would have loved to know we were back together. Mom always liked you."

"I liked her, too. Where is she buried? I'd like to pay my respects."

Reggie managed a strained smile. "You know Mom. She was ever the non-traditionalist. She was cremated. If you want to pay your respects, I scattered her ashes at the lake."

"Ah, yes. The lake."

She sighed. "I suppose that's sort of ruined for us now. It would be hard to get into the mood with the idea of my mother watching in the back of my mind."

"We could still have a picnic there," he suggested. "I could show my respects."

"That does sound nice." Reggie rolled from her stomach to his chest and snuggled in. Just being here with him soothed her nerves.

They'd been living in the cabin for a week. Gabe had told Adam not to bother arranging a new house, when they moved her out of the old one. Half of her belongings were in storage at the manor, and the other half had been delivered here. They'd already started referring to the cabin as "home."

"It's nice to have you home early," she stated.

"We have time tonight."

Reggie didn't have to ask what he was talking about. He'd been suggesting it for the last three days, and she'd begged off every time.

She laughed heartily at his persistence. "You're not serious."

"Never been more serious."

She knew that was a lie. "Is it safe?"

"I'm offended." His tone said he was teasing.

Who am I kidding? Gabe wouldn't hurt me, and he does want this. "Okay."

Gabe raised his head from the pillow and looked down at her. "Really?"

"I trust you." That was probably what it was about, after all.

He smiled widely. "Now?"

Her heart stuttered, and she talked herself out of the spike of outright fear she felt. "Yes. Now."

Gabe lifted her to her feet beside the bed, then handed Reggie her lap desk and computer. While she put the computer back on the charger, he plucked his weapons belt off the dresser.

Reggie took his offered hand and let Gabe lead her into the bathroom. He undressed her slowly, reverently. By the time she was naked, she was shivering in anticipation instead of fear.

"Relax," he breathed. "All Maher Warriors learn how to do this."

She raised an eyebrow in challenge.

"On ourselves! Good gods, no."

"Well, as long as you're not making a habit of this," she conceded.

"First time on someone else," he assured her.

"I don't know whether to be honored or nervous."

His smile made her heart skip in excitement.

Gabe got Reggie settled on the heated tile bench, retrieved a steamed towel from the drawer, then placed it over her midsection. She relaxed there, soothed by the heat, while he mixed up some of the oatmeal shaving cream he liked.

He moved toward her with the mug and brush in hand. Reggie held her breath, releasing it in a rush to return his smile.

"Relax," he reminded her.

Gabe removed the towel and dropped it on the bench next to her. Then he started spreading the shaving cream up her mound. She moaned at the touch of the brush.

"I knew you would like it."

But this was only the first part.

When he was satisfied with his job, Gabe set the mug and brush aside. He retrieved his weapons belt and pulled out one of the palm-sized throwing blades.

Reggie broke down in giggles.

Gabe looked from the knife to her, issuing a silent question.

"I thought—" She burst into laughter again.

He frowned. "I could do it with the full-sized sacred weapon, if you prefer. It's more difficult, but we're taught complete control over every weapon."

Reggie glanced at his half-erect cock. "I know you have complete control of your weapon. And no, I don't prefer you use the full-sized weapon."

His smile returned, then widened, and his cock surged up. Gabe stepped into the tub, taking his place at her knees.

She tensed as he brought the knife up. It skated along her skin, firing her nerves pleasantly. Gabe wiped the knife on the towel and brought it back for the next swipe.

Reggie moaned, reminding herself not to move. Her nipples came to hard points. Though she knew Gabe wouldn't hurt her, there was an edge of danger in this endeavor that made it more potent.

Gabe's single-minded attention made her heart pound. He shaved, cleaned the blade, and moved along, working his way across and up her mound.

When she thought he was done, Gabe trailed his fingertips over her, finding areas to neaten up. At last, he set the knife aside. He folded the towel to place the mess of cream and hair inside it, then used the clean side to wipe her down.

He wasn't done yet. Gabe pulled down the Kama Sutra Kissable oil from the highest shower shelf. The scents of coconut and pineapple teased at her nose. He massaged the oil into her sensitized skin, making her squirm and gasp.

Gabe went to his knees in the deep tub. "Now to test it."

His tongue and lips danced over her shaven mound, moving downward at a maddening pace. Reggie thrust her hips up, and he took the hint. Gabe ate ravenously. She grasped at his hair, urging him on.

It wasn't enough. Reggie begged him for more, begged him to fill her. Gabe ignored her, driving Reggie toward release.

"Fuck me," she cursed.

Gabe drew away slightly, his breath fast and hot against her core. "Never."

"I didn't mean—"

He resumed eating, forcing a shout of pleasure from her.

Reggie worked at that encounter. "Make love to me."

Gabe rose to his feet between her parted legs, his expression hot in sensual promise. "That's more like it."

In the next breath, he was lodged inside her. Gabe grasped Reggie by the hips and thrust in earnest.

It was exactly what she wanted, and Reggie went into sensory overload. Her mind registered a patchwork of touches and sounds, scents, and the alluring sight of Gabe's nude form in motion.

She came with a scream, and he followed her over. Gabe levered her legs up, stroking at her thighs, setting off aftershocks.

"Next time," he whispered.

She chuckled. "Yes?"

He groaned, and his cock bucked inside her. "Next time, I'm shaving your legs, too."

Reggie clenched down her inner muscles at the thought of it, setting off another moan from Gabe. She smiled. "I think you need to shave."

His brow furrowed. "Five o'clock shadow?"

She stroked her fingertips down his abdomen to the damp curls around his erection. "No. How...controlled are you?"

Gabe took a calming breath. "Tell me what will happen if I do."

Oh, this is appealing. Seducing Gabe would be so sweet.

It was also fair play. He'd teased her for days with what he intended to do to her if she let him shave her.

"Reggie?"

"After I wash you down, I'm going to stroke you up with the oil."

"You won't need to," he promised. "I'll still be hard for you."

She levered herself back and forth against his length. "I'm going to find out how sensitive you are."

"How?" It was a gasp of sound.

Oh, yes. He's already convinced. Convinced wasn't good enough. "Lick you like you licked me. Suck on your smooth balls."

He jerked, spurting more cum into her.

"Suck your cock until you beg me to stop."

"Oh, yes!" His muscles tightened down.

"Then we find out what your oiled skin feels like rubbing against mine."

He nodded frantically. "All our skin. Every millimeter covered in oil and stroking against each other."

"I like this plan."

Gabe left her body in a rush and settled on the bench beside her. He pressed the mug and brush into her hands.

She stared at them, confused. He wasn't suggesting *she* try to shave him with one of his blades, was he? Accelerated healing or not, that was taking a huge risk.

"Mix the shaving cream," Gabe requested. "I want you to lather me up."

Reggie smiled. "I think you should mix it."

"But I—"

She leaned across his body, drawing Gabe's gaze to her bare chest."While you mix it, I'll get the steamed towel. I want to work you up with it before I lather you up."

Gabe dropped a kiss on her lips, grabbed the mug and brush, then jumped out of the tub.

Chapter Twenty-Seven

May 30th, 2051

Reggie floated toward consciousness, trying desperately to hold to the last vestiges of her dream. Gabe trailed his fingertips from just below her breast to her mound, and she licked her lips.

"Are you awake, Reggie?" he whispered.

Wisps of heat played against her lower abdomen. She shifted toward him in a haze.

"Are you awake?" There was something of a tease in that.

"No." She smiled, trying to decide if he was part of a dream or reality. She'd fallen asleep while he'd been hunting. Reggie didn't remember him coming home or getting into bed with her, though she'd stayed awake until at least two in an effort to meet him when he returned, so either was possible.

The answer came in the form of the press of his lips to the soft, smooth skin beneath her navel. Reggie was freshly shaved, and her body was ultra-sensitized.

She shivered in response, parting her thighs for him. "If you're real," she hinted.

He worked his fingertips against her clit, circling lightly. She pressed up against him, begging for more silently.

"If I was a dream, this wouldn't be torture, Reggie."

"You're being a bastard," she muttered.

Gabe laughed heartily. "Nope. Not even Joseph can legitimately be called that." He slid one finger inside her, moaning as her muscles clenched against him. "Wake up, Reggie. Please."

She opened her eyes, seeking out his heated gaze. "Mmmm. You *are* real."

He was rock hard, both his cock and his body in general. Every muscle was strung tight.

"What is it?" she asked.

Gabe hesitated for a moment. He shot her a wry smile and laid his cheek to her abdomen. "I don't want to rush you."

Her heart stuttered. "Gabe?" Was he saying what she thought he was?

"I told you I was likely to say it, Reggie."

"Say it then."

"I want you. I need you. I want you to be my mate. Seal with me." His expression was starkly serious, and his muscles tightened against her, as if holding tight to her.

She nodded dumbly.

"Reggie?"

"That was fast. Last time—"

"If you're not ready—"

"I am."

Gabe jerked his head up, his eyes going wide. "You mean that?"

Reggie smiled widely. "I believe there is another step. First you ask. Then..."

He levered himself over her and captured Reggie's mouth with his own. He didn't thrust into her; neither did he rush toward what he so desperately needed.

Gabe moved his hands up and down her body, caressing her, making her feel like the goddess he had proclaimed her their first night back together. At last, he rolled to his back and pulled her over him.

Reggie stared down at him, questioning Gabe silently.

"I'm not rushing you," he repeated.

"I said 'yes'."

"When you're ready, take me in."

She nodded. Reggie didn't want to rush what they were doing either. Instead, she lowered herself over him and went back to the kiss.

In minutes, they were at a simmer. Hands trailed up and down. Bodies shifted against bodies. Mouths explored. Reggie nipped at Gabe's chest, prompting a gasp.

At last, she straightened, coming to her knees over him. Gabe met her gaze, and she nodded. He levered his cock up, and Reggie lowered herself around him.

He pushed his hips up, seating himself deep inside her. Reggie rocked back and forth, working him to the hilt. Gabe's hands closed on her hips, and he guided her up and down, taking much of her weight for her to help Reggie ride him with ease.

Reggie let her eyes slip shut, rocketing into climax. Sparks of sensation danced along her nerve endings, making her feel weak and spent. She expected Gabe to follow her over, but he didn't. He went still beneath her, letting Reggie come back to Earth.

She stared at him, trying to make sense of what he was doing. "Gabe?" *Please tell me this wasn't some lame test to make sure I was willing to accept him.* Reggie would be hard pressed not to hit him if he'd played that game with her.

Gabe feathered his fingertips down the edge of her jaw. "You realize what this means to me."

"Of course."

"I want you to enjoy it as much as I do."

"I think it's safe to say I've enjoyed it quite a bit so far."

A smile curved his lips up. "Tell me you want to be my mate. I'm asking, Reggie."

"I've already said 'yes'."

He tensed slightly, forcing his cock further into her.

"But I'll say it again," she hurried to add. "Yes."

Gabe tucked Reggie to his chest and rolled her beneath him. Before she could question him, he was thrusting into her, hard and fast. She rolled her head back, licking her lips. One thing she could count on with Gabe was that he always knew what she liked. This position and his urgency... She'd always gotten off quickly this way.

This time was no exception. It didn't take long to force her to a second climax. Reggie lay, dazed, when Gabe roared out his climax, pouring into her in hot waves that ripped a gasp from her.

He dropped his head to the pillow beside hers, groaning as if he was in pain. That made Reggie's heart stutter.

"Are you okay?"

Gabe laughed harshly. "By the gods, I don't think I've been this good in years."

She furrowed her brow in confusion. "You sound like you're in pain."

"More like the release of pain."

"I don't get it," Reggie admitted.

"Printing is a painful thing. Breaking printing is a *very* painful thing. Even reaching *Endspiel* is really painful. Sealing printing? Good gods, I've never felt anything so pleasurable in my life."

She smiled and buried her hand in Gabe's hair. A moment later, she sobered. They'd sealed printing, but that didn't mean Adam Maher would like it.

Gabe tensed against her. "Reggie?"

"So...what happens now?"

He smiled, snuggling down against her shoulder. "I say we get a shower and go to lunch." His tone made it clear he had more in mind.

"Be serious," she chided him.

"I am serious. I know a great little restaurant. It's owned by Dale's mate. You'll love it."

"I'm sure I will, but—"

"And they will love you. So it's settled. Shower and lunch."

"What will your father say?" That was the real problem, she was sure.

"That I'm not starving. Marie makes great food."

It was a poor way to change the subject, at best. Reggie wasn't in a redirection mood. "He just won't get over the idea that I'm bad for you, you know."

"He has to. The Rules of Sanction do not give him much choice." Gabe seemed to think that ended the discussion.

Reggie laid a smack on the back of his skull.

He chuckled. "And what was that for?"

"Rules can't force someone to change their mind. Your father hates me. Whether he says it aloud or not, he's going to keep hating me." She was being peevish, she knew, but she couldn't help herself.

"They can force him to pretend to like you long enough for him to get to know you, at which point, he really will like you." Gabe laced his fingers through hers, tickling her palm with his thumb. "If there's still a problem, we'll live somewhere away from the manor. It's a big range, and there are only seven Warriors to cover it."

"Your father controls your movements. He's not going to let us live too far away. Besides, I don't want to cause a rift between you." It was true. While she would dearly love not to have to deal with Adam, she didn't want Gabe to turn his back on his family for her.

"If he shows you disrespect, he answers to me as his judge. The Rules of Sanction say that. Very clearly, as a matter of fact. He's not even allowed to defend himself, and I can definitely make him pay, in that case."

"Gabe, you're impossible."

"Only on an empty stomach. I expended a lot of energy hunting."

That made her crack a smile. "Well, I suppose we should have lunch, then."

"Knew you would see it my way."

****

Gabe jumped from the truck and trotted around it to open the door for Reggie. She placed her hand in his and slipped out, perched on stiletto heels. He smoothed the little black dress down her back, taking a moment to cup her ass between their bodies.

Reggie laughed and pulled away, batting at his hand, but her cheeks were an alluring shade of deep red, and her eyes were crinkled. He lunged for her, and she squealed and danced away.

"We could," he teased.

She shook her head, laughing harder.

"I ghost us. You be quiet, so no one hears us. Marie won't mind if we're a little late."

Reggie backed off another step. "I thought you said you were hungry."

"Oh, I am." In more than one way.

He'd proven that. The shower had turned to more. In specific, Reggie had ended up pressed to the shower wall, while Gabe thrust into her. The outfits they were wearing were the second they'd donned. The first had ended up very rumpled when he'd lifted her to the edge of the bureau and indulged in his mate again. Then they went back to bed...at Reggie's request. Lunch had quickly become an early dinner.

"Well, well, well, Cousin," Dale drawled. "What are you doing here?"

Reggie turned abruptly, barely keeping her balance. Gabe wrapped his arms around her and nestled to her back.

He nuzzled her neck, then met Dale's smirk head on. "Treating my mate to an early dinner. I called Marie, and she agreed to serve us before the dinner hours start."

Dale raised an eyebrow at the announcement. Then he offered an antiquated bow. "Congratulations to you both. I assume a private table is in order?" He opened the door and waved them inside.

Gabe took Reggie's arm and escorted her inside. "A private table would be perfect. This is my cousin, Dale. Dale, I would like to present my mate, Regina."

"Reggie is fine," she corrected him.

"Now why would I want to call such a beautiful woman Reggie?" Dale replied.

"Down boy," Gabe ordered. "You have a mate of your own. No charming mine."

"Agreed," Marie chimed in. She offered her hand. "Welcome to the family, Reggie."

Reggie took it with a strained smile. "Thanks."

Dale's mate wrapped an arm around her and guided Reggie further into the nearly-empty restaurant. Marie pointed out the touches of Warrior culture she'd added to the décor.

Dale held back and walked with Gabe. "Going out tonight?" He clearly meant hunting and not date night.

"I think printing entitles me to at least one night off."

"One? I don't think Marie and I came up for air for three days."

"Marie was fertile and willing." Gabe nodded toward the curve of his cousin's son in Marie's womb. "And *your* father isn't Adam Lord Maher."

Dale winced but didn't comment further. Whether he was thanking Tes he had Bryant for a father or was taking silent bets on exactly how *un*happy Adam was going to be about Gabe sealing printing with Reggie, at least he kept it to himself.

Marie pulled back a lush velvet drape in Maher blue. Behind it, was a cozy table for two. The two women ambled inside, chatting about the old-fashioned setup.

"Do me a favor," Gabe whispered.

Dale snorted. "For the newest mated man in Maher range? It would be an honor. Name it."

"Once they deliver the food, ask Marie to give us privacy."

His cousin's arched eyebrow took a moment to sink in.

Gabe glared at him. "Not what you think."

"Really?" he drawled out.

He put his fingers on either side of the ring box in his jacket pocket.

Dale gaped, shot a sideward look at the ladies, then nodded. "Done." He smoothed his expression before the two women turned back toward him.

Reggie came to his side and pressed a kiss to Gabe's cheek. "You were right. I love it."

Marie ticked her finger at Reggie. "You haven't even eaten yet. Wait until you taste the food."

Dale stepped in. "Make yourself at home. I'd like to spend a few minutes with my mate before I head out."

Gabe pulled out all the chivalrous stops: taking Reggie's wrap, pulling out her chair, and even kissing her hand while they waited for the server to show up.

Gabe tried to still his trembling hands. His nervousness made no sense. They were already mated. Whether or not she married him didn't make any difference.

Somehow it does.

****

"Close your eyes," Gabe whispered to her.

Reggie complied, trying to swallow down a laugh at how juvenile it felt.

"Keep them closed."

"They are."

He brought her hand to his mouth and laid a kiss in the palm. Reggie shivered in delight. Gabe laid a kiss on the tip of her little finger. He moved on to her ring finger. Just when she expected him to move on to the middle finger, he worked a ring down the ring finger.

Her lungs seized in surprise. Gabe shifted. From the sounds and the change in angle of her hand, Reggie guessed he was going down on one knee.

He can't be proposing. There's no need for this. She hadn't expected this. Few Warriors *married* their mates; most stopped with sealing printing.

"Open your eyes, Reggie."

She did, moving her focus from his tense smile to the square-cut diamond with two smaller diamonds on each side. Words deserted her; a gasp was the most she was capable of.

"You always said you wanted a big wedding," he reminded her. "I'm offering the full package: a beautiful little church I know, one of our protected priests, whatever you want for decorations and dress, flowers, reception...even a honeymoon."

"But...we've already printed." He didn't think she'd leave him without a wedding, did he?

Gabe pressed a kiss to her knuckles. "You can have whatever you want, Reggie. I don't want you to feel you've sacrificed a single thing for me."

"I don't. You're the one who's—"

"Or your father."

"What?" What was he talking about?

He sighed. "You're his only child. Won't he want to see your wedding?"

"He might." *Probably not, but it was worth a try.* Reggie wanted the chance, but the expense of it hardly seemed warranted. "I guess we could have a small wedding."

"Whatever size you want, but I want you to promise me you won't skimp, for any reason. I'll even fly your father back and forth to attend."

"I don't understand," she admitted.

Gabe's jaw tensed. "Printing makes sure no other Warrior in the world will make a pass at you. I want to make sure no human man who values his life will either."

What he'd said was sweet and charming. Reggie was caught between the urge to laugh and the urge to cry.

"Will you marry me?"

"Yes. Yes, I will."

Gabe got back in his chair and leaned around the table edge to kiss Reggie. "So, do you like it?"

She wiggled her ring finger, watching the rainbow refractions in the diamond, at a loss for words

"Reggie?" His voice waivered slightly.

She threw her arms around his neck and kissed him, gasping as Gabe lifted her into his lap. His hand slid beneath her skirt, teasing at her inner thigh.

He broke away, his eyes hot in promise. "What do I get for a honeymoon in Hawaii? You've always wanted to go to Hawaii."

Reggie bit back a laugh. "I don't think we'll ever leave the room."

His hand inched higher. "We can do that at home."

"Yes, we can." Her voice was ragged.

He stroked at the crotch of her panties, teasing at the seam. Reggie bit at her lower lip, trying not to make noise someone would hear outside the curtain partition.

His lips nestled to her ear, and his voice rumbled against her. "Here and now, Reggie," he invited.

She shook her head, refusing. This was a public restaurant.

Gabe slipped his fingers under the edge of the panties, stimulating her directly. He thrust two fingers inside, twisting and stroking, driving her toward release. "Oh, yes. Come for me, and we'll go home."

He couldn't do this. Still, she made no move to stop him.

"We'll discuss our wedding in bed." Gabe shifted, skating his lips along her cheek. "We'll discuss...everything."

His meaning was painfully clear. She wasn't on birth control, and Gabe used condoms when they were needed. He was thinking about children, the children she'd dreamed of all these years.

"Yes." She'd already decided to give him those children, when he was ready to ask for them.

"Yes, you want a honeymoon in Hawaii?" he prodded.

"I want..." Her climax neared, making thinking difficult.

"Want?" His lips covered the corner of hers.

"A baby." As long as it was with Gabe, she would have as many babies as she could.

"What?" His rhythm faltered a bit before he resumed in earnest.

"Plan Hawaii for when I'll be..."

He quickened his pace, his breaths rasping in and out. "Go on."

"Fertile," Reggie managed. She rose against him, seeking climax. "Bring me home pale and pregnant."

Gabe captured her mouth, adding massage to her clit to send her over. Reggie whimpered into his mouth, meeting his tongue avidly as she contracted around his fingers.

When it was over, he caressed her lips, again and again, devouring her in between. "Next time, I'll be eating you while you come."

She looked at the curtain, nervous.

"Not here," he assured her. "We'll get dessert to go."

Reggie considered the long drive. "Five minutes?"

Gabe smoothed her dress and lifted Reggie to her feet. A smile lit his midnight blue eyes. "Be quick."

"I will," she promised. Reggie slipped through the curtain and strolled down the hall toward the restrooms.

The realization that someone was moving close behind her came an instant too late. In fact, it came a split-second before a hand covered her mouth and a gun pressed to her ribs. Reggie froze, a cry of alarm catching in her throat as he dragged her toward the kitchen doors.

"Keep quiet," he ordered gruffly, shouldering past the swinging doors.

Marie and another kitchen worker looked around from dinner prep. Both their eyes widened, and Marie's jaw dropped in shock.

"Not a sound, or I kill all three of you," her attacker warned. He guided Reggie toward the back door.

Reggie planted her feet, desperate to delay him. He could force her along with him, but if she slowed him down, Marie could get Gabe before they were out of range.

The attacker released her mouth and closed his fist around her amulet. "One more thing, sweets." He yanked forward, nearly pulling Reggie off her feet before the chain snapped.

The pain across the back of her neck made Reggie's eyes water, and Marie grasped at the counter between them, looking tortured. The older woman went still, as his gun came up under Reggie's chin. Marie backed toward the cooler, and her assistant stepped between her boss and the weapon.

The amulet landed on the counter. "If I know what that means..." he hinted, letting the obvious hang between them.

Beasts! He's a minion. The game wasn't over. He meant to use her to get to Gabe, probably to kill Gabe, in an attempt to kill Adam.

He wrenched her toward the door again.

No! I have to stop him. Reggie met Marie's gaze and offered silent apologies.

Marie nodded and took another step backward, putting her within jumping distance of protection within the cooler. Reggie swept a set of nested metal bowls onto the floor, praying the minion wouldn't have time to shoot them. Or maybe even that he would run now that she'd called his bluff.

The gun retreated, and Reggie held her breath, letting it out in a rush as Marie dodged into the cooler and her assistant took her place, blocking the door. She had just enough time to wonder if the other chef was also a bodyguard Dale had hired for his mate before blinding pain exploded across the side of Reggie's face. The world went dim to the echoes of the clatter of metal and a shout of protest.

Chapter Twenty-Eight

Gabe slid his jacket on, his body humming in anticipation. He'd been trying not to rush Reggie. He hadn't dared ask for a child yet, due to her reasons for leaving him last time. But Reggie wanted one. For once, the gods were looking out for him.

At the discordant crashing of metal, his muscles tensed. Marie's shout of 'no' had his *Blutjagd* burning merrily, and he launched through the drape and down the hall toward the kitchen. Whether it involved Reggie or not, Marie was a woman of his family. A bearing woman, at that.

Marie bolted at him from the kitchen doorway, Kyra at her heels, most likely protecting her back. His cousin's mate was wild-eyed; she grasped Gabe's hand and pressed an amulet into it.

He took a moment to examine it. The sturdy chain had been snapped. He recognized it immediately. "Reggie." Realization was a moment behind. "A minion." He rounded the two women.

Kyra turned with him, nodding, a cell phone in her hands. Most likely, she was texting Dale. "Out the back. Be careful, Gabe. He has a gun. Reggie didn't stand a chance."

"Call in my father." Gabe didn't wait for her reply. He tore through the kitchen and into the back alley.

He didn't need to be slow about tracking them. There was only one way out of the alley for a human man hampered by an unwilling woman. Gabe surged into the parking lot the restaurant shared with the neighboring shop, scanning for them.

The squeal of tires pinpointed his adversary for him. He vaulted into a truck bed, over the cab, and then down again in the next traffic lane. The truck he sought was already speeding away.

Gabe realized he had no chance of catching them on foot, even as he laid on speed. He sought out the tiny, razor-barbed blades in his belt pouch and let three fly, praying to Ani and Tes for one solid shot.

The truck jerked to the right onto the main street, and Gabe came to a halt at a glint of metal, noting one of the barbs. He pulled out his tablet and opened the tracking program. Gabe squatted and returned the last barb to his pouch, barely breathing while he waited for the program to link with the active barbs.

It synched, and he breathed a sigh of relief. *Now you learn what it means to cross a Maher tracker.*

Gabe sprinted to his truck, settled the tablet in its cradle, and started following the map lines GPS was drawing from the two-per-second synch rate with the barbs on the other truck.

His cell rang, and Gabe answered it without taking his eyes off the readout. "Yeah?"

"How's it going?" his father asked, his voice gruff.

"I have dual barbs on them, and I'm in motion."

There was a moment of silence. "I see it. Unless the minion tries to—"

Gabe's *Blutjagd* went off the charts.

"Gabriel," his father barked. "Unless he does anything further to harm her, stay ghosted and wait for us."

"Are you insane?" he growled. "Reggie is my *mate*."

"I know it, but this is Dubrae. We have to kill him off, or Reggie will never be safe. Dubrae doesn't care that he's marked. He'll keep trying until he's dead or she is."

"You're using *my* mate as bait." Protected were never used as bait, especially not a Warrior's mate or intended mate. What the hell was Adam thinking?

"If the minion had been ordered to kill her, he would have done it the minute he had a shot at her. He took her amulet away to make her prey for Dubrae. *That* is the one we have to kill. This is your duty, Gabriel."

"She's. My. Mate!" What part of this didn't his father understand?

"Before we take them down, I'll get you next to her. You can get the amulet on her before they have a chance to touch her. I promise it."

"But the minion—"

"Would have done a hell of a lot worse than hit her, if he had his beast's leave to do it."

Gabe swerved, then brought the truck under control again. His breathing was labored, and his *Blutjagd* burned merrily. The metal phone body groaned a complaint as he tightened his hand around it.

Kyra didn't tell me he hit Reggie.

She didn't have time. Keep your eye on the ball, Gabe.

"Gabriel? Gabe!"

A deadly calm came over him. "The minion is mine. No one kills him but me. When we have Dubrae, if he doesn't harm her again. If he lays a hand on her before that—"

"Agreed."

****

"Goddammit! The fucker killed my tire."

Reggie winced, moving tenderly. She couldn't seem to piece together where she was or how she'd gotten there, but she was in a cramped space, and she hurt all over.

A rush of air accompanied the sound of a truck door opening. Reggie squawked in surprised protest as she was hauled out of the truck onto a gravel road. The heel snapped on one of her shoes, and she went to her hands and knees. The pain cleared her head a bit more.

The sunlight was blinding, and her head spun. The entire right side of her face was on fire. The dark cameo of a short, muscular man loomed over her, the light behind him rendering him an indistinct blur.

The faint copper taint of blood fouled her mouth, and her lip protested her attempt to open her mouth to ask a question. Just as the word 'minion' formed in her mind, he moved. His hand closed in her hair, and he yanked her up and away from the truck.

Blessedly, his next tug turned her away from the sun and toward a cabin. A sob caught in her throat. This cabin wasn't a safe place, and the slowly sinking sun was an even worse omen. She resisted the urge to look back at it.

There was a decided chill inside the structure, a lack of warmth that she'd always found in Warrior cabins. It didn't surprise her, but Reggie wished it wasn't so. It might have been easier to delude herself into a cocoon of perceived safety if she had at least been comfortable.

Comfort wasn't on the minion's agenda. He pushed her down onto a high-backed wooden chair with sturdy arms, then proceeded to use duct tape to secure her wrists to it. He silenced her request to use a restroom with the threat of his gun.

Minutes passed...then hours. The sun started disappearing behind the hills, and her hopes sank with it. If Gabe had been able to track them, he'd have been there long ago.

****

The hours passed as torture for Gabe. He could see Reggie through the window; he could see the occasional sob or shudder as she watched the sun disappear from the sky.

The first time had been the worst for him. When he'd arrived, Reggie had had her face lowered, her hair hiding the damage the minion had done from him, save the abrasions on her knees. Then she'd tipped her head up and looked out the window, through his ghosted form, at the sun beyond.

Her split lip and the red-purple bruises... It had been all Gabe could do to maintain his ghosting and not kill the minion that instant. He had given his word not to move unless he was forced to.

Much as Gabe hated to admit it, his father's plan was rational. They had to snare Dubrae. After the attack at her old house and this move against her, he couldn't allow Reggie to live in fear that the beast would try for her again the moment she was out of Gabe's sight.

If he let his ghosting slip, even to reassure Reggie he was with her and protecting her, Dubrae might be close enough to sense a Warrior nearby. If that happened, the beast would flee, and this insanity would be wasted. *Worse, Reggie would go through this and still be in danger.*

His father's hand closed over Gabe's shoulder. He didn't have to ask who it was. No one else would dare touch him in this near-mad state.

Reggie raised her head again, and the hand squeezed in comfort. There were no words between them. There was no reason for them; Adam knew what version of the Christian Hell this was for Gabe. Mere words could never do it justice, so they didn't waste them.

Warmth at his other shoulder let Gabe know another Warrior had joined them. He didn't ask who it was. In truth, he didn't care. As long as the other Warrior did his job and they left the minion for Gabe, their names didn't matter...for now. When Reggie was safe, he would thank them properly.

The sun sank behind the far hills, and the Warriors prepared for battle. The hand left his shoulder, and the heat dissipated.

The minion moved toward the door. Gabe took one last look at Reggie, then mirrored his motion. If the minion opened the door, Gabe wasn't going to miss his chance to slip inside.

The door swung wide, and the dark-haired human beast sauntered out, stretching his arms as if to embrace the darkness. He stepped onto the crushed stone walk and strode past Gabe.

The urge to kill him was strong, and Gabe stamped it down. *After. Reggie and Dubrae come first.*

He'd already scanned for electronics, so Gabe knew there were no traps he couldn't avoid. That a given, nothing was going to stop him from protecting his mate. He joined her silently, wincing at the pungent smell of urine.

She was going to the restroom when the minion snatched her. Reggie had no choice but to loose her bladder.

His cheeks burned in sympathetic embarrassment. *I will make this up to you, Reggie. I swear it.*

Gabe noted the arriving beasts in anticipation. It was ironic. The predators had just become prey for the Warriors again. *And they don't know it. Yet.*

****

"You fool!"

Reggie cringed, cowering as far back in the chair as she could with her wrists bound as they were. Dubrae was back, and she didn't have an amulet to protect her.

The door flew the rest of the way open, and the beast and minion stalked in. Two other beasts followed. She swallowed a cry of alarm as they converged on her.

"You fool," Dubrae repeated. "She belongs to them now."

"She'll be dead before they find her. Kill her and Gabriel of Maher dies. That's what you wanted," the minion pleaded.

"We'll be marked," another beast snapped.

"We would be for killing a Warrior anyway," the last beast reasoned. "Or for killing a protected."

Dubrae turned on them, snarling curses. "You have never seen marked as a mate killer is marked. Veriel learned that. For fifteen centuries, he was hunted. A mate killer knows no peace. Warriors expect to die in battle eventually. It is war to kill a mate."

Reggie watched the argument, her heart pounding in terror. Even if Dubrae and the beast who agreed with him abandoned this right now, it was clear the minion and the other beast intended to press on.

She gasped at a touch on her hair. The feeling of an amulet against her throat was unmistakable. The chain closed around her neck, and she bit back a sob of relief.

The voices around her faded into the background. Fingers trailed up her cheek, then brushed down her forehead to her eyes, urging them closed. Reggie complied. Whatever was about to happen, she didn't want to see it.

She jumped at the sounds of shouts. The acrid smell of beast blood filled the air.

"Keep them closed," Gabe whispered. The hand left her face, and the tape on her wrists ripped away, forcing a yelp from her. "I'm here. You're safe now."

Reggie nodded, moaning as he laid a gentle kiss to her split lip.

"Gabriel?" Adam asked, his voice devoid of emotion.

"Keep your eyes closed, baby." His jacket settled around her shoulders, and Gabe lifted Reggie into his arms. "Joseph," he called out.

She reached for Gabe as he transferred her into his brother's arms, disobeying him to see him. His face was tense and haggard.

Gabe pried her hand off his shirt gently, then kissed her knuckles. "For a minute," he promised. "Close your eyes, baby."

Reggie did so, reveling in the warmth inside his jacket. She was safe with the Warriors, though she smelled horrible and felt worse.

Then she was whisked away into the chill night air. A scream pierced the night, and she echoed it, her nerves strung to their breaking point. Reggie buried her face in Joseph's chest. She gasped for breath, trembling in the combined stress of the hours she'd been held hostage. She slid into unconsciousness.

****

Gabe watched Joseph's retreating back, until the black of his outfit blurred into the black of the moonless night. His *Blutjagd* boiled over. *How dare they touch my mate! How dare they batter her!*

If Reggie's safety hadn't been compromised, Gabe would have killed them all himself. As it was, his father had killed Dubrae and Sulter, and Joseph had killed Geralt.

A sound brought his head around. And now, the minion was Gabe's to deal with.

The foul creature fought Adam's hold on the scruff of his neck, beating ineffectually on the Warrior's chest. From the look on Adam's face, it was by force of will alone that he hadn't snapped the minion's neck or slit his throat already.

"Gabe?" his father prompted him.

"He's mine."

Adam nodded and shoved the minion toward Gabe.

His first punch knocked the minion solidly against the wall, and he doubled over, gritting his teeth and wheezing. The second punch was designed to do roughly the same damage he'd done to Reggie. The minion screamed, clapping a hand to his shattered nose.

From somewhere beyond the walls, Reggie echoed the scream. Gabe looked up in surprise, tensing, listening for sounds that she was in danger, despite Joseph's presence.

"She's scared," Adam offered. "Finish it quickly."

As much as he'd like to take the minion apart a joint at a time, Reggie came first. He pulled his weapon, grasped the back of the minion's hair, then dragged him up.

"The Rules of Sanction are clear," Gabe stated. "You abducted a Warrior's mate. *My* mate. You beat her, and you intended to kill her. Moreover, you threatened to kill my cousin's *pregnant* mate. Be glad my cousin isn't here right now."

The minion's eyes widened, and his face went pale behind the splatter and flow of blood.

"You will never endanger my mate or the mates of my brother Warriors again."

Mindful of Reggie, he slit the minion's vocalis muscle at the top of the trachea. Before he had a chance to do more than gasp, Gabe slit the minion from navel to breastbone.

Gabe stood over the dying thing, transfixed, unwilling to look away until the human beast was dead. He shifted away just far enough to avoid the spill of foul blood.

His father handed him a damp cloth, and Gabe wiped his hands and weapon, his gaze locked on the last twitching movements.

"It's over," Adam stated. "Time to go. I'll light the fires."

Gabe felt oddly tired. "Yes. It is. I'll meet you at the SUV."

The walk to the vehicles seemed to take much longer than the trip out had. Gabe climbed into the back of his father's SUV and took a cool cloth from Joseph's hand. He bathed Reggie's bruised and cut face, tucking the blankets his brother had covered her with around her body.

Joseph fished the truck key from Gabe's pocket. "I'll drive your truck back."

"Thanks," he managed.

His brother eased out of the vehicle and closed the back hatch. Gabe looked up at the sound of his truck starting. He stared at the flames licking at the night sky.

Adam appeared, silhouetted in the firelight. He took his place in the front seat without comment. In heartbeats, they were in motion. The vehicle bumped along the back roads. Gabe laid down beside Reggie, needing the reality of his mate in his arms.

****

Adam nudged Gabe's shoulder, pulling his hand back as his son tensed. "We're home. Your mother is waiting."

Gabe mumbled his thanks, gathered Regina to his chest, then headed for the door.

For a burdened complement of men, things moved quickly. Joseph had driven ahead in Gabe's truck and was already inside. He threw the door open before they reached it.

"Mom is in your room and set up."

Gabe nodded and trudged on, tucking Regina's head beneath his chin.

Joseph shut the door, then took his place at Adam's side, guarding their backs as they made their way upstairs. He stayed in the hall, closing the bedroom door behind them.

"On the bed," Jo ordered.

But Gabe was already there. His son placed a gentle kiss on Regina's swollen lips. He held himself over his mate for a long moment, looking as if the day had aged him a decade.

"Gabe," Jo soothed him.

"Yeah." He pushed up off the mattress and stuffed his hands in his pockets, making room for his mother to render medical aid.

Jo was all business. She cleaned the wounds on Regina's face, then the ones on her wrists and knees. "When was the last time she had a tetanus shot?" she inquired.

"I don't know," Gabe admitted. He winced, most likely blaming himself for not knowing something so vital about his mate when the information was needed.

"Probably when she was bitten before then," she guessed. "It won't hurt her to have another." Jo prepared the shot and administered it.

"No broken bones," Jo reported. "The cuts are minor. She'll heal up, but it will take a week or so." That established, she started packing her gear.

"Would you mind leaving?" Gabe asked.

Adam looked at his son, surprised that the request seemed to be aimed at himself. "Why?"

Gabe's *Blutjagd* flared. "Because the minion kept her taped to a chair until she pissed herself. I intend to change her clothes and clean her. I *don't* intend to do that with you standing over her, watching."

He put his hands up in surrender and turned toward the door.

"Do you want my help?" Jo offered. She was a woman. There was no reason for Gabe to refuse her.

"No. This is my burden to bear."

Adam winced at the pain in his son's voice.

He feels responsible for Regina's pain and degradation, even though most of the damage happened before he got to her. He's wondering if killing Dubrae was worth it.

Gabe will get over it. He'll realize it was the only reasonable decision to make.

Adam walked away, certain that Gabe would calm down once Regina woke and he saw there was no lasting damage.

Chapter Twenty-Nine

May 31st, 2051

Reggie buried herself under the blankets, enjoying the warmth. She turned to her side, wincing at the slice of pain down her cheek.

"Reggie?"

Gabe's voice was laced with concern. She tried to figure out why it would be...and why her cheek would hurt. The answers fought emerging from the muddled thoughts circling in her mind. She turned toward him without opening her eyes, reaching out for him in the bed.

He wasn't there. Gabe took her hand and wrapped it in both of his. Reggie tugged at him, urging him to join her. He settled to the mattress beside her and drew Reggie to his chest. His breath warmed her scalp through the curtain of her hair.

A niggling of unease settled in her gut. Gabe was dressed in his t-shirt and jeans; she could feel the length of his armored boots through the blanket. Running her hands down his body, she encountered his weapons.

Why is he armed and dressed in the bedroom? Why isn't he in bed with me?

For that matter, Reggie was half-dressed. She wore a Warrior's button-down shirt with no underwear. If she wore anything to bed with Gabe, it was lingerie. Normally, she wore nothing.

"Reggie. Oh, gods, forgive me," he pleaded.

Her mind slogged along, trying to make sense of that. Forgive him? Why should she forgive him? Gabe wouldn't have hit her. If he had, his own family would have killed him for it.

"I was there with you. I swear I was. I... There was no way to show you without letting Dubrae know."

Her mind rebelled as the memories assaulted her. She'd been kidnapped by a minion. Dubrae and two of his cronies were going to kill her. Gabe and his family had saved her. She grasped at Gabe's ribs, her breathing ragged.

A sob escaped his throat, and his arms trembled. "Dubrae wouldn't stop," he whispered. "If the minion had touched you again— I wouldn't have waited, I swear, no matter what promise I made to take Dubrae down."

"P-promise?" Reggie was abruptly cold. Colder than she'd been in that damned cabin. *It's shock.*

For a long moment, Gabe didn't answer her. When he did, tortured was the only appropriate description for his voice.

"I had to end it. Dubrae would have kept coming. I didn't...want to..." His arms tightened. "I wanted to gut the minion the minute I reached you."

She snuggled into his chest, sharing Gabe's body heat. Reggie wished they were skin-to-skin.

"I promised my father to end it now, if I could."

"End what?" What he was saying made a limited amount of sense to her, now that her mind was clearing again.

"Dubrae. End the threat to our family. But...I swear, if the minion had touched you again or threatened you directly, I'd have ended him, Dubrae or no Dubrae."

Reggie nodded, numbly fitting the pieces together. "Your father used me as bait." If Gabe didn't want to wait, there was only one person who could have forced him to make that vow.

Gabe shuddered. "I hated it. I watched you every minute I was there. I never took my eyes off of you. Not for a second."

Realization of what he needed from her came slowly, about as long as it took her to follow Gabe's train of thought. Being forced to use his mate as bait would be traumatizing to any Warrior. And Adam had forced Gabe to make that choice. "I forgive you."

His armor cracked. In the next instant, Gabe was sobbing into her hair, being comforted as much as he was comforting her. He choked out something that sounded vaguely like he didn't believe he deserved her forgiveness.

Reggie smoothed his hair. "I forgive you," she repeated. *But I don't forgive your father.*

****

Reggie settled into the chair Gabe pulled out for her, biting back the urge to tell Adam off first thing. A glance around the room showed concern and a strained smile—Jo, discomfort—Joseph, and cool disregard—Adam, of course.

"Feeling better?" Jo asked

"Well enough," Reggie answered simply. "How is Marie?"

"She's fine," Joseph offered. "Dale insisted on closing last night, but Marie is ready to go back in today. Good idea with the bowls."

She nodded.

Jo motioned to the kitchen. "If you need anything for the pain—"

"Not necessary." They might as well learn she was tougher than they thought, right now.

Gabe settled his chair closer to hers, leaning close to her uninjured cheek. "If you'd like *anything*," he hinted.

Reggie took advantage of his proximity to brush her lips against his. "I have what I need, and I do like it."

His sappy smile made Gabe appear like the seventeen-year-old Warrior she'd fallen for half a decade earlier.

The rest of the meal passed in much the same way. Reggie offered one and two word answers to Gabe's family, but she showered her mate with affection. Gabe didn't seem to notice it, probably too relieved that *he* was in good favor with her to care about anything else.

Adam and Jo noticed, though. There was no question of that. The lord's frustration and his mate's confusion spoke volumes of a brewing 'discussion'.

True to his reputation, Adam showed little patience. They'd no sooner stood to leave the dining room when his voice stopped them in their tracks.

"Regina? May I have a moment?"

Gabe shot his father a narrow-eyed look.

Reggie placed a hand on Gabe's arm and nodded him away. Then she turned to Adam. "Of course."

The few Warriors who'd eaten with them trailed out, leading their families and Gabe with them. Jo lingered a moment longer, but a nod from Adam, similar the one Reggie had offered Gabe, sent her away as well.

The door closed behind them, and Reggie raised her chin in challenge.

"Regina—"

"Let's get this over with," she interrupted him.

That seemed to confuse him. "I only wanted to put you at ease."

"You should have thought of that...oh...say six o'clock yesterday or a little earlier."

He winced. "I know what you must be thinking, and—"

"This isn't about me. Okay, yes. You broke your own laws and used a protected as bait, but that's small potatoes, compared to—"

"I owe you an apology for that," he soothed her. "It was a chance to turn the tables on—"

"I know *why* you did it."

Silence fell between them for a tense moment. "But?" he prompted her.

"I know you don't want me in your family." That was the real issue, after all.

"Who Gabe prints on or marries is his business." His tone made it clear he'd still like to make it his own business. "As a Warrior with autonomy, I have no right to—"

"Oh, you're just *all* over breaking Warrior law when it suits you to," she challenged him.

Adam took a calming breath. "You're right again, but Gabe has chosen you. He's tied himself to you, and—"

"And you need to quit screwing around with that," Reggie informed him.

That left him stunned...for a few heartbeats. "What?"

"Whether you like it or not, I'm here to stay this time."

"Whether I like— I would *never*—"

It was time to make herself clear. "No matter how much you hate me, you have no right to take it out on Gabe. You want a fight? Come to me directly."

He paled several shades. "I don't want a fight, and I'm not taking anything out on my son."

"Save it," she ordered. "You dared to lecture me about hurting Gabe, then you pulled this shit on him? Worse, you made Gabe fear I wouldn't forgive him, that I would leave him. You know and I know that would kill him. Worse, he knows it. Lord or no lord, I won't stand for it. You have laws to keep you accountable. You *will* be accountable, to me if no one else."

Adam's jaw dropped in shock.

"Would you have used your own mate as bait?" she continued.

He ground his teeth, abruptly the lethal man she saw most often. "No," he growled. "I wouldn't."

Reggie forced her feet to the floor when she wanted to take a step back. She was done retreating from Adam. Instead, she relaxed her arms, limbering for a fight, though she didn't anticipate one. Reggie was fairly certain Adam wouldn't break that particular rule.

"Why not?" she pressed him. She knew she was pushing it, but Reggie wasn't going to stop until Adam got her meaning bludgeoned into his thick skull.

His muscles tensed, and his eyes narrowed.

She pretended to be oblivious. Reggie raised an eyebrow and tapped her foot, demanding an answer from him. When he didn't offer one, she affected a sigh. "Gabe is *my* mate. I may not be a Warrior, but I'm as fiercely protective of my mate as any Warrior is. You hurt Gabe, you answer to me, and you won't like answering to me. Get used to it."

Reggie turned on her heel and marched away. Warriors turned to stare at her when she breezed into the foyer. They shot nervous looks the way she'd come.

Gabe met her at the foot of the stairs. A frown marred his face. "Everything okay?" he asked.

She didn't have to turn back to know Adam stood in the doorway, glaring at her. She didn't need a Warrior's senses to feel his *Blutjagd.* "I think we understand each other now," Reggie replied simply.

Gabe's gaze shifted between Reggie and his father several times. "Maybe we should go upstairs," he suggested.

"Best idea I've heard all day."

****

"So tell me what happened," Jo invited.

Adam closed his hand in a tight fist, at a loss to cork his *Blutjagd*.

When he didn't answer, his mate sighed. She wrapped her arms around him and nestled to his back. His anger faded somewhat at her touch.

"Better?" she asked.

"Much."

Jo kneaded at his shoulders, digging her hands in to smooth knots. "I doubt that."

Adam winced. "You know me too well some days."

"It's impossible to know your husband too well," she teased. "I simply know you better than you *want* me to some days. You can't bullshit me."

He turned toward her and scooped Jo into his arms, gathering her flush to his chest. "Gods, I don't know what I would do without you."

"You think you're going to find out soon?" she asked in surprise.

"I pray to every god I know that's not so."

Jo twisted his ponytail around her index finger. "What does this have to do with Reggie?"

Oh, she does know me so well. There was nothing to do but give her the truth. "Regina called me on a breach of honor. Actually, three breaches of the Rules of Sanction."

Her shock would have been comical under other circumstances, he was sure. "You?"

Adam nodded sheepishly. "And she's right. Syth help me, she's called it right."

Jo darkened, her expression going hard in rebuke. "Because you suggested using her as bait."

"I *did* use her as bait, but that's the least of it."

"I'd offer to—"

"Don't," he pleaded. "I don't even want to consider it."

Jo nodded, a clear acknowledgement of how much the idea of it tortured him. She pressed her cheek to his shoulder. "I see. She called you on forcing Gabe into that choice, on urging him to risk losing her in the crossfire." She didn't question it.

"She's right."

"He could have refused."

"Could he? I ordered him to do it, Jo. I made him give his word to me, before either of us had a handle on the situation. And I stood there and watched them both hurt."

"For good reason," Jo reasoned.

"Maybe not good enough." Adam had to admit that he hadn't considered what making that choice would do to Gabe. He hadn't considered his son's feelings, only his duty.

She sighed. "What was the third?"

"Third?" In the aftermath of a raging *Blutjagd*, he was tired, nearly in a stupor.

"You said it was three breaches of honor. I count two: using a protected as bait and forcing Gabe to do it."

"Actively standing in the way of Gabe printing on Regina. This time, of course."

Jo didn't respond to that, but she stiffened in his arms. That left Adam in terror and with no clue of what she was thinking.

"This is probably bad," he muttered.

"I can't argue that she's judging you unfairly, Conan."

He winced. "I've really fucked up, haven't I?" Jo hadn't uttered that nickname in almost two decades. If she was using it now, it was a safe bet that she was furious with him.

"You have to ask that?" Jo didn't wait for his answer. "She probably thinks all sorts of ridiculous things about you, Adam."

He squeezed his eyes shut, replaying the argument. "That I hate her. That I don't want her as a part of the family."

"You see?" she challenged.

"She's right," he admitted.

Jo went still, then her fingers left his hair. She eased away from Adam, spearing him with a calculating look. "What did you just say?"

Adam reached up and rubbed one of the remaining stiff spots in his neck. "Well, I'm stuck with her now. It's probably better for Gabe that I am, but I don't have to like it."

"Don't have to *like* it?" Jo turned on her heel and stormed away with a growl of frustration.

"Jo?" he called after her.

She stopped at the door and turned to glare at him. "You are lord of Maher range, and Reggie is your daughter-in-law. You will find a way to make peace with her."

378

"She won't give me a chance to," he argued. Much as he hated to admit it, Regina had made that more than clear.

"Figure it out. And just to spur you to actually trying... Sleep somewhere else until you do."

"You can't mean that," Adam protested.

Jo didn't hesitate. "You sleep somewhere else, or I will. And make it good, Adam. Lip service isn't going to cut it."

Then she was gone, leaving an overly-obvious cold spot in his soul.

****

Gabe looked around the dinner table, his unease growing. He hadn't seen his father since the glaring session after breakfast.

His mother was clearly livid about something, and that didn't bode well, on the best of days. Despite the title of 'lord', the lord of a range wasn't in charge of a manor if he had a mate. The manners and social rules of the house were the lady's domain. Whoever had pissed Jo off was surely regretting it and would regret it worse when Adam got ahold of him or her.

Reggie shifted uncomfortably, picked at her food, and darted glances at Adam's vacant place at the head of the table. Yet again, Gabe wished he knew what was said between the two, but his father had been in no mood to question and Reggie had assured Gabe there was nothing to worry about.

Since the rest of the family was either distinctly nervous or confused, he wasn't sure Reggie had called that right.

When it became abundantly clear no one else was going to ask the loaded question, Gabe decided to address his mother. "Where is Dad tonight?"

Jo tensed, then took a mouthful of her milk. She set her glass on the table with precision that spoke of thinning patience. "On trail."

Two words. No elaboration. No details. Did they get into a fight about something? If they had, it would be the first in his memory.

Reggie stared at her plate, pushing food around with her fork instead of eating it.

Gabe squeezed her free hand. "You okay?" he asked, well aware that she wasn't, no matter what she was about to say.

She offered him a strained smile. "Fine. Just...thinking."

That seemed to brighten his mother's mood somewhat. "About the wedding, of course. I'm sure you'll want to do some planning with Gabe, but I'd love to help as well, if you'll have me."

Reggie offered a relaxed smile. "Sure. Why wouldn't you be welcome?"

"Good. Now, when are you planning to hold it?"

His mate shot Gabe a potent look. "The sooner the better, I guess."

He didn't miss her meaning. She'd promised him a child on their honeymoon, and Reggie didn't intend to make him wait.

Of course, he didn't intend to spend the entire time in Hawaii in the room, no matter what teasing they'd exchanged. Gabe did the mental math and came up with a rough estimate. "Six weeks?"

Reggie planted a kiss on his lips, then nodded furiously.

"Six weeks it is," Jo announced. "And no expense to be spared."

That lightened the mood around the table, and everyone started offering help and advice. It was almost enough to cause Gabe to miss the underlying tension still brewing in the manor house.

Chapter Thirty

July 16th, 2051

Reggie fidgeted in the overstuffed chair, offering a weak smile in response to Jo's chuckle.

"You'll be fine," Gabe's mother assured her.

"It's not that."

Jo's hand covered hers. "What is it?" Her tone spoke volumes of her intent to gut anything that made Reggie uneasy today.

Forcing the words out was difficult. "Adam isn't here. I know Gabe wants him to be, and I imagine you do, too." It was bad enough her own father had passed on the chance to attend, but she'd driven away Gabe's father as well.

"Reggie—"

"No. Wait. It's my fault he's not here. I said—"

"I know what you said and why you said it."

Her heart ached. "No. You don't. You really don't."

Jo sighed. "That Adam broke several of Rules of Sanction. That he has no choice but to get used to your presence in our lives," she rattled on. "Need I go into specific comments about his lack of tact and honor? About how he hurt Gabe, in the process?"

Reggie winced. "I just wanted him to back down and consider—"

"Gabe. I guessed that."

She nodded miserably. "I didn't expect him to leave."

"That wasn't your fault."

Reggie sighed. "You're too forgiving."

Jo offered a wry smile. "Not at all. You didn't chase Adam away. I gave him an ultimatum, and he chose to go. He'll be back when he comes to his senses and swallows his pride enough to admit he was wrong."

Reggie twisted the engagement ring on her hand. "Maybe... Maybe we should postpone this," she suggested.

She paled. "You would do that to Gabe?"

"We've sealed. This can wait if it has to." Though just the thought of postponing made her heart sink.

"If Adam doesn't show up, he doesn't deserve to be here." The glint in Jo's eyes left no doubt that she believed what she was saying.

"Does Gabe deserve to remember that his father hated his wife so much that he shunned them both on their wedding day?" *Does he deserve to think his father thinks no more of him than mine thinks of me?* She knew well enough how much that hurt.

"Does Gabe deserve to remember you calling off the wedding over his father's temper fit?"

Reggie had no answer to that. She didn't want to call off the wedding, but Adam... She cleared her throat. "Maybe just an hour or two? If I called him and apologized and he was close enough, he could—"

"Believe me," Jo offered drily. "You have *nothing* to apologize for."

"It doesn't feel that way," she admitted. Tears pricked at Reggie's eyes, and she blinked them away.

Jo laid a hand on Reggie's shoulder. "None of that. You go out there and be happy and gorgeous and loving. You and Gabe both deserve it."

"And Adam?" she asked nervously.

Jo headed for the door with a backward glance and a roll of her eyes. "Adam will get whatever misery he heaps on himself."

With that, she headed out the door, leaving Reggie alone with her rioting thoughts. Should she cancel? Delay? Try to call Adam? Or just forget Adam and try to enjoy the day without him?

"I should talk to Gabe," she whispered.

"It's bad luck for the groom to see the bride before the wedding."

The rumbling voice took her by surprise. Reggie launched to her feet and turned toward Adam. He stood on the opposite side of the dressing table, his long leather jacket and sunglasses in place.

Reggie scanned for an entryway, aside from the door Jo left through. It had been closed before she exited the room, and it was closed again. There was no way he came in while she went out.

Her face went hot in embarrassment and outrage. "You have been in here the entire time." *You bastard.*

He scowled. "I turned my back at the appropriate times, Regina."

384

"You're still spying on me." Reggie postulated on what Jo would think of that. Adam might become the first Warrior in history to find himself divorced.

He sighed deeply, shaking his head. "No. I just wanted to talk to you alone."

"Because that worked so well last time?"

Adam winced.

"So you had to sneak up on me to accomplish talking to me? Likely story, but you could have just asked to talk to me." *I'd certainly be less pissed at you that way. Oh, Jo is going to hear about this.*

"You don't exactly make it easy." Adam darkened, shifting as if discomfited. "And Jo is right. I'm creating my own misery here."

For a moment, Reggie seriously considered that she was hallucinating. "You're saying you want to play like we're a happy family?" Even if it wasn't real, that would be better than what they had going now.

Adam stared at her, fine lines appearing at the sides of hi downturned lips. "I'm saying I want to *be* a happy family."

"I'm definitely hallucinating," she decided. "Or I'm dreaming. I'm not sure which."

He dropped to one knee, which still placed him chest and above over the top line of the table. "I've wronged you, and I've wronged Gabe. I'll judge myself due a blow from Gabe for every offense...plus one for every injury you suffered." He grimaced. "Plus one for every hour you suffered at the hands of the minion and every hour Gabe had to watch you suffer. By my count, we're up to ten now. An even dozen sounds fair. After the festivities, if that's acceptable to you."

Reggie forced her mouth closed, fighting for words and for breath at the same time.

"Regina?" His voice was hesitant.

"I... I think you went light on Gabe's suffering. I was unconscious all night. He was in agony." It was a good start. Adam was trying, but Reggie wanted him to appreciate what he'd put Gabe through.

Adam sighed, then nodded. "Two dozen," he conceded.

"You're serious?" He couldn't be.

A wry smile pulled up at his lips. "I may spend your entire honeymoon in bed, but I deserve nothing better."

"You are serious." Reggie couldn't sort out how she felt about that. Part of her wanted to let him off the hook. *Jo won't stand for that.*

"I'm sorry, Regina. I'm asking you to forgive me."

"Okay. I can do that." She hesitated. "Does this mean you're staying for the wedding?"

"Would you like me to?" he countered.

"I know Gabe would—"

"No, Regina." He paused, seemingly pained. "Do *you* want me here?"

Reggie considered that. "If it will make Gabe happy, it will make me happy."

Adam removed his sunglasses, dumbstruck. "Then you're a better person than I am. If I'd said that...believed it in the beginning, we wouldn't be in this mess."

She nodded, at a loss for anything more poignant to say. A glance at the clock had her pulse racing. *I'm going to be late for my own wedding.*

Adam's voice shocked her into motion. "We'd better hurry. There's a wedding waiting for us."

She turned to find Adam folding his coat over the dressing table, revealing the immaculate morning coat beneath.

"Wow," Reggie breathed. "You come prepared." *And clean up well.*

A blush darkened his cheeks. "I would have left, if you'd asked me to. Or... Well, I probably would have ghosted, so you wouldn't know I watched. It *is* my son's wedding, after all."

Reggie smiled at his honesty. "You know, only members of the wedding party typically wear morning coats," she pointed out.

Adam didn't look back at her, and his shoulders tensed. "Your father not being here...I thought, maybe—"

"You want to give me away?"

"Can we just say give you to Gabe?" he pleaded. "It is sort of symbolic of me embracing your marriage."

"Do you?" It was stupid question. This was obviously borne of whatever ultimatum Jo had posed to him.

He met her gaze, head on. "Yes. I do. Completely."

Reggie headed toward the door, and Adam strode to her side. She offered her hand; he placed his forearm beneath it and his opposite hand over it. Even in her heels, he towered over her.

Adam reached out and opened the door, then guided her through. The hallway passed in a blur, her eyes on Adam more than the beautiful church Gabe had arranged for. At the head of the aisle, she met Gabe's gaze, watching his shock melt into a wide smile.

Then they were moving; Adam whisked Reggie to his son's side. The Lord Maher leaned to plant a kiss on her veil-covered cheek, then offered Gabe his hand. After they shook hands, Adam lifted her hand and placed it into his son's.

"You take care of her," Adam ordered gruffly. "And take care of my grandson, while you're at it."

Reggie's laugh at Adam's advance plans for them choked off at the sight of Gabe's guilty expression. She started counting days, the mental math making her dizzy. She'd been so busy with wedding preps, she hadn't realized Gabe had gone more than a month without wearing condoms.

Or that I should have started my period days ago.

Her balance deserted her, and both men reached out to steady her. Adam called for a glass of water, and Jo rushed forward, taking her pulse at the wrist. Shana came running with the water; she raised it to Reggie's lips, but Reggie motioned for a moment of peace.

"Gabe?" she asked. "Am I?"

He went dark, and his gaze shifted from Adam to her. "What's Hawaii without *some* sunshine?"

Adam glared down at his son, and Gabe offered a sheepish grin. Shana tipped the glass up to Reggie's mouth, urging her to drink, before she could figure out what to say.

"You owe me a couple of blows for that breach of the Rules of Sanction," Adam informed his son.

Reggie managed a laugh. "But you take yours before you give any."

The End

Questions from the Beta Readers...

Q: *Why didn't you write Lewis's story?*

A: I asked Lewis for his story, but he insisted his life was largely uneventful, until the time period in *Will of the Stone*, which we've already seen.

He met his mate when he saved her, like many Warriors do. She presented him with three strong sons, and the A-B-C naming was her idea, not his. They had nearly two decades together, before Colleen died of an aggressive form of breast cancer. Since that was the worst day of Lewis's life, he chooses not to tell the tale of nursing his mate through her illness or how she died in his arms.

Q: *Why don't we hear about Julia in* Will of the Stone *and* Hunter's Moon*? Did she die, too?*

A: On the contrary, Julia didn't die until after Kord did, but after facing down the Council of Lords, Julia tended not to spend time with visiting Warriors.

The Mahers were another matter entirely. Julia took an active hand in raising Curtis after Colleen died, and Curt—of all the younger Maher men—visited her often, until she died. Julia's involvement in raising Curt explains a lot about his personality.

Q: *Did Jack ever print?*

A: He did, shortly after he became Lord Farmer, but this isn't his story. In fact, the Farmers were lucky in love. Four of Julia's five brothers found mates and produced children. The unlucky brother was Alan, of course.

Q: *What was Adam talking about at the beginning of* Twice Printed*? What was Brandon Lord Hunter reporting to Adam?*

A: Ah... The answer to that lies in the next book in the series, *Bear's Women*. Since it would be a spoiler for me to explain it now, you'll just have to wait to find out when that book releases.

Q: So...*do* Warriors regrow teeth?

A: That is up to the Stone's whim. When Warriors lose teeth in battle, they regrow them within about six months. Since Falken lost his tooth as punishment after insulting a woman, the Stone made him live without it.

Also by this Author

KEIF'S DEN AND PACK
Keif's Pack
Mother of the Keif
Keif's Den (Coming Soon)

PROPHECY
Prophecy: Revelations
Prophecy: Rapture
The Prophet's Mate
Prophecy: Rampage - Meet Gavin
Prophecy: Rampage (Coming Soon)

RENEGADES SERIES
TYGERS
Renegade's Run
Max Sec

THE FANTASY CLUB
The Consort

INSTINCT SERIES
Animal Instincts

KEGIN SERIES
Earth-Born Lord
Graham: Training the Earth-Born Lord

NIGHT WARRIORS
Claiming a Lady
Stone Lord
Mother's Son
Night Warriors
Will of the Stone
Bearing Armen

Cubed

STAR MAGES
Written in the Stars
The Master's Lover

DAN AIDAN FAIRIES
Fairy Dreams
Monsters of Myth Anthology

XXAN WAR
Daahan Rising
Raashh Decisions

MYTHOS SERIES
The Punishment of Phoebus Apollo
Black Sail

IT'S ALL GREEK TO ME...
All's Fair...

SANCTUM
Dream Walk

GRELLAN WAR
With Great Power

BLOOD MAGES
Enslaved

CARSON COUSINS
All I Want for Christmas is You

FATES WAR
Fates Magic

Beyond the Veil
Mine for the Night

Once in a Blue Moon
Overtime Pay
Stay With Me
The Fire God's Woman
Nevermore
Bride Ball
Undead in Blue
Mama's Tales
Unexpected Daddy
We Shall Live Again
May the Best Man Win
Marked
And It Was Good
Monsters of Myth Anthology

Available from **Under The Moon**

Evil Overlords Union Issue #1 Anthology
Undead Embrace
"Playing Games" in *Forbidden Love: Bad Boys*
"Marked" in *Forbidden Love: Wicked Women*
"The Master's Lover" in *Forbidden Love:*
Sacred Bands

Available from **Logical Lust**

"Mine for the Night" in *The Cougar Book*
Anthology

Available from **Coming Together Charity**
Anthologies

INSTINCT SERIES
"Foundling" in *Coming Together: Into the Light*
Anthology

"Claim Mate" (available separately and as
part of the *Coming Together: Against the*

Odds Anthology)
"The Fire God's Woman" in *Coming Together:*
Under Fire Anthology

Available ***self-published***

Snapshots from a Poet's Life

Award-Winning Books

EPPIE/EPIC eBOOK AWARDS WINNERS
Coming Together: Against the Odds- 2010
Time Currents- 2010
Coming Together: Into the Light- 2011

EPPIE/EPIC eBOOK AWARDS FINALISTS
Fion's Daughter- 2004
Collected Poems: Book One- 2005 (now titled
Snapshots of a Poet's Life)
Renegade's Run- 2005
Rites of Mating- 2006
All I Want for Christmas- 2006
Phaze in Verse- 2008
"The Fire God's Woman" in Coming Together:
Under Fire- 2009
Three Wishes- 2010
Matchmaker's Misery- 2010
The Cougar Book- 2011
The Master's Lover- 2011
Bride Ball- 2011

DREAM REALM AWARDS FINALIST
Last Chance for Love- 2003

PEARL HONORABLE MENTION
Night Warriors- 2004

PEARL FINALISTS
Schente Night- 2003 (now included in *The*
Last of Fion's Daughters)
König Cursebreakers- 2004 (now titled *Will of*
the Stone)

JOYFULLY REVIEWED BEST BOOKS OF
2010
Written in the Stars- 2010

SPINETINGLER'S BOOK OF THE YEAR 2007
NOBODY: An Anthology of Dark Fiction- 2007
(Brenna's pieces of the anthology can be
found in *Beyond the Veil*)

TRS's CAPA FINALISTS
Ultimate Warriors- 2004 (Brenna's portion is
now available as *With Great Power*)
Written in the Stars

LOVE ROMANCE AND MORE CAFÉ BOOK
OF THE YEAR RUNNER UP
Last Chance for Love- 2008

ROAD TO ROMANCE REVIEWERS' CHOICE
AWARD
Prophecy: Revelations- 2004

LOVE ROMANCES REVIEWERS' CHOICE
AWARD
Black Sail- 2003

ROMANCE JUNKIES BOOK CLUB STAFF
PICK
TYGERS- 2003

FALLEN ANGELS ROMANCE
RECOMMENDED READ
Devon's Price-2005 (now available in *Bearing
Armen*)

JOYFULLY RECOMMENDED READ
Fairy Dreams- 2008
The Last of Fion's Daughters- 2009

TREBLE HEART FINALIST
Prophecy: Revelations- 2003